MOTOR CITY ALIEN MAIL ORDER BRIDES COLLECTION

INTERGALACTIC DATING AGENCY

ELLIS LEIGH

ISBN: 978-1-944336-30-1

Looking for love in all the wrong solar systems? Tired of traipsing from galaxy to galaxy hoping to find that perfect match, only to be disappointed? Want a little direction on what planets have the most available singles so you can point your ship and fly? Sign up for the Intergalactic Dating Agency newsletter!

And now is the perfect time as we launch our best customer offer ever!

We've recently discovered a treasure trove of amazing candidates for your every mating need. An entire planet populated by beings brand new to our records awaits your attention. This newly discovered species is soft to the touch, has the capacity for independent thought, and emits very little slime. And no death rays!

Not sold yet? Want to know more of what you're getting into with these creatures? Afraid you'll enter rest period with a shiny comet and exit to find yourself in a black hole? Don't be! Let our experience guide you to the perfect candidate! But you'd better act fast—even a ripe, new planet has limited sustainable occupancy. Don't miss your chance to find that one true love you've been searching for.

Contact us today to request an interview with one of our expert matchmakers. We guarantee you'll find a suitable mate or your money back!*

———

** Money-back guarantee not valid if suitor accidentally maims or otherwise damages mate due to alien life form transition. Limited time offer. Matchmakers are not responsible for the accommodations on host planet, nor can they be held liable for any damages the planet's atmosphere may cause. Travel at your own risk. Amount of slime emitted varies from subject to subject and cannot be quantified.*

Cutlass never thought he'd be stuck on some backward planet in a solar system with only one sun. Earth wasn't his home, but he'd find a way to survive there if it meant finding a mate. He could put up with their ancient mechanical devices and a name that wasn't his own for the right woman.

Chloe never imagined she'd sign up to be some sort of modern-day mail order bride. But too much wine and an internet connection were a bad combination, especially when the life she imagined seemed so much greater than the life she was living. Everyone stretches the truth on those dating websites, right?

One ad in a space station, one night of too much drinking, and one hotel room that will never be the same. What would you do if you found out the man from your fantasies was actually the man from your science fiction?

CHAPTER ONE_

CHLOE

Application 247E
Lead Generator: Referral
Species: Human
Planet: Earth
Breeding Rank: Receptacle
Intake Office: Detroit, Michigan, United States
Original Content: With a degree in chemical engineering, I probably should have gone into some sort of manufacturing, but the call of my true love was too strong. I found myself behind the lens instead. As a successful photographer, I've lived a life most people would dream of, but there's always been something missing. Something more I needed. Perhaps it's you.
Translation: Human female seeks adventure and excitement, in and out of the mating bed.

You ever do something that year-ago-you would have refused? Something so horrible and terrifying, you never would have thought you'd even think about trying it? Yeah. That was my day.

"Welcome to the IG Dating Agency, Chloe. Ms. Ampetheia will be with you shortly."

I did my best to smile, though it felt way forced and tight. As if I was showing my teeth to a dentist I knew was going to be all root-canal crazy. "Yeah, okay. Thanks."

The lady behind the desk's face fell, and she sniffed. Visibly sniffed like a dog scenting something on the wind. *Crap.* I hurried across the room to one of the chairs along the wall and curled into myself, trying to be subtle as I ducked and inhaled. God, I really hoped I didn't smell like hot dogs. That particular predicament was something to worry about whenever I had to go someplace directly from the Coney Island where I worked. The scent of hot dogs, fried onions, and grease tended to follow me around.

Everyone loved the smell of greasy food, right? *I wish.*

Ugh, this whole dating agency thing was such a bad idea. Who the hell would match to someone like me? As much as it killed me to admit, my life was shit. It might always be shit. And my love life? Ha. Such a joke. I hadn't even been on a date in almost two years, let alone had any sort of love in my boring, shitty life. To be honest, I hadn't even tried, not after my last boyfriend cheated on me with his boss. Working late all the time, my ass.

But I'd agreed to try this bullshit agency thing, even though I thought it would never work. I was going to kill my best friend Amelia for pushing me into it, too. Not that I could blame the girl for trying, though. Happy people in good relationships tended to want to spread that joy around. After two years of listening to me complain about battery-operated boyfriends and the craziness of multiple servings being listed on the side of a pint of ice cream—because let's be real, those little things aren't making it back into the freezer once they're opened—Amelia had talked me into trying a matchmaker service. I'd scoffed at first—and scoffed hard—but with Amelia living some sort of happily-ever-after crap with a man she met through the service and me only hanging out on the weekends with Ben and Jerry, I figured I didn't have anything better to do. So one night, under the covers as if hiding from the imaginary people who might possibly see me, I looked up the IG Dating Agency. And then I almost fell out of bed. Two weeks. That was what they gave you to accept or deny a match. Two weeks of being together every day, then you had to get married or...not. And the best part? I would be matched to my very own Mr. Right based on a letter I had to write.

Some real, honest to goodness mail order bride shit with a two-week shelf life.

"This is crazy," I'd yelled at Amelia when I'd finally crawled off the floor. Dealing with a matchmaker and only getting fourteen days to get to know my future husband? What year was I living in? Besides, with my luck, the guy they picked for me would have sweaty palms and a micropenis even if he did write the prettiest words I'd ever read. So not appealing.

But Amelia had sworn these people were experts, and her new husband treated her like a princess, so I got a little tipsy and wrote up a wonderful story about my life. Well, really, a life that would have been great had it been mine—everyone exaggerated on those types of things.

I'd clicked the send button with my eyes closed, as if the internet would explode under the pressure of my stretched truths. Sadly, nothing that exciting happened. Well, unless you count my inbox pinging like a slot machine in Vegas.

Yeah, my letter and fake life were a winner.

Within a few hours, I had fifteen emails from the agency, all with letters from possible matches attached. I didn't know any of their names, but I knew they were all new to the area and adjusting to the culture. My brand of culture featured hanging out at the Eastern Market on the weekends and arguing over whether National or Lafayette had the better coney sauce. I doubted that would be part of their adjusting.

"Chloe? Ms. Ampetheia will see you now." The lady at the front desk smiled, her head at an angle that made her seem somehow friendly and inquisitive all at once. Interesting. Was there training for stuff like that? Some sort of union for pretty, intelligent employees with the ability to put even the most skittish of customers at ease? Professional Head-Cockers United?

"Chloe?"

Get it together.

"Sorry. Just...lost in my thoughts." About head-cocking. Brilliant.

I followed the head-cocker down a long hallway that reminded me a bit of *The Shining*. Not for the décor, merely for the fact that it scared the shit out of me. All over the walls, on just about every surface, pictures of happy couples doing the things happy couples did seemed to mock me. As if I couldn't ever be as happy as they were. Why were they so smiley, anyway? It couldn't be because they'd found the loves of their lives. No couple I knew grinned that hard. The pairs in the pictures looked more like models for dental upgrades than real couples.

Meet a man, get veneers!

"Pardon?"

Shit. I must have said that out loud. "Nothing. Just...thinking of my dentist."

An eyebrow furrow joined the head cock, and I knew I was done. Ugh, I should have grabbed a cup of coffee before this meeting. I was too tired to use my verbal filters. These people were going to throw my application in the trash when they figured me out.

Head-Cocker just shook her head as she ushered me into an office in the back. It was small but neat, with a high ceiling and nice, thick carpeting. The perfect place to discuss your nonexistent love life without being humiliated by other people with nonexistent love lives overhearing.

"Ms. Ampetheia will be here in a moment."

"Yeah," I said as she hightailed it back down the hallway. "Great."

Ridiculous. This was totally and utterly ridiculous. I was going to kill Amelia for letting me do this. I should go home instead of—

"Chloe, I've been looking forward to meeting you."

Trapped.

Ms. Ampetheia swept into the room and directed me to a chair before taking the seat across the desk. I recognized the paperwork the lady laid out—my application, copies of my ID, and *the letter*. The very good, very not-quite-accurate letter.

Did the heat suddenly kick on?

"Don't be nervous," Ms. Ampetheia said, as if the thought of being nervous wouldn't make me even more nervous. "We're almost done with the process. Just a few things to go over."

Oh God, I was going to be sick. That stupid, stupid letter. I'd wanted to write something that would attract a man—or at least not scare anyone off—so I'd really put my heart into every word. My drunken heart. My lying, drunken heart. Most of the letter was accurate, but I may have fibbed a bit on income and where I lived. On what I did for a living.

Ms. Ampetheia made a noise like a purr as she read over my information. Odd, that sound, but not as odd as the muddy, baby-poop color of her beady eyes. I'd swear she was wearing brown contacts over light eyes if I didn't think that'd be ridiculous. Who wanted baby-poop brown eyes? "A photographer. I love matching creative types—you're never limited by what you see before you, but you're freed by the possibilities instead."

Okay, so fibbed was being gentle. I'd lied right through the skin of my teeth. If they found out...

"Good, good." Ms. Ampetheia nodded with a look on her face that set me slightly at ease. "Your health scans came back fine. No diseases or genetic markers for anything that would cause us to deny your request."

Huh...bonus. Still. "You deny people?"

The woman smiled, which made me recoil on instinct. The slight squint of her amber eyes and the baring of her teeth were a bit too spidery for me. An odd sensation for sure, considering the woman I sat across from was dressed in a brown cardigan. Who could be dangerous in a librarian's sweater?

Apparently a mail order bride matchmaker, that was who.

"Our gentlemen expect the best." Ms. Ampetheia leaned over the desk, growing more serious and looking only slightly more dangerous. "We don't set a match unless we're sure the union can last. These aren't dates, Chloe. They're full relationships with commitments guaranteed within two weeks. These men want a partner, someone to share a life with, to have a family with, and they don't want to wait."

Partner...family. Yeah, I hadn't found a man who wanted either of those things on my own. My last boyfriend claimed he saw forever with me, but apparently, he'd only wanted his cock sucked in the copy room. Lucky for him, the woman setting his raise every year was more than happy to do that while I sat at home alone. Ugh, what the hell. Maybe these guys *were* a different breed, after all. Amelia was superhappy with her match. Like, Disney-princess happy. It couldn't be all bad.

"Okay," I said, unable to stop my eye from twitching. "If you think you can find me someone, I'm ready."

"Good, because you've picked the perfect time to apply. Our flyers have been a huge hit! I've got a load of new males coming to apply this week and the letters from the women are beginning to clog the mailbox. You beat the rush for sure, you lucky gal." Ms. Ampetheia slid a piece of paper—a contract by the looks of it—across the desk. "We don't want to make you wait through the crowd, though. So if you can just sign the acceptance letter today, I'll get you all set up for what is potentially your last first kiss."

Oh, God. Hand shaking just enough for me to notice, I signed on the dotted line to accept the terms of the contract. *Sold to the highest bidder*...sort of.

"Excellent," Ms. Ampetheia said once I was finished, almost hissing the word. "We'll call you with the details once we find your perfect match."

"Yeah. Okay." I hurried to my feet, suddenly ready to escape. I was doing this. Diving headfirst into a full-blown relationship with a man I'd never met who was matched to me based solely on a letter. A letter filled with lies on my part.

This was going to be such a failure.

"One more thing," Ms. Ampetheia called, stopping me in my tracks half in and half out of the office. "We've found that a full immersion in the beginning of the relationship is really the best way to handle the partnership."

"Full immersion?"

"Yes. To keep the territory neutral, we set you two up for a weekend at a hotel in the city. You'll be alone enough to really get to know one another, but someone from IGDA will be nearby just in case."

Well, that didn't sound ominous. Nope, not a bit...so long as you didn't watch the nightly news.

"In case of what, exactly?"

Her smile didn't falter, though there was definitely something close to a warning in her unusually colored eyes. "In case the match doesn't take."

"And women do this? Go off and share a hotel room with a man they've never met? Because, really, that's like the perfect setup for a horror movie."

"Our applicants are fully vetted, as are you. You'll be safe with your match."

Fully vetted? *With a degree in chemical engineering, I probably should have gone into some sort of manufacturing, but the call of my true love was too strong. I found myself behind the lens instead.* I had no degree, I failed high school chemistry, and I had no idea why I'd picked a photographer for my faux profession in the first place. Yet I'd been matched and was being sent off to start a relationship with some man I'd never met. We were fully vetted all right.

I'd better remember to pack my Mace.

CHAPTER TWO_

CUTLASS

Application 5749SL
Lead Generator: Advertisement at Space Station PF456-G2
Species: Reithhar
Residence: Former planet Xouthhgros, Former planet BHG489
Breeding Rank: Inseminator
Intake Office: Space Station PF456-G2
Original Content: Strong, healthy Reithhar machinist fighter from planet
Xouthhgros available to care for female as mate. Master hunter status
ensures female will never go hungry.
Translation: Tall, handsome warrior available to fulfill your every damsel
in distress fantasy.

"No, no, no. That won't do." Ampetheia, the female with the sharp claws on the tips of her fingers, made a cooing sound as she looked over my application. "We need to simplify how your name is spelled so the *hue-mens* know how to say this. Can you pronounce it, please?"

"Cutthlaise, Reithhar Warrior of the planet Xouthhgros and Master Machinist for the former BHG489-2140 Colony."

"No, just your name."

Their language must be broken on this planet Earth. "That is my name."

Ampetheia stared for a long moment with eyes as bright and orange as the three suns of my home. Her deep, intense watchfulness ignited instincts I hadn't felt in many seasons. Instincts to run, to protect myself from a threat. The plan to kill Hohddshoun for pushing me into this process began to unwind in the back of my thoughts even as I plotted how to escape her clutches.

Before I could decide if smashing through the wall or tossing her desk on top of her would be a more effective distraction, Ampetheia sat back and released me from her hunter's stare.

"You're heading to planet Earth, to a colony called the United States," she said, speaking slowly as if I didn't understand the words. As if my communication core were somehow damaged or malfunctioning. An impossible idea. "They speak a language your name won't translate to, which means you'll stick out. You cannot stick out, or you risk being discovered. If you're discovered, every other non-earthling we've brought to the planet through our mate-finding program is in danger. Your name is not worth all those lives." Her lips pulled up in a way that bared her teeth. I jerked back with a snarl, ready to fight her if need be.

But Ampetheia didn't attack. In fact, she cooed again, this time a bit more loudly as she pointed at her mouth. "It's called a *schmy-ell.*"

"The *hue-mens*...they *schmy-ell?* Why?"

"Oh, good grief. It's not hue-mens. Humans." She stressed the word, making her lips purse as she sounded it out in the new language. "One word, no pause. And it's a smile, an expression of happiness and joy. You'll need to learn their emotional reactions before you head down to the planet. All you warriors have so much to learn."

I doubted her words, though. I had been taught for many seasons by the best of my tribe. I could fix almost any ship, hunt any animal, and beat any foe. I was through with my learning phase.

Ampetheia tapped her claw against the screen a few times before once again baring her teeth at me. I controlled my initial need to destroy the threat and tried to mimic her facial motions. My upper lip shook, and my teeth ground together. A smile, she'd said. How painful.

"Let's go with Cutlass." Ampetheia gave me no say in the matter, so

I grunted my acceptance even as my instincts balked at the different sound. I would need to kill Hohddshoun to make up for this idea. Being part of a matchmaking service that paired various species with the beings on Earth seemed odd enough. Matching mates based on nothing more than a few antiquated communications and Ampetheia's intuition? Worse. What being would fall for this? What type of female would even apply to meet a mating partner via written words? I'd always thought I'd find my mate the same way Reithhar warriors always had—by meeting someone my esehhnce crooned for and giving in to that attraction. But this farce of a dating agency? This was nothing like I'd expected.

Hohddshoun...definitely dead for pushing us to sign up.

There was nothing wrong with the process according to Ampetheia, though. The female tapped her pen against her desk in some sort of pattern before giving me another smile, one that instantly made me want to move farther away from those sharp, white teeth.

She was not one to be taken lightly.

"I have to admit, your application is quite good other than the name," she said. "So long as you agree not to use any of your Reithhar powers around the humans, I believe we'll find a match for you in half a Xouthhgros lunar cycle."

"That fast?" Her estimate was impossible in my world. It took most of my kind many seasons to find a mate, while some never did. Half a lunar cycle on Xouthhgros would pass far too quickly for such a search.

Still, I peered at the images on the walls, the female humans. The couples standing close together or embracing as if mated. Most everything about the beings seemed similar to my own kind—two eyes, proper auditory sockets, no tentacles, biped anatomy. Very similar, indeed, though they looked so much smaller than my kind. Softer, even. A thought that intrigued. After the strong, hard bodies of the Reithhar females, what would it be like to press my cock deep inside such softness? Would I need to be gentle with my ruts, or could I seek my pleasure fully? All questions to be asked, but not of Ampetheia as she was neither Reithhar nor human. Still... "How can you find a suitable mate for a Reithhar Warrior like myself in such a short time?"

Ampetheia didn't seem surprised by my doubt. "We match quickly and accurately at the Intergalactic Dating Agency. Earth is ripe with females hungry for a strong, willing male to be their mate, so we have more human applications than I can match, which is a wonderful place to be."

"But my Warrior brother, Hohddshoun. You have not matched him or Maivehricck."

The matchmaker frowned and slid her finger over her computer screen. "Ah, yes. Their applications are still in process, but no worries. We'll find someone for them. We have an 85% successful first-match rate, which is much higher than we usually start out with on a new planet. Human women are hungry for strong, sexy, take-charge men in their beds, and the Reithhar species, in particular, has always been known for their decisiveness when it comes to their mates. "You'll be snatched up in no time, as will the other two warriors." She leaned over her desk, those orange eyes glowing, only slightly off-color from my own bright yellow ones. "But this won't last. Males and nonbinary maters are coming from just about every galaxy to find their perfect mate. We wouldn't want you to miss out."

Those words caused a prickle of worry to run over me. No, I wouldn't want to miss out. My people were gone, and only the other hunters and crewmembers who'd been on the exploration trip with me the day our colony was destroyed were left. My chance at a Reithhar mate had ended with a single explosion on planet Xouthhgros. This was an opportunity to continue my species, to find a female who made my esehhnce croon. With luck, Hohddshoun and Maivehricck would have their own opportunities. This was mine, and I couldn't pass it up.

"What do I do?"

Ampetheia tapped one of her claws on the tablet she slid my way. "You touch here, lover."

I didn't even attempt to decipher the black symbols on the screen before grabbing the tablet and pressing my fingers where Ampetheia pointed. The tablet glowed blue for a moment before letting out a quiet beep.

"Done." Decision made and contract approved, I tossed the tablet back on the desk. "You may find me a mate."

"Perfect. Now, the letter for your human female. We write that for you because there's no way the translation would come out perfectly. Their language is a bit clunky. Besides, we would never expect you to learn to read any human dialect. It'd be a waste of time unless you and your match choose to stay together and on Earth. Spend the two weeks you promised to participate getting to know the human instead of the language, I say."

"Two weeks?"

"Oh, did I forget that part?" This time, the teeth-baring didn't seem so innocent. "You have two Earth weeks to finalize your mating. After that, we plop you back in the pool and reassign a match. Hopefully, if we get this right, we won't need to do that. Eighty-five percent first match success rate, remember? Even after the humans learn our clients aren't earthlings. Though, I do recommend waiting until the end of that two-week period to bring that up." She leaned forward, lowering her voice as if not wanting others to overhear. "Some of the humans get a little funny about the whole non-Earth being thing. We try to filter those types of humans out of the pool of candidates, but one or two sneak through. We're working on the process."

"Fine," I said. "I won't tell the human female."

"Great. And we'll get you some lenses to cover those eyes."

"Why do my eyes need covering?"

"Oh, honey. Consider yourself lucky. Eye coverings are no big deal. I cover mine whenever I deal with the humans. Be thankful you're not one of the ones with some sort of rainbow skin color or non-biped shape." She leaned forward as if telling me a secret. "The ones with tails are the worst. There's just no hiding that." A visible shiver rocked her shoulders before she sat back and bared her teeth at me again. "But eyes are simple. No one on Earth has such bright eyes as we do. The earthlings will think you're the son of a *skuule buhhs* or something if you don't cover them up."

The pictures my translator showed for *skuule buhhs* did nothing to hold back my ire. Still, I managed to growl out my last question without any direct threat to the female. "What else?"

"Right, the letter. Let's see." She eyed me up and down, an entirely different sort of predatory inspection. "Tall, handsome warrior available to fulfill your every damsel in distress fantasy."

CHAPTER THREE_

CHLOE

Two days, three bottles of wine, twenty-four panicked texts to Amelia, and about forty-seven miles walked as I paced around my decrepit loft was all it took to receive the magical call I'd been promised. The match was accepted, which meant I was sort of engaged. To a man I would meet for the first time in a few days. A man I knew nothing about except that he had some sort of damsel in distress fantasy, which I found hilarious. *Come home with me; see the shithole I live in. You can rescue me anytime, sir.*

What the hell had I done?

"So you'll be meeting Cutlass this Friday at the Atheneum Suite Hotel. He'll join you in the room." Ms. Ampetheia practically crooned as if this was the greatest thing ever. Meanwhile, I was caught up on the whole he'd meet me in the room line.

In. The. Room.

Room…singular. Not so much with the plural.

It had to be a joke.

"Wait, we're sharing a room?"

"Of course," Ms. Ampetheia said, almost laughing. "All our couples start out this way. You'll love it."

You'll love it—all the cool kids are doing it.

As I'd waited for that call, I'd vacillated between being ready to jump into something and wanting to run away screaming. With the whole single-room-with-a-stranger plan laid out for me, I told myself no, that I wasn't going to do this, that it was insane. I was adamant I would withdraw from the process. Regrets, be damned.

Yet somehow, the words that came out of my mouth went something more like, "Great. Thanks. I look forward to meeting him."

So long as he isn't a serial killer.

And that's how I ended up on the ninth floor of the Atheneum Suite Hotel on a Friday afternoon, my hands shaking almost uncontrollably, and my one and only dressy top practically sticking to my skin. I was a nervous sweater, and meeting my future husband—*don't heave, don't heave*—for the first time was apparently an anxiety-inducing experience. This would not go well.

What was I thinking, anyway? This was a bad plan. A horrible plan. Just because cobwebs were growing in my vagina didn't mean I should hook up with some stranger. This was a horrible, bad plan, but I'd thrown caution to the wind and let the agency decide who my perfect match would be...sight unseen. And to compound matters, I'd let them talk me into spending a weekend alone with him.

I had never felt so stupid.

Still, there was no turning back. My mind was made up, and I could be a stubborn bitch when I wanted to. Even to myself. So I took a deep breath, tossed my hair over my shoulder, and opened the door. Yes, I was stupid...but apparently, I was also determined to follow through on my stupidity. Such a great combination.

First impression of the hotel room? There was only one bed—*one*—and I was going to share it with someone named Cutlass. Like the car.

"Why is there no air in this place?" I waved a hand in front of my face and tried to talk myself down. At least my future husband—okay, seriously, stop thinking that word—wasn't in the room to see me freak out. The lady at the agency had said Cutlass would be arriving after I did—something about me maybe needing time to prepare. I didn't know what I was expected to prepare for. It wasn't as if I was going to slip into something more comfortable for a man I'd never met. Though, I'd brought *more comfortable*. Technically, less comfortable, but really, in case this guy turned out to be some Gerard Butler or Channing Tatum look-alike, I was ready with the lace and sheer. A girl had needs.

And right then, I needed some motherfucking AC, but the thermostat would not let me change the temperature.

"Stupid, defective room."

With my stomach tight and my heart racing, I paced. What if he wasn't attractive? What if he was? What if he didn't find *me* attractive? Oh God, the chill on my skin suddenly felt like needles. Why was I sweating so badly?

I glanced at the bed.

Oh, yeah. *That.*

I picked up the pacing again, staying far away from the bed in a loose arc. I needed a plan. Or two, really, because there were at least two ways I saw this thing happening. My mom had always said to give yourself options so you weren't disappointed. Those words had never seemed more important than at that moment. So I sat—not on the bed because I really didn't want to throw up on my own shoes—and I plotted.

Plan A: The guy who walked through the door was more of a Danny DeVito than a Channing Tatum. Upside, I wouldn't have to worry about sweat or shaving or figuring out how to get my curves into something strappy. We could talk, then I'd leave to go back to my apartment for the few days I might have left living in it before being evicted and moving in to my car. Awesome plan.

Plan B: The guy who walked through the door was attractive and attracted to me. Upside, I would get laid. Hopefully, he'd be good in bed. Hell, this was totally my plan and my imagination—he'd be phenomenal in the sheets. Downside...

I thought and thought, but nothing came to mind. All win, that plan. I mean, sure, if I did happen to want more than a night or two, he might not be down for that. Fine. The matchmaker claimed this great rate of successful marriages after the completion of the two-week trial period, but no one agreed to forever from the start, right? It wasn't as if we were going to run down to the courthouse and get hitched before Monday morning. Maybe I could get a single, dirty little rendezvous out of this. Possibly a date or two. Yeah, that was all I needed. One night of hot, sweaty, toe-curling...

I swear the bed was leering at me, and the room was a fucking oven.

Okay, back to pacing. My head spun, my breath coming faster with every step. Why couldn't I stop and relax? This was nothing—a dalliance. I hadn't been honest with him, and he probably hadn't been honest with me. Who could be in letter-form? We'd meet, exchange pleasantries, and then I could choose to stay or go. Done.

But my nerves... Maybe I should have hired an escort instead of writing a letter with all my deepest secrets and fears in it. Maybe I should have tried hitting up the bars and clubs to find a man, instead of relying on an agency to find me some sort of personalized Mr. Right. Not that I could afford an escort, though I might end up having to be one if I couldn't figure out how to pay rent. There was always my landlord's son. He'd been propositioning and catcalling me since the day I moved in. He might exchange sex for rent, which should probably be looked at as a real possibility considering where my life was at.

Shit, it really was hot in the room, and the thermostat was as broken as my future.

Plan A, I ended up homeless. Plan B, I got laid then ended up homeless. Either way, screwed.

A quick knock was the only warning I had before the door swung open. A man walked in, and I finally stopped pacing. In fact, I damn near froze in place. Holy shit. Plan B it was.

CUTLASS

The hotel teemed with people when I walked in. Humans in all their shapes and colors filled the meeting area and crowded the doorway. Just what I wanted. I grunted as I stalked through the chaos, scowling at the ones who dared to look my way.

Try to be nice. The humans scare easily.

Ampetheia's words from when she gave me my match assignment picked at my memory. Be nice...how? Reithhar warriors were not built for nice. We were built to hunt and kill, to either break things or fix them. We were designed to survive the harshest of elements and the most dangerous of threats. Humans were small, weak, soft, and easily frightened. Exactly what I didn't need in a mate.

And yet, I had hurriedly accepted my task from Ampetheia. Meet my match in a hotel—a building filled with sleeping quarters for traveling humans—and work to attract her. Fine. If I could get a mate out of this assignment, perhaps it would be worth the trouble. Doubtful, but perhaps.

I did my best not to scowl at the little beings running every which way and hurried to the box Ampetheia had called an *ellah-vaddohr*. There was nothing to tell me how to use the box, of course. Apparently, humans didn't need instructions for the things. While I was not human, I was a Reithhar machinist. I could figure this machine out.

With one last glance at the scattered humans, I placed my hand over the metal panel with the small, round lights and let my Reithhkoneccs find the right parts and pieces to make the thing work. Ampetheia had said no powers on Earth, but that was almost impossible. My Reithhkoneccs, my sense of how small pieces were meant to work together, was not something I could turn off. I was a fixer and had been since my earliest days. Asking me to hold that back was akin to asking me not to protect myself during a battle. Ridiculous.

My Reithhkoneccs worked just as I had expected it to. Every tiny switch and wire pulled together under my guidance to move the box. The doors popped open before a single human seemed to notice me pressing my hand to the panel. Perfect.

The box smelled unpleasant and shook as if untethered to the building, but I entered it as directed. Ampetheia had given me a piece of paper with a shape on it and told me to touch that shape in the ellah-vaddohr. It took me far longer than I'd like, but I found the strange intersecting lines and touched the one on the panel. The doors slid closed, trapping me inside, and the entire machine shook and groaned. If I died in this moving box, I would still find a way to kill Hohddshoun for this idea. He deserved it.

But a hand on the control panel told me everything was working as expected, so I restrained myself from breaking through the doors to escape. At least for the moment.

As the ellah-vaddohr rose with me in it, I rubbed my eyes, the thin lenses provided by the agency gritty and irritating. Ampetheia had demanded I wear them to cover my so-called unusual eye color. Unusual on Earth, not on Xouthhgros. But I wore them without complaining... much. There was no way I could hunt with these things, though. If this mating didn't take, if the female I was assigned to did not make my esehhnce croon after these few days together, I was going to talk my team into leaving this Earth behind. Find a hospitable planet with a more advanced technological footprint. Somewhere we could be of service. Our machinist skills were always in demand, and our hunters were lauded throughout the galaxies. We could move on.

But first, I had to go through with this whole match process.

The contraption came to a rough stop, and the doors opened without request. Silly machinery, really, but effective. Again, I had to hunt down a series of squiggles and lines to locate the proper door. All too soon, I stood in front of the entry to the room Ampetheia had said housed my match.

And then I froze.

What if this didn't work? What if my esehhnce refused to croon for her? If the match didn't take, I'd feel like a fool for attempting it.

But my matched partner was behind that door, so I needed to stop stalling. I was a warrior, a hunter, and a master machinist. I had fought battles far greater than Earth had ever experienced, across galaxies they didn't know existed. I would not be afraid of a simple female.

With a single deep breath, I pressed my hand against the metal latch of the door. In no time, the lock popped. I almost bared my teeth and made the smile. Too easy, this place.

I knocked twice, as I'd been told to do, and walked inside. The human woman across the room spun, her long, dark mane flying out behind her in a mesmerizing wave. And when she faced me, when her gaze met mine, I nearly stumbled back out the door. She had the biggest eyes I'd ever seen. Eyes staring right at me and framed with a deep, dark fringe of some sort of fur. Intriguing.

But she was so small. Gentle and almost weak in her appearance. The warrior in me stood at attention, ready to protect her. Ready to keep her safe as we completed the mating dance to determine compatibility. The male in me, well, he stood at attention too, for an entirely different reason. Small, soft, and carrying a scent of sweetness, this female definitely had my attention. Still, I pushed aside the thoughts of rutting and mating and the needs my hard cock tried to burden me with and gave her one of her beings' smiles.

"*Klow-ee?*"

She flinched, the act of frightened prey. Was I scaring her? I'd practiced the facial movements to bare my teeth as her kind did. Perhaps I'd gotten the move wrong. Before I could try again, the female stood a little taller and stiffened her shoulders.

"Are you Cutlass?"

Her quiet, sweet voice called to me, initiating a warmth through my body I'd not experienced before. Even though Cutlass was not my real name, I liked the way it rolled off her tongue. Experienced much pleasure from watching her lips form the different sounds. Something to tuck away and think over later.

I nodded, inspecting her as she seemed to do the same. My instincts wanted me to go to her. To touch that silky looking mane, run a finger along all that smooth, golden skin. To find out how she felt under my hands. But Ampetheia had been very clear on that aspect of this odd ritual—the human female initiated the touching. I was not to stun her, drag her, push her, or force her to do anything she did not express interest in first, even though my kind tended to lean toward the aggressive side of the mating spectrum. But she was not Reithhar, she was human, so I would wait for her interest. Ampetheia had said to have patience, to hunt as if she were skittish prey. Earth females were apparently easy to bed once you were able to master something called the *woo*.

I would woo her, all right. Woo her straight onto my cock so I could experience the softness of the human form.

The female took a deep breath, seeming to shake off some of her fears. "Hey. I'm Klow-ee."

She stepped closer and held out her hand in an odd gesture. I had seen pictures of such customs in the pamphlet on human habits. There had been one about meetings, with an image of two hands coming together. Something about...shaking. I could do that.

Trying my hardest to match her movements, I reached for her, sliding my hand into hers. The moment we touched, the moment her skin met mine, an electric tingle shot up my arm and down to my gut. That tingle, the attraction, the way my cock grew painfully hard with a single, simple brush of flesh, was all the sign I needed. This was a good match, one I could work with to see if there would be crooning from my esehhnce.

A chance.

"I am Cutlass." I moved our hands up and down, pulling her slightly closer as I did. Unable to resist. "Many greetings."

Her deep, wide eyes stayed on mine while a lovely, darker color rose along her neck and up her cheeks. And her scent—she wasn't just sweet, she was aroused. One touch, and I'd made her want me.

Maybe Hohddshoun wouldn't need to die, after all.

Klow-ee pulled her lips up in a smile, her small, blunt teeth shining. Not nearly as worrisome, though, as when Ampetheia had made the same expression.

"Many greetings to you, as well." Her words came across as a weird sort of double whisper in my ear as they were translated through my communicator core. A distracting quality, but workable. At least I could understand her.

"I am glad to be meeting you, Klow-ee," I said, letting my voice rumble just a bit. The sound of a hunter on the prowl. "Should we get to the eating out now?"

CHAPTER FOUR_

CHLOE

Inky black hair, dark eyes, and a body that made me want to bite my fist came strolling through the door, and I was gone.

Woman down!

Christ on a cracker, the man was gorgeous. He was tall and thick, with more muscles than I knew what to do with. I mean, I knew what *I* *wanted* to do with them, but I wasn't sure he'd be down for me licking all over those dips and swells. One could only dream.

Oh, my God, I'd been staring at him forever. Time to—you know—do something.

"Hey. I'm Chloe." Without thinking, I offered him my hand. Such a ridiculous way to start what would possibly end up in a marriage, but I didn't know what else to do and my hand was already out there. Hanging. Waiting for him to take it or not.

He took it. He took it real good.

"I am Cutlass. Many greetings." His words came out almost on a purr, the sound going straight to my clit. How did he do that? And could he keep doing it? Like, could I have him read the phone book while I shook and twitched and basically got off on nothing but sound? That wasn't wrong, was it?

I grinned, unable not to with him so close. With our hands clasped together. With his warmth practically blanketing me. "Many greetings to you, as well."

Cutlass pulled me closer, leaning over my smaller body. Jesus, he was really, really tall. My breathing sped, my heart thumping hard. I hoped something else was hard or close to it. I hoped he felt the same tingle from our hands joining that I did. I hoped—

"Should we get to the eating out now?"

Record...scratch.

I jerked back, staring up at him with what had to be a surprised expression. My damn forehead hurt from the furrowing I couldn't seem to stop. "Excuse me?"

Cutlass looked confused in an adorable sort of way, not that I was falling for it. Not at all.

"You are my Klow-ee. Yes?"

Okay, the accent was oddly intriguing even if the *my* rubbed me the wrong way. Normally, I'd tell him I belonged to no one, but he didn't seem to be lording anything over me.

Or at least, I hoped that wasn't the intention behind the my.

"I *am* Chloe, but I'm not really sure about being yours yet."

That cute, confuzzled expression deepened. "You are not the female chosen for me?"

Okay, yeah. Confused for sure. "IDGA selected to introduce the two of us, but that doesn't mean I'm all 'let's jump in the sack so you can...eat me out.'"

Though, really, I sort of wanted him to. Like...a lot. Cutlass looked like excellent one-night-stand material.

"Ampetheia matched us," Cutlass said. "And you agreed to this meeting, but you don't want to be eaten out? The agency said the eating you out was expected."

I could barely speak. How did he make pervy and questioning so attractive? God, if my cheeks got any hotter, I'd explode. I wasn't even going to think about how wet my panties were from his oddly dirty words. Nope, totally wasn't thinking about it.

I pressed my thighs together, not thinking. "I...don't know you."

He hummed, and I damn near came from the sound. Holy shit, it really was hot in here. Needing a distraction, and to stop clinging to the man's hand like some sort of koala in a tree, I rushed to the thermostat to turn the AC lower.

"Shit," I hissed when the damn thing still wouldn't work.

"What is shit?"

I spun, pressing my back to the wall. "It's hot, but this thing is broken."

Cutlass glanced from me to the thermostat before coming closer. He pursed his lips and squinted a little as he brought his hand to the broken hunk of plastic. His big hand. Those fingers were seriously long.

The scent of ozone struck me a moment before the whirring of a fan kicked on. A cold wind blew through the room, chilling me in the best possible way. Finally.

"Better?" Cutlass asked, staring down at me with a look in his eyes that made me want to melt.

"How'd you do that?"

He shrugged. "I fix things. Now, how about the eating you out?"

Eating you out. Yeah. My panties were wet at the thought, but come on. He'd just walked in the door, and even I wasn't that hard up. *He fixed the thermostat, too,* my inner hussy reminded me. Not that I would be listening to her. I couldn't be all naked and spread out for him so soon.

Maybe in a few hours.

"You read my letter," Cutlass said, still sounding as if he was somehow purring those words.

I nodded, keeping my back to the wall. Wishing there was something to hold on to so I didn't throw myself at the poor man. "Yes. I read your letter."

"Then you know I'm interested in the eating you out and the learning you."

Stop. Fucking. Blushing. "I have no idea what you're talking about."

His brow pulled down, and his lips did this sort of pursing thing that made my knees weak. "Am I...is this not the way to woo?"

"What's a woo?"

He huffed. "The agency said I would need to woo. Am I not doing it correctly? They told me women here liked the eating out as part of the wooing."

Yeah, they did. They really, really did. But maybe not with a complete stranger. "Look, buddy, I don't know who you think you are—"

He grinned, and all my words died a silent death. How was he so... pretty? "My name is Cutlass."

Surname: Too Damn Hot For Words.

I had to bite back a return smile so we could stay on course in the conversation. One distraction, and I might do something stupid. Like jump him and let him do the eating out. My vagina could be awfully demanding at times.

I backed away, forcing myself to retreat. "Okay, Cutlass. I think we need to slow down."

"Slow?" His measured steps as he followed me weren't what I'd had in mind, yet I couldn't help but enjoy the view. He was a man on a mission, a hunter stalking his prey. His prey being me, and I'd never been so happy to be hunted in my life.

"Slow," I whispered as I bumped into the desk. Trapped...and I liked it.

Cutlass sighed, his breath making my hair flutter as he nearly surrounded me. He was so close, so ridiculously overwhelming. And hot. Gloriously, unendingly hot. Fuck, what was I running from again?

"I am trying to do the wooing," he said, his voice doing that purring thing again. "So, if no eating you out, we could do the eating you in. The agency was clear that I should feed you."

Feed me? As in...food? Like forks and spoons and meat of the nonsexual variety? Oh, hell. Language barrier, meet humiliating innuendo.

"Is that what you meant by...eating me out?"

A head cock...of course. "Yes. What did you think I meant?"

My cheeks burned, and my ears positively tingled. I couldn't speak, couldn't think of a single word to say in response that wouldn't embarrass me more.

Cutlass moved closer, staring in a way that made me want to whimper. "The *cow-lo*r rushing under your skin is attractive."

Don't. Jump. Him. "It's embarrassing."

"So, so wrong, dear Klow-ee. May I?" He held up a hand, staying an inch from my face as he asked permission. As he gave me the option to touch or not. I liked that a lot, so I nodded. Cutlass ran a single finger down my cheek in the lightest touch possible. Almost a whisper of skin on skin. I'd never known my cheek could be an erogenous zone, but it had to be because I could have sworn I felt that touch right on my clit as well.

"The flush is warm and brings added life to your skin," Cutlass murmured, ignorant to the restraint I was showing by not attacking him like a lioness in heat. "Lovely."

"Thank you," I whispered as I trembled before him. He nodded, taking a single step back to give me room once more, not that I wanted him to do that.

"Let me feed you." His demand was so soft, so quiet, there was no way I could turn him down.

"Yeah. Okay."

That made him smile. "Eating you out or eating you in?"

Oh, hell. "Out, but here's the thing—you can't call it eating you out."

"Why not? We're eating outside of this room."

"Yes, but eating you out has a...non-food cultural meaning."

There was no mistaking the interest in his eyes at that statement. "What is this *mee-neng*?"

My cheeks burned again, hotter this time. I couldn't have stopped that blush if I'd tried.

"More *cow-lor*," Cutlass said, offering another touch of my cheek. "Whatever this eating out is, I want to speak of it often so I can see this flush on your face."

Oh Lord, I was going to die. Implode from sexual desire, and he'd only touched my cheek. "Going out to eat. We're *going out* to eat."

He hummed. "Then what is eating you out?"

Hopefully, I'd get the chance to teach him that a little later. Speaking of which...

"I need to change into something a bit more comfortable before we go."

CHAPTER FIVE

CUTLASS

Klow-ee had that warm glow again as we left the hotel. The flush of her skin, the way the rush of blood darkened her neck and cheeks, was attractive, to say the least. Though I still wasn't sure what I'd done to garner such a reaction. Something about the turn of words the translation core provided obviously excited her. I could smell it, see it, practically taste it—I just couldn't figure out the cause of it. My translations had been off before, especially with a new language such as this Earth's *Een-gllisch,* and the lack of proper communication could be entirely too frustrating. As it was right then.

But, really, I couldn't complain. My cock was hard, my senses firing on full blast to monitor the lovely female at my side, and my esehhnce happy. Not yet crooning, but in tune with Klow-ee's. This might be a good match, after all. Perhaps Hohddshoun wouldn't need to die.

We had walked a short distance when Klow-ee turned suddenly and smiled at me with a look of joy on her face. I stood stunned for a moment, unable to pay attention to the fact that she was speaking. She took every ounce of my cognitive function away from me. Her beauty radiated in a completely arousing way. Her eyes bright and attentive, her smile wide and excited. A total trap for my senses. I wanted to stay in her presence, to absorb some of that happiness. To bask in the light of that expression.

I wanted this little human in ways that were far too carnal for being in public.

Her smile faltered, though, when I didn't answer her. I nearly kicked myself—I'd totally lost focus and missed the conversation.

"My regrets," I said with a small nod of my head and slight baring of my teeth. "Your smile distracted me. What did you say?"

Her head tilted, a wary sort of look in her eyes. My prey back on guard. "I asked if you liked *scee-fued*."

The translator core worked out the unknown word in record speed, not that it helped much. *Scee-fued* didn't quite translate. The core filled my mind with images of various sorts—from small critters with multiple legs scuttling across the ground to large creatures with no legs, black eyes, and sharp teeth. Now those intrigued me. Great beasts who ruled the waterways on this planet would be a hard-fought prey, it seemed. I understood from my cultural training that I wouldn't necessarily be hunting my own food here, but that didn't mean I couldn't enjoy the spoils of someone else's hunt.

"I'm curious about this *scee-fued*," I said. "I'll try it."

With a shrug of her delicate shoulder, Klow-ee led us into a building with many tables and people all around. The volume of the chatter, the press of bodies in the cramped space, made the hunter in me nervous. I inched closer to Klow-ee, wanting to hold her sweet body against me. To keep her safe amid the chaos around us. To use physical connection to ground any worries she had. But Klow-ee didn't seem worried. She stood tall and calm in the crowd of humans. Brave, my little female was.

Looking around, I catalogued the various ways males and females interacted. All the computer-led cultural training in the world was no match for immersive education. Everywhere, couples stood together, some talking loudly while others silently looked at the communication devices they held. Still others touched and bared their teeth, obviously enjoying their partner. Those were the ones I watched the most, the ones I would imitate. They would be my teachers.

I leaned closer to Klow-ee, ready to initiate the communication required to woo, but before I could say anything, a male approached her. A human male.

"Table for two?" The male's smile dropped when he saw me, and his steps faltered. There was even a bit of a nervous warble to his voice that denoted him as prey instead of predator. Good.

"Please," Klow-ee said, sounding happy and relaxed in front of this other male. Perhaps not a direct threat, then. I followed Klow-ee as the male led her across the space.

"I used to come here a lot when I was younger," Klow-ee said as we sat at a table in the middle of the room.

"This is close to where you grew?"

"No, but my mom worked downtown, so we'd sometimes end up here on a weekend. This place was her favorite." Her smile and her eyes dimmed. I reached across the table and grabbed her hand, ignoring Ampetheia's advice to let her touch first. The look on Klow-ee's face meant she needed comfort, and I would be the male to offer it.

"Why are you sad?"

She didn't even bare her teeth at me as she wove her fingers through mine. "My mom passed away a number of years ago. It's...still hard."

Passed away... The translator showed pictures of dirt and containers, which didn't make sense. But then it showed other pictures. Ones of mourning and grief. Of fallen warriors and family. Of loss.

I knew loss well. Too well. "I am sorry your mother fell. There is no greater pain than losing someone close to you."

Her eyes locked on mine. "You're a kind man, Cutlass."

I wasn't a man at all, not in the human sense, but she would learn that soon enough.

Klow-ee ordered something called *tiil-ah-peeahh* when the human male came to the table, and I chose to order the same. The idea that this place would bring the beast to me appealed. I didn't want to trek far from Klow-ee, but I still enjoyed the spoils of a good hunt. I'd been a machinist, a fixer, for many seasons, but I'd hunted with Hohddshoun and the others when opportunities to take a break from the ship came up. Taking down prey on the inhospitable moons of Xouthhgros had been one of my favorite things to do with the other males of my ship.

But what arrived at the table was not at all what I expected.

I scowled at the circular disk the male placed in front of me, my eyes locked on the slab of pale meat in the center. Where was the great beast? Why was this so...small?

"What's wrong?" Klow-ee asked, holding a pronged weapon in one hand.

"Nothing." I followed her lead again, grabbing the cold metal dagger. The translator threw Een-gllisch words at me. Apparently, the item was a *forck*. Odd word indeed.

"Do you not like it?" She used her pronged tool—her *forck*—to separate a chunk of flesh from the rest on her plate and brought it to her mouth. Aha, an eating utensil.

I stabbed the flesh with my *forck* and yanked a piece off, far less graceful than my companion. The meat was sweet and flaky against my tongue. Delicious. And without any effort expended. So odd, these humans, but so smart.

"I like it very much," I said, going back for more pieces. "But I was just expecting something larger and with far more teeth."

———

CHLOE

I did my best to hold in the giggle threatening to escape. The language barrier was a bit more than I'd expected, but we were getting by just fine. Except for the whole eating you out thing. Lord, I needed to get him to stop saying that before I jumped him and showed him exactly what *eating you out* meant in my sex-driven culture.

Taco Tuesday...every day.

Cutlass dove into his dinner as if he enjoyed his food, and I definitely enjoyed the view and conversation we carried on throughout the meal. Still, in the back of my mind, my thoughts spun out of control. Dirty thoughts. Horrible, naughty, perfect thoughts. Maybe Plan B was the right choice now—the old dinner, drinks, and mattress dancing. Considering how attractive Cutlass was and how charming, I figured I should at least further evaluate the option. Plan A was out for sure. He was interesting enough for me to want to get to know him. Perhaps a Plan C—dinner, drinks, mattress dancing, *and more*. Maybe. I hadn't really been thinking of *more*, but there was no denying I felt an attraction to Cutlass. Maybe *more* was just what I needed.

I almost started to sweat again. *More* was a bit terrifying. We had two weeks to decide on the *more*. Two weeks of being in a relationship with this man didn't seem like a hardship.

That dating agency lady would be getting a lovely letter of recommendation if *more* happened.

When dessert came, Cutlass again looked a little lost.

"What is it?" I asked as I grabbed my fork.

He frowned, peering at the dessert as if it might jump up and bite him. "I don't know. I assumed you did."

I'd ordered a lava cake for the two of us, all dark, gooey, and warm, with ice cream melting on top and falling over the side. He'd told me to pick. Perhaps I'd chosen wrong.

He glanced up at me, a disgusted turn to his plump lips. "Why is it this *cow-lor*?"

His accent turned the word into an interesting bastardization of itself, but I understood what he meant. Though, really, in my world, not understanding why a dessert was brown was impossible. Almost afraid of the answer, I asked a question I'd never had to ask before.

"Do you not like chocolate?"

His eyes went a little unfocused, and his brow furrowed hard. "I don't understand. What is *chow-koe-lahte*?"

It took me a solid ten seconds of staring to realize my mouth was hanging open. Did he just... How could he... Oh, that poor, poor man.

I kept my words steady and weighted as I stated the unbelievable truth. "You don't know chocolate."

"No, I don't."

That pensive, almost disgusted look on his face just wouldn't do. I loaded my fork with a small bite of the best parts of the dessert and held it out for him.

"Try it."

He glanced from the fork to me, his eyes questioning. "For you, Klow-ee."

God, I loved the way he said my name. As did my pussy, but we'd get to that later. Chocolate took priority.

I held the fork, and his eyes held mine, infusing the moment with so much more intimacy than I'd expected. This was no simple bite. Oh, no, this was foreplay. And I was definitely down for that.

Not breaking the intense stare down, Cutlass slowly opened his mouth, giving me the green light to feed him. Trusting me, even. A fact I didn't take lightly. His tongue darted out and his lips closed around my fork, his eyes still on mine. That intensity almost a physical thing. Intimate? Feeding him was downright sexual.

Cutlass held that searing look for about half a second once the dessert hit his tongue, but even he was no match for the angel that was chocolate. I could see the moment he registered the flavor. He closed his eyes as he chewed, moaning in pleasure.

Oh, holy hell.

"I like the feel of this on my tongue," he murmured, looking at the dessert plate with far more interest than before. And me? I had pretty much jumped into the "screw dessert, let's go back to the room" camp for the first time in my life. My legs shook and my body burned as I watched him. Jesus, I was going to implode from sexual desire, and all he'd done was try chocolate for the first time.

"Yes," I said, trying—and probably failing—to keep my voice steady and free from that lovely phone-sex vibe I knew would come out if I talked while aroused. "It's my favorite."

"It's mine as well."

I grinned at his almost boyish excitement. Couldn't help myself. Now if only I could get my thoughts back into the PG arena.

———

After dinner and the sexiest dessert-sharing incident known to man, Cutlass once again proved the cultural differences between us were greater than just a few misspoken words.

"You need to write in the tip and sign, sir."

Cutlass held the pen in his fist, like a weapon of some sort. "I apologize. I'm not fluent in your currency exchanges. Tip?"

The waiter damn near rolled his eyes, a fact that didn't escape my notice. "Just sign on the line. The bill is being taken care of by an IGDA Corporation, but you have to decide the tip and approve the expense."

Cutlass huffed, the sound a little deeper than expected. A little almost growly. God, that was hot.

"Does *he* have to sign, or can I?" I asked, already irritated with the guy hovering over Cutlass like some sort of watchdog.

"No, not him specific—"

"Great." I grabbed the folio and pen from Cutlass, smiling to let him know I wasn't mad. At least, not at him. "I'll deal with this."

Cutlass grunted and eyed the waiter hard, shooting daggers with a look. Also hot. Of course, everything about this man seemed to turn me on. It was as if I'd been given some sort of aphrodisiac along the way to the restaurant. Or I'd gone too long without sex and was ravenous for a little smack and tickle.

Probably the second.

I signed the bill with a flourish, putting my *fuck-you-asshole* in the curves of my name since I couldn't say them. Well, I could, but that would be rude. What wasn't rude was giving the guy a 10 percent tip. As a waitress, I tended to tip higher than most people because I knew how much the job sucked. But really, all the guy had to do was be nice. He'd failed when dealing with my date. No big tip for him.

"All set," I said, smiling up at the waiter and handing him the closed folio. "You have a nice night now."

He startled as if not expecting that. "You both as well."

As soon as the guy disappeared across the room, I sighed. "Let's go before he sees what I tipped him."

"Why?" Cutlass stood and offered a hand to help me up. Such a gentleman.

"It's no big deal, but I only tipped him 10 percent. He seems like the type to confront me about that."

Cutlass moved to my shoulder, shooting a scowl across the crowded restaurant to where the waiter stood at a service station. "He won't get close to you. But I need you to explain what a tip is."

My God, he smelled good. I sort of wanted to roll around in that scent. And I might...later. Wait, what was the question?

"Um...oh, right. Tip. It's like a bonus? You give servers a little extra for doing a good job."

"And you gave him extra of your monies?"

"Technically, I didn't, the IGDA did. But, yes."

Cutlass huffed that growly sound again, sending a shiver straight down my spine. "He didn't deserve it. I would have given you just the tip instead."

Just...the tip. Yeah, my mind went there. "Hopefully, I'll get more than the tip a little later."

His confused expression only made him seem that much sexier.

Cutlass walked me out of the restaurant with his hand at my back. That move was such a guy thing to do, but I liked it. In fact, I sort of loved it. That contact made me feel safe and protected. Almost cherished.

Cutlass might be getting some tonight.

Maybe.

Okay, probably.

As we strolled back toward the hotel, another couple walked the same path about ten yards in front of us. They were leaning into one another, whispering, holding hands—obviously together. Cutlass watched them with a thoughtful look on his face. I watched him, wondering the whole time what he was thinking.

When the man leaned down to kiss the woman's temple, Cutlass glanced at me instead. I smiled, hoping to be encouraging, and he reached for my hand. His skin was soft and warm, and a shiver flew up my spine at the contact. That touch was electric, intense, and the perfect end to such an amazing meal.

Yup. Probably getting laid.

We inched closer the longer we walked, me ending up pressed against his arm and him clinging to my hand when we finally made it to the room. The tension between us was luscious. I almost didn't want to open the door or do anything to break that sort of anticipatory sensation. Almost. Because the idea of throwing him down on the hallway floor wasn't as appealing as getting him naked behind closed doors.

Even my hussy self had some standards.

"Oh," I said, reaching for my purse. "I don't know if I have my card."

"That's fine." Cutlass ran his palm over the lock, and the door clicked open. No card that I noticed...just his hand and the scent of ozone on the air. Like when he fixed the thermostat.

I was going to ask him about that, I really was, but the second we made it inside, Cutlass pushed me against the door, pinning me in place and making my pussy positively weep with joy.

"We're alone, Klow-ee." My name was a whisper on his tongue, a breath of longing and desire tinged with an accent I couldn't place. Plus, he smelled like chocolate, a fact that made me want to taste every inch of him. So fucking arousing.

Key? What key?

I wrapped my arms around his neck and pulled him closer. Ready and willing for more. Our noses touched as he lowered his face to mine. A slight nuzzle. Warm skin on warm skin. A total tease.

"I had a great time at dinner," I whispered, letting my lips brush against his chin as I spoke. Cutlass moaned his agreement, his tongue peeking out to lick his lips. I wanted to feel that. Taste it. I wanted it so much.

"Klow-ee," he murmured, the tone of his voice pure sex.

"Yes?" My eyes were heavy and almost closed, my desire something fierce and unrestrained.

"May I mate with your mouth?"

Ice bucket...thrown.

I recoiled, hitting my head on the door as I did. "Huh?"

Cutlass gave me that adorably confused look again. "I'd very much like to mate with your mouth."

My thoughts scattered, my brain too foggy to put those words together properly. "Are you...asking for oral sex?"

His brow pulled down in what could only be confusion or frustration. Or both. "I don't understand that term."

"Oral sex. Fellatio. Blow job."

"Blow...what? From the pictures I've seen, blowing doesn't seem to come into play."

Okay. Language barrier totally in the way. "Pictures? Of what?"

"Let me show you." He pulled me closer, his movements slow and measured as if giving me the chance to refuse him. Looking at my lips the whole time.

"My mouth against yours. My hands" —Cutlass slid said hands to my ass and grabbed some serious booty— "here."

I melted a bit. An ass-grab and a desire to kiss me? I was in.

"Oh, yeah?" An impressive package pressed against my hip, and I purposely arched into it. Teasing.

"Yes." His nose nuzzled mine again. His lips so close. "May I?"

"Kiss," I whispered, letting our lips brush. Sinking into the sparkling reality of being completely surrounded by this man.

He inhaled sharply. "Kiss?"

"That's what it's called. Not mouth-mating. Kissing."

"Ah." He leaned in, dragging his lips along my jaw. "May I kiss you, Klow-ee?"

Deep down, I'd like to say I did something suave and sensual, something awesome in response. That I said some damn sexy words and really played up the tension.

Nope.

I grabbed him around the neck and yanked the two of us together instead. Our lips met, and a fire exploded within me. Hot. He was so hot to the touch. So hard and muscular as he fell into my body. The door bit into my back, but I didn't care. I had Cutlass against me, his mouth on mine, his cock pressing into my hip. A few bruises would totally be worth it.

Cutlass sucked on my bottom lip before plunging his tongue into my mouth. In a good way, not like a gag-reflex-initiator way. Tongues sliding together, breathing harder than if I was running a marathon—or so I assumed—I gave as good as I got. Moaning, grabbing, pulling, nibbling on that plump lower lip and all-out attacking his mouth with mine. Again, in a good way. Not like some sort of nasty kissing, openmouthed, licking-all-over-each-other's-faces way. That wouldn't be hot, and the moment with Cutlass was definitely—*definitely*—hot.

And Cutlass? He held his own. God, he was a good kisser. All heat and soft and pressure and small nibbles when he needed to break. I liked that. Liked him. Liked both a lot.

"Cutlass," I groaned as I pushed myself away from the door. He followed my lead, allowing me to direct him toward the bed. The perfectly situated king bed.

God bless the IG Dating Agency for the brilliant plan of shoving us together in a hotel room with just one bed.

Cutlass totally let me direct the progression, which was good because he was big enough that I doubted I'd be able to move him without help. And when his knees hit the mattress, he sat down. Well, technically, he sort of fell. I wouldn't call him out on that, though. He must have been so distracted by our awesome kisses he didn't realize where I was leading him or what I had planned.

Yeah, that sounded like a good excuse.

Cutlass stared at me, looking all hot and bothered and only slightly confused, as if he hadn't been prepared to stop with the kissing. His hair had lost some of that perfect wave, and his lips were even plumper. Sex-tousled, I'd call him. Soon-to-be sex-tousled, really.

"Plan B time." I grinned before grabbing the bottom of my dress and dragging the fabric over my head, leaving me in the sheer and strappy shit I'd thrown on before dinner.

Way to think ahead, past me.

Cutlass' eyes heated as he took me in, as he devoured me with just a look. As he licked his lips in what had to be anticipation. He ran a single finger along the lace of my panties, his eyes dark and hooded, his lips kiss-swollen. If a look could set a person on fire, I'd be burning. A lot.

I'd be ash.

"I don't know what a plan B is," he said, reaching for me. His warm hands circling my hips. "But I think I might like it."

Oh, this poor, misguided man. "Trust me, you'll love it. I'll make sure of it."

CHAPTER SIX_

CUTLASS

The needs of a Reithhar Warrior were quite simple. Beyond food and a place to hole up away from the sun, we needed little else. Our wants, though, were varied. Some hunters wanted soft skins to wrap around them when they slept or a large tribe to be a part of. Me? I wanted to claim Klow-ee with my words and my cock.

Not necessarily in that order.

She's so beautiful, my soft, sweet human.

Klow-ee dropped to her knees, fingers strong and sure as she unbuttoned my shirt. No shaking, no sign of fear or nervousness. Her eyes met mine, so heated, her stare sexy enough that it made the head of my cock slick. Made me crave her touch in a way that caused an ache deep within.

She wanted me to fulfill her needs.

"Klow-ee." My guttural whisper caused her flesh to prickle and flush. There was no greater temptation than that soft, warm skin all dark and ready for my attention. But I wanted to keep mouth mating with her. *Kiss-sing,* she'd called it. I liked kiss-sing her a lot. There was something so intriguing about sliding my tongue inside her mouth, about the press of her lips against mine. I also wanted to slide my cock between her legs and rut her until she screamed my name. Simple needs, all of them.

"I'm probably not ready for full-on sex yet," she said. Still smiling, still undressing me with care. "But I want to *plae* with you."

The word didn't quite translate to my language, and the visuals from the translator confused me. "*Plae?* What is this *plae?*"

I growled as her fingers brushed my skin, as she rubbed my hard nipple through my shirt. The sparks that move caused were new to me. Reithhar females ignored such things, choosing to focus solely on the cock instead. I'd never once felt as if I was missing out on anything during my exploits, until Klow-ee. This human knew how to entice me for sure.

She pushed the fabric off my arms and ran her fingers over my bare chest. "It's play, as in to have fun. You know. Everything but."

I didn't know, but as long as she kept touching me the way she was, I'd play with her all night.

When she reached for the fastenings on my pants, I grabbed her around the waist and yanked her close, falling back on the bed so she was draped across me. Klow-ee laughed, and the sound was a blessing to my ears. This woman, this human female, was much more than I had expected. She was beautiful and soft, funny and charming. And ignorant of my true self. I needed to tell her, and soon.

But then she pulled her legs up and straddled me, putting her weight right on my aching cock, and all thoughts of telling her anything other than *yes* and *more* flew out the window. Especially when she rubbed herself against me—gyrated that warm, wet cunt on the head of my cock just once. My control officially snapped at that touch.

"Klow-ee." I grabbed her hips, moving her against me in a rhythm I hoped we could both find pleasure with. I definitely did. Already, my cock twitched and leaked, ready to delve into her soft, slick depths. Needing release and wanting to garner that inside of her. But she wasn't ready, she'd said, and I would honor that. It would be so hard—because I was already *so hard*—but I'd honor it. I could only hope that this play led to something more.

As I pressed harder against her soft sex, Klow-ee leaned down, kissing me deeply. With her lips against my mouth, her cunt warm and soft against my cock, she groaned and rode me toward that point of pleasure where release was inevitable. I watched her, amazed at how beautiful she was in the throes of her passion, how her body moved so well over mine. How her softness begged for my touch. My sac tightened and my cock positively screamed for more, but Klow-ee wasn't through. Not yet. The human had more tricks for me.

In the huskiest voice I'd ever heard, she whispered, "I'm so wet for you."

Kill shot. Hunt over. Prey destroyed.

I groaned, my fingers clutching her thighs so tight, I knew I'd leave marks. "I can feel your wet cunt against me. You have no idea how much I want to be inside you right now."

I wanted to do more than feel her, though. I wanted to taste that cunt. Wanted to feel her juices on my tongue and savor every drop of that precious arousal. Wanted to know what sliding inside that wetness would do to me. But my Klow-ee only wanted to play, so I would do the next best thing to pressing my cock inside her. I would fulfill at least one need of hers—and one want of my own.

As Klow-ee moaned, I grabbed her thighs and pulled her up the length of my body until her sweet cunt was directly above my face. The women of my kind didn't mate unless fertile and ready for a cub, but that didn't mean they didn't seek pleasure. I was well skilled with my hands and mouth. I could satisfy my female, and I would. For as long as she'd let me.

With one finger, I moved aside the thin fabric between me and her swollen cunt, and then I dove in.

"Cutlass," Klow-ee gasped, clinging to the pillows under me as she rode my face.

"What is this?" I asked, taking a long swipe through her beautiful cunt. Licking the length of her before pulling away once more. "Is this the mouth mating that kiss-sing is not?"

Klow-ee groaned, her legs shaking under my hands. "Oral...oral sex. It's called oral sex."

"Is that all?" I flicked the little ball of flesh I found at the apex of her sex, loving the way she jumped and moaned. "Oral sex doesn't roll off the tongue well. I prefer licking your sweet cunt. Can we call it that instead?"

Her moan was more than the answer I needed. I dove back in,

spreading her lips with my fingers and working my tongue over her softest flesh. Her taste ran down my throat, and her scent positively smothered me. If this was Klow-ee's version of play, I'd definitely do this all night. And all day. Every second.

I flicked the little ball again. The feel of it against my tongue brought me much pleasure, and Klow-ee twitched when I licked it. Moaned when I circled my tongue around it. She positively jerked and screamed when I sucked it between my teeth. Interesting.

"Fuck, Cutlass. Do that again." She trembled in a way that told me paying attention to that little flesh brought her much pleasure, too. So I flicked it again, then brought it between my lips.

Klow-ee slammed her hand down on the headboard. "Yes, fuck."

I'd be doing that again, but not yet. First, I needed to tease a bit more.

"What else is it called?" I gave that little ball another swipe, unable to pull my mouth away from it or her. "What am I doing to you? Teach me your words."

"Cunnilingus. Going down. Fuck, giving me the best..." Klow-ee shook and moaned as she grabbed my mane and pulled me even closer. "Eating me out."

Had I not been devouring the taste of her need, I would have laughed. No wonder she'd flushed so pleasantly when I'd offered to *eat her out*. The translator had put the words together in that order, but apparently, it was wrong. I'd have to remember that.

But we could laugh about that miscommunication later, because right then, I had Klow-ee's cunt on my tongue, and I wasn't giving that up. Wouldn't take the time away from her sweetest taste to talk more.

I licked a single line from back to front, suckling the little ball of flesh before diving back inside her with my tongue. I couldn't contain the purr, the sound of pleasure my people gave when close to sexual release. Klow-ee gasped and jerked, falling forward as she quivered all around my tongue.

"Coming, coming... Oh, fuck. I'm coming."

The translator images were extreme and filthy, adding to my enjoyment and perfect inspiration for finishing off my female's rush to release. But I wanted more from her. I wrapped my arms around her thighs and pulled her closer so I could pay more attention to the little ball between her flesh. She screamed, pulling and yanking my mane as she orgasmed on my tongue. As I pushed her over that edge two more times. As I drove her through her sexual releases to the point she could no longer sit up on her own. And when I was done, when Klow-ee lay beside me groggy and sated, I finally searched for my own release. Three strokes of my hand was all it took, and I spilled with her name on his lips. Her taste on my tongue. Her flesh against my side.

Next time, I could only hope to spill my seed with my cock inside of her. But only after I told her my truth.

CHAPTER SEVEN

CHLOE

I was pretty sure I'd died at some point. Killed by cunnilingus. The joke of *what a way to go* flitted through my mind but I was too tired to give it the time it deserved, so I tucked it away for next time. Because there would definitely be a next time. I'd found the oral-sex jackpot with Cutlass, and unless he turned out to be an axe murderer or someone who hated puppies, I was keeping him around.

He was nice, too. It wasn't *just* the oral sex. Though...the oral sex was good enough on its own.

But I still needed to tell him my secrets. And man, I was not looking forward to that admission.

Hey, I totally lied about everything. Still want to snuggle?

Ugh.

Yeah, that wouldn't be dealt with quite so soon. The man had just rocked my sexual world... Deep thoughts could wait for the morning.

I pulled Cutlass closer and rested my head against his chest, blocking out all possibilities of futures and lies and secrets. And I slept.

———

There was something warm and solid against my back when my sex-addled brain came back online. Something soft but weighty over my waist, too. Odd. I opened my eyes and blinked against the golden light of a sunrise that definitely wasn't coming through one of my loft's filthy windows. Jesus, this place needed to invest in better curtains or something. I closed my eyes and recoiled from the brightness, but that same something hard held me in place.

Hard...weighty...with a blanket.

I was in a bed.

The hotel...the man...the hussiness of my vagina.

Oh lordy, I was in a bed, under the blankets, and with Cutlass at my back. At first, I was sure he'd wake up and be shocked to find me next to him. I knew that look—the wide eyes and momentary fuzziness of a man trying to figure out why his one-night-stand hadn't stood and left. But then I sank into his hold. Cutlass didn't seem to be that sort of guy, plus the agency had said we'd both be given two weeks. He'd had to come into this knowing he would be stuck with me for fourteen days. There should be no surprise. Not for him, at least.

For me? Yeah. The feel of warm skin and cotton against my skin—*all* my skin—gave me the surprise for the morning. I was naked. *Surprise!* I remembered riding Cutlass's face to orgasm—remembered that particularly well, if I was being honest—and I remembered all the dirty, nasty things he'd done with his tongue. Remembered and loved. What I did *not* remember was taking off my bra and panties. Which meant Cutlass removed them.

He undressed me while I slept.

I kind of wanted to be pissed about such a ballsy move, but really, that fucking lingerie was uncomfortable. I was glad it was all off and I wasn't waking up with underwire poking me in the breast. Good thinking, possible future husband.

That thought nearly killed my morning mojo. One night with the man treating me to a little Taco Tuesday, and I just accepted this could be something real? Just one? Where was my independence? My sense of self-preservation? I knew nothing of the man other than he was apparently the pussy whisperer. He could still hate puppies.

As my brain began to spiral into panicked thoughts of chains and rings and things I'd have to sign, Cutlass slid a warm hand across my waist. Pulling me even closer. Resting his head against the back of my neck in a comforting, secure sort of move that calmed me in a way nothing else could have. That stilled my brain, turning my thoughts from frenzied to sexual in the space of a second. Crisis averted...for the moment.

"I can hear you thinking. Sleep, my Klow-ee." He pulled me into the cradle of his pelvis as his lips pressed against my shoulder.

But I couldn't sleep. Cutlass was hard where my ass met his hips, hard and hot while I was already wet with desire. With thoughts of his fingers and lips, his dirty mouth and all I knew he could do with it. I wanted more than to ride his face again—though, I'd happily mount up at any point in the future. But first, I needed to explore a bit. To give him as much pleasure as he'd given me. I needed to know what that big dick felt like breaking me open. And I needed it immediately.

"Cutlass." I grabbed his hand and dragged it between my legs to where I was so ready for him. Leading his fingers to where I was already hot and wet. Letting him feel what he did to me. Letting him know what I wanted.

Cutlass took the hint well, rocking against me as he chuckled at my back. "Is my Klow-ee in need?"

"Yes," I whispered, moaning as he slid his thick, blunt fingers along my pussy. He zeroed in on my clit on his second pass, the pressure harsh but welcomed. The rub of those rough hands something to be thankful for.

"You want this?" he asked in a scratchy sort of voice, one filled with carnal promise. The Sam Elliott of the dating agency candidates, perhaps.

I jerked and moaned when he gave my clit a little pinch, just enough to make me gasp. Just enough to make me clench. "More."

He released a noise like a growl in response, rolling me forward a few inches to use his weight against me. To overtake me. "More how? Tell me what you want."

I rocked back, wanting to tease him as much as he teased me, pressing my hands against the nightstand for leverage. Rolling my ass into his hips and finding complete and utter joy when he hissed at my hips meeting his cock again.

"Tell me," he said.

I moaned, unable to deny that demanding tone of his. "Inside. Need you...inside."

Cutlass took that direction like a champ, sliding his other hand between my legs to slip a finger inside me. That meant I had one arm underneath me, one over, and much of his weight leaning on my back. I was surrounded by him. Captured in a way that left me little to no room to move. And I loved it.

"What is this?" he asked as he slid a second finger deep inside me. As he made me moan with the way he refused to let me go. "Teach me your words, Klow-ee. What am I doing to you?"

I rocked on his hand, loving the stretch of his fingers. Still ready for more. "Finger-bang, Cutlass. Fuck, you're...fingering or finger-fucking or finger-banging."

"Hmmm, interesting." He pressed deeper, still rubbing circles on my clit with his other hand. Still holding me against him. I spread my legs a little wider, looking for more, hoping for it. I needed him to fuck me. Had to have him inside me.

Had to.

As much as I hated to do it, I pulled on his wrists to get him to let me go. My pussy made a wet, sucking sound as he removed his fingers from it, but I didn't care. I was too far gone to give a shit. Besides, that sound proved he'd been doing something right. Long live the squelch.

Cutlass didn't try to hold me in place. Instead, he followed along, tracking my movements, matching them like a dancer follows their partner. Once I grabbed a condom from the nightstand drawer—I totally came prepared for this weekend—I rolled over completely. Sheathing him took less than ten seconds, then I pulled Cutlass with me until he was lying between my thighs, ending with his face barely inches above mine. The weight of him, the solidness, had my legs shaking and my pussy clenching on nothing. I needed to kiss him, wanted to pull him down and take his mouth with mine. That kiss was a must, a craving. An undeniable desire.

"Cutlass."

He grunted, rocking his hips and teasing me with the slow slide of his cock against me. Breathing hard even as he pulled back. "I should tell you..."

His body shook with what had to be his desire, his restraint obviously cracking. I wanted to break that willpower, to watch him let go and get all animalistic with me. I wanted him to be a little rough and demanding like he'd been the night before.

So I leaned up, biting his earlobe before whispering, "No more talking. Just fuck me."

He jerked back, his eyes darting to mine. That look, that need. I felt it, too. Understood it. I wrapped my legs around his hips and pulled him closer. Let his cock run all along my pussy, let him feel the heat and the wet he caused in me. Gave him permission.

Cutlass slid a hand between us to grab the base of his cock, keeping his eyes on mine. Looking like a man about to explode from need. I liked that look, his expression. It made me feel powerful and desired. Sexual.

He lined himself up just so, nudging the tip just inside, and then he shot me a cocky grin. "Hold on to me."

And I did. I grabbed hold of his shoulders and dug my fingers deep as he thrust inside. Every muscle tensed, every nerve ending fired at once. My moan when he bottomed out was something dark and gritty and altogether filthy, but I didn't care. He was huge. Long and hard and so much thicker than the other men I'd been with. And he used that girth to his advantage, splitting me open in ways no one ever had. Making me feel things no one before him could have. Good things. Dirty, intriguing things. Things I never wanted to end.

"What am I doing to you, Klow-ee?" he asked, his words punctuated by soft, guttural grunts as he set a pounding pace. "Teach me the words."

I groaned and pressed my feet against the mattress, lifting my hips to take more of him. Wanting every inch, every bit. Wanting every part of him. "Fucking me. You're fucking me, Cutlass."

And he did. He fucked me well.

———

"I wonder why they matched us." I dragged my finger along the carpet, the afternoon sun shining a little more white than the morning glow.

"Our letters," Cutlass said after a tense sort of pause. He placed a handful of openmouthed kisses along my shoulder blades, his hips cradling mine. "Your words matched mine somehow, and mine yours."

My arm stilled, my head heavy as I stared at the floor from where I hung precariously over the edge of the bed. That fucking letter.

"What if it wasn't the letter?" I asked, keeping my voice soft. Almost afraid of the answer.

"What else could it be?"

I rolled over, feeling somewhat hopeful. "Maybe something else. Like a feeling or a sense of something. Maybe Ampetheia just knew we'd be good together."

Cutlass pulled me in closer, his voice almost hesitant as he answered me. "Maybe. But the agency said it was the letters they used. They told me I would want to meet you from the first time I read your words."

I stared up at him, my heart heavy with guilt. He watched me with wary eyes of his own, as if the talk of the agency and the letters would somehow taint our day. As if we should forget how we came to be.

After a few silent moments, his lips greeted mine in a kiss that made my toes curl, but my mind was stuck on what he'd said.

...from the first time I read your words.

But what if all those words were a lie?

———

My dream was outstanding. There were hands and mouths all over my body, teasing me, bringing me closer and closer to the edge. I didn't attempt to escape, though the heavy weight across my thighs wouldn't let me anyway. Instead, I dreamed, floated, enjoyed the paradise around me. Warm beaches and gentle waves of the ocean. A handsome man rubbing sunscreen on my thighs. His head buried between—

I woke with a start to find my dream was partially reality. No beach, but Cutlass was between my thighs. I'd take that over sand in my bathing suit any day. As I groaned and grabbed hold of his hair to direct him, he worked his tongue against my clit like a champ. Like an expert. Like a man who knew exactly what I wanted.

Best wake-up call ever.

"Oh, God." I arched into his touch, wanting just a little bit more. Needing it. Biting my lip as that tension built in my lower gut. "Cutlass."

He didn't answer with words. No, that would be too easy. Instead, he reached up and grabbed my hand as he suckled my clit. Wove his fingers between mine as he wrapped his lips around me in what had to be the greatest move ever in oral sex. I crashed right into my orgasm, not building up to that point of almost painful anticipation. Nope. This was a full-on, assault-type O.

"Ffffffuuuuuuucccccckkkkkk."

My moan only spurred him on. He didn't let up for a second as I clenched and trembled. Oh no, he dove right back in. Thick fingers slid inside my still-quivering pussy, and he moaned against me as he continued to lick. That was just about the greatest feeling ever, and I fell right back through that pleasure wall into a second orgasm. Softer and smaller than the first time, but still so damn good. Cutlass kept going. Kept licking and thrusting and sucking and all-around being the greatest man who ever thought "huh, I wonder what would happen if I licked right there" the world had ever seen.

Or maybe that was the multiple orgasms talking.

CUTLASS

Her taste was like nothing I'd ever experienced. Warm and sweet, distinctly her. Addictive.

I would have liked to lap at her cunt forever, would have chosen to bury my tongue inside her and work her little ball of flesh with my fingers until she shook again and again and again. But my Klow-ee, she had other plans.

She pushed me away, almost growling when I tried to refuse her.

"Want more," she whispered.

And how could I deny her? I did as she directed, letting her go and rolling onto my back. Watching her. My cock hard and leaking as I waited for whatever *more* she needed.

She crawled over top of me, straddling my hips and letting her full breasts hang in my face. Such a teasing sight.

"Am I to suckle you, my Klow-ee?" I grabbed both breasts, rubbing hard, flicking her nipples with my thumbs. So soft, so perfect for my hands. I brought my mouth to one nipple, licking it carefully, watching her face for a reaction. She closed her eyes and rocked into my hold for a moment, obviously enjoying my attentions. But before I could pull that flesh between my lips, she smacked me away.

"Quit trying to distract me." With a quick kiss and a laugh, she sat up. Sat right on top of my aching cock. I'd never had a female mount me before, never been the submissive partner in bedgames. And while a small part of me resisted, the rest was ready to see where she would take this. What she had planned.

It didn't take long for her to show me.

She wrapped my cock in something thin and plastic again. Some sort of barrier. I didn't ask, though. I let her do what she wanted just as I had the first time she let me inside. She had me completely at her mercy, and I was thrilled to be there.

With a hand still wrapped around my cock, she placed the head right at her entrance. The tip slid in—just the tip—a total tease.

"What are you doing, sweet Klow-ee?"

"Payback." Klow-ee rocked slightly, letting me slide inside a small amount before retreating. Not pulling me all the way inside. Not giving us both what I knew we wanted. And doing so with a smile on her face.

"Klow-ee, please." I grabbed her hips, trying to pull her down on me, trying hard not to as well. This was her moment, her lead. And I had to follow at whatever pace she set. Even if it did feel as if she was trying to kill me.

"Am I driving you crazy?" she asked. The pictures from the translator made no sense, so I just nodded. Biting my lip as my hands clenched on her thighs. So tight and warm, and still too far away.

"Good." She sat back, sliding down my cock with a groan, both hands coming to rest on my chest. I grabbed them, hanging on to her, holding my breath as her cunt squeezed my cock like a vise.

"Have you ever had a girl on top?" she asked, rocking her hips over me to take more of my cock inside. I shook my head even as my eyes rolled back. The pressure was delicious, the weight of her on top of me an added bonus.

Deeper yet, her heat burning me in the best way. "Let me show you."

"Teach me," I said on a gasp as she pinched my nipples. "Teach me everything."

And as she settled deep, as her body allowed my cock to push in farther than it ever had before, as my eyes rolled into the back of my head at the heat and the pressure, I surrendered to her. And I died just a little bit with every move of her hips.

"I want to make you come," she said, moving in a way that caused my sac to pull up almost painfully. Such a wonderful pain, though.

Hands on her hips, thrusting up into her tight cunt, I gave her what she wanted with her name on my lips.

———

"What was she like?" I stared at my Klow-ee's shoulders, the way the light played across them. Warmed them. The single sun here may not have given off enough heat for my preference, but the way the glow changed colors as the planet moved about in its orbit was fascinating. Especially when mixed with my mate's stunning skin.

"Beautiful, strong, amazing. Strict. She worked hard, and she expected me to do the same."

I ran a hand up her thigh, not sliding anywhere interesting. Just giving her an affectionate sort of stroke. An I-can't-keep-my-hands-off-you touch. "How did she pass?"

Her muscles tensed, and I spread my fingers wider. Grounded her in my touch. I knew bringing up her mother would be difficult, but the shadows around us, the intimate feel of the night falling as we lay together, had made me slightly nostalgic over my own lost tribe. I wanted to know my human, and that meant discussing the bad and the good.

Klow-ee sighed, hiding her face from me. "*Drrunck drrie-vrr.* She was coming home from a midnight shift at the plant, and the guy claimed he never saw her car. I was fifteen and alone when the cops came to the door."

The pain in her voice gutted me, left me flayed like a beast of prey. I wanted to ease that, but I didn't know how. Didn't know the words to offer comfort, so I held her tightly and wrapped my body around hers instead. Holding her together.

"What about you?" Klow-ee asked, hitching her leg higher against his hip. "Where's your family?"

I grunted. "Gone."

"All of them?"

All of mine and then some, but she still didn't know who I was. What I was. She had no idea what life off of planet Earth was like. And this wasn't the time to explain. "Yes. I have two of my kind with me, but we're not kin. We are the last, though."

She was silent for a long moment, and I'd begun to think our conversation was over. Apparently not.

"The last of what?"

I pulled her closer, clinging to her soft body in silence. If she knew, if I told her the truth, would she still be willing to stay in my arms? Would she fear me as an unknown? Or would she accept me, us, our fragile bond? I couldn't know, and I wasn't ready to risk what I'd found. Not yet.

Without answering, I moved us so she rested almost on top of me once more. The warmth and weight of her body soothed a part of me. Brought on feelings of sleep and rest, even though we'd spent most of the day in bed. Not sleeping, of course. At least, not all the time. Still, the hour was growing late on her planet. It was time for animals to begin their long night of stalking prey in the shadows. Or lovers to play bedgames.

"Cutlass," she whispered as I rolled her onto her back and fitted my hips between her legs.

But my mind was still stuck on other things. On truth and facts and possible loss. I clung to her, rocking softly. Needing to claim her over and over again to prove my worth as a potential mate. "There is so much to tell you."

But instead of talking, my mate grabbed my neck and pulled me down to her lips. Kiss-sing me. Giving me her body as she spread her legs wider and rocked her hips to take me inside.

Words weren't always necessary, and some secrets could keep until the light of a new day.

CHAPTER EIGHT

CHLOE

If ever there was a time when I wanted to puke and cry at the same time, it was walking out of the hotel with Cutlass at my side. Okay, so walking was a stretch. I meant limping. The man had dicked me down for two solid days after a very long dry spell on my side. Muscles I'd completely forgotten about ached, and every inch of my pussy was overly sensitive.

Best weekend ever.

But all good things must come to an end, including our weekend immersion program. And my fantasy life.

"You could come with me," Cutlass said as we reached my car. My beat-up, junker of a vehicle that I had no idea how to explain if he asked why I drove such a piece of shit if I was a successful photographer. Oh God, this was such a bad idea. I should have told him. I needed to tell him.

"I have to work tonight," I said, my voice too soft, too weak. I swallowed hard, trying to keep my eyes on his, trying not to look like the liar I knew I was.

Being an adult was way too hard sometimes.

Cutlass pulled me into his arms, smiling down at me. Clueless that our fledgling relationship was based completely on lies. "Reschedule your clients. We have a lot to discuss and very little time to do so."

"Twelve days," I said, running my hands up and down his arms as visions of eviction notices and sleeping in my car danced through my addled brain. Along with what he'd look like once I admitted my truth. How angry he might be. "But I can't cancel. I...need to work."

He sighed in the most adorable way, still smiling, still clueless. "Okay. But I want to see you soon. I need to woo you more."

I nearly jumped when his hands landed on my ass. He gripped hard and pulled me close enough to feel his thick cock. Showing me his woo. Jesus, did the man ever go flaccid?

"I think we wooed enough this weekend for at least a month."

"Never," he murmured, giving me the softest kiss I'd ever had. "I will never get enough of you."

I melted...right around the rock lodged in my gut. Why wasn't I honest? If I could go back and rewrite my letter to the IGDA, I would to keep from having lied to Cutlass. But then, would they have placed me with him? Would we have matched? Would I have formed a connection with another man instead?

Knowing what I did, having spent two days alone with the man in front of me, that thought made me ill. I didn't want another match. I wanted Cutlass. But to get him, I'd have to be honest. Soon. Tonight.

"Tell you what," I said, pulling up my figurative big-girl panties and preparing to be a real adult. "How about you come by after I get off work? It'll be late, but we can talk. At my place."

At my shitty, disgusting apartment that in no way says successful anything, I thought but didn't say. No sense giving away the ending.

Cutlass answered exactly as I knew he would. "Tell me when, and I'll be there."

"Where's your phone?"

"Phone?" His head cocked.

"Yeah. Your cell phone."

I swear, the man shook his head as if he didn't have one. Ridiculous. With a shrug, I grabbed a pen from inside my bag and scribbled my phone number on his hand. Nineteen-ninety-two style.

"Call me later, and we'll set it up."

He nodded, diving in for one more kiss. Pressing me against the side of my junker in his fervor. Not that I was complaining. I was too busy trying my hardest not to drag him into the car and have a little high school style make-out session on the backseat.

"Okay," I gasped when he finally released my lips. My God, I needed to change my panties after that one. "I'm going."

He gave me a look of pure want, as if he hated letting me out of his sight. A turn-on for sure. "If you must."

"I must," I whispered almost to myself. Because I had a long day of slinging hot dogs and making myself sick with worry over what would happen when I finally told him. I gave him one more kiss, a final good-bye, and hurriedly escaped his roaming hands.

But when I slid into the car and turned the key, nothing happened. Not a rev, not a whine, not a thunderous backfire. Nada. *Fuck.*

"What's wrong?" Cutlass asked as I swore at the old beast.

"My battery's dead." I left off the *again* on that statement. The damn thing had given me trouble for months, but I'd been putting off buying a new one because...well, money. Hopefully, Cutlass would give my car a jump so I could get back to my side of the city. If not, I'd have to hunt down someone who could help. And I hated asking strangers for anything.

"Let me see." Cutlass, looking more than just mildly concerned, walked to the front of the car and pressed a hand against the hood.

I leaned out the window. "Actually, if your car is close—"

But my brain went completely blank as the scent of ozone overtook me. Staring, my eyes wide, I watched him raise the hood. The locked hood. The damn thing *popped up* without me having to pull the unlock lever. That was next to impossible on my old beater. I knew; I'd tried it a few times when I was alone and in a hurry. That lock was almost older than I was and wasn't easy to release, so there was no way he managed to unlatch it without me releasing it from inside the car. A fact that reminded me of other instances where things worked for Cutlass as they wouldn't for me. The door to the room, the thermostat. How was he doing these things?

Cutlass bent into the engine compartment, almost completely hidden behind the raised hood. Almost. There was a gap at the bottom where the hood met the actual car. I slouched in my seat so I could see him through that thin opening. Trying to be sneaky so he didn't notice I was spying.

But he wasn't looking at me; he was staring at the engine with a frown on his face. When he seemed to zero in on something—what, I had no idea—he glanced around as if someone could be watching him. An odd thing to do for sure, and something that made my blood run a little cold. Then he placed his hand on some part in the mass of mechanical things I'd tinkered with myself to keep the car running when I had no money. Parts that needed replacing and cleaning. Parts that he couldn't fix with just the flat of his palm. And he waited.

The air grew thick and hot, the smell of ozone heavy. Just like when he fixed the thermostat. Just like when he opened the hotel room door. Just like when he popped the locked hood.

And then the car started all on its own.

CUTLASS

The components making up Klow-ee's vehicle engine needed to be sent for scrap. I wasn't even sure my Reithhkoneccs could save the decrepit thing. But I had to try.

I glanced over both shoulders to verify I was not watched, just in case. Ampetheia would be angry if I was caught using my powers by a human, but I had to help Klow-ee. I didn't want her stranded or worrying over things I could easily solve. Usually solve, really, because her engine looked as if it was ready to be melted down. If I couldn't fix whatever was wrong with it, Maivehricck probably could. Hohddshoun wasn't as skilled as I was, but Maivehricck was the best of the three of us. He could repair almost anything without a lot of strain. Me? I wasn't as strong, so this was going to take a lot out of me. Something I didn't mind because it was Klow-ee I helped. I just couldn't let her actually see what I was doing.

With no humans in sight and Klow-ee behind the metal lid, the timing was as perfect as could be. I placed my hand against the filthy hunk of metal and let my Reithhkoneccs flow. Small parts and pieces fell into position, wires and sensors all aligning properly. It took only a few seconds to find the broken part. The unit, a power-keeping device, would need to be replaced, but I had enough energy to give it a temporary boost so Klow-ee could get to work. I'd bring Maivehricck with me later tonight so he could work on it while I wooed my new mate.

With a great rumbling grind, the engine finally fired and began to run. I dropped the lid, happy with the repair but knowing things were about to go bad for me. My own efforts to stay on my feet seemed even greater than what it took that motor to start. The power unit had completely drained me, leaving me feeling slightly foggy and offline. A bad spot to be in for sure as a non-earthling stuck in the middle of an all-human population. I needed to get back to my rented room, back to where I could recover out of sight. And that need only got worse the moment Klow-ee stumbled out of the car, staring at me in what I could only describe as fear.

"How'd you do that?"

She saw. I knew it, could tell by the surprised sound to her voice. She saw...she knew my secret. Or part of it. The agency had said to wait to tell her about what I was. To give her the full two weeks to get to know me so I could woo her.

The time to woo was over.

Still, words were hard with my body so drained. "I can fix things."

"Yeah, so can a mechanic, but they need tools and things. How'd you do—" she waved at the car "—all that. With nothing."

"I told you—"

"And the door to the room. And the thermostat. You fixed those things, too."

The translator unit released images for her words but slowly. It took me longer than it should have to answer her. "The door wasn't broken."

"Don't try to distract me," she yelled, looking fierce and ready for battle as I struggled to stand up. "The door was locked, and you *unlocked* it without a key. The thermostat was broken, and you fixed it. My car wouldn't start, but you made it. How did you do all that?"

Hadn't I already told her this? "I fix things."

"You said that."

Apparently, I had, but I couldn't remember through the fog in my mind. This was it, my one chance to explain myself to her, and I was blowing it because I couldn't keep my thoughts straight. That wouldn't do. Readying myself for a battle I absolutely had to fight and win, I took a deep breath and held out my hand in her Earth greeting. "I am Cutthlaise, Reithhar Warrior of the planet Xouthhgros and Master Machinist for the former BHG489-2140 Colony."

She retreated a step. "Planet...what?"

When she didn't take my hand, I let it fall back to my side. My esehhnce felt as if it was breaking inside, as if it was being torn in two. I'd wooed her, claimed her with my cock, and spent hours learning how to please her. Could she be so afraid of me now simply because I fixed things?

"Klow-ee," I said, trying to keep my voice loud enough for her to hear me. Exhaustion quickly weighing me down. "I'm not from here."

"No shit," she said, a rough laugh escaping her. "But not from here and magically fixing a car are two different things."

Calm. Detailed. Explain the process, and the answer will be found. "My kind, we have skills that yours do not. Power seems to be the word from your language, though it's hard to know for sure right now." I ran a hand through my mane, my head beginning to ache from the effort of speaking. "My power is as a machinist. I can fix things—get parts to work when they shouldn't any longer."

She paced the length of her car, staying far away from me. "Where are you from?"

"Planet Xouthhgros originally."

"So you're...an alien?"

I was too tired to control my words. "Non-earthling, yes."

She fell back, retreating farther from me and inching closer to her vehicle as her voice began to shake. "What is this? Some kind of joke? Aliens aren't real. Are you here to make me fall for you and then lie like this?"

"No. This is me." My words were low and deep, holding a promise I didn't know if she would understand. "I don't know your *joe-cke*, but I'm definitely real. I'm Cutthlaise, Reithhar Warrior of the planet Xouthhgros and Master Machinist for the former BHG489-2140 Colony. My planet was destroyed many seasons ago, so I moved to a colony on the planet BHG489 with the few of us who were left. I was on a hunting trip when that colony was also destroyed. Those of us who survived have been looking for a place to reside ever since."

Words were hard with my body so depleted. I fell back against the car, catching myself on the edge before I crashed to the ground. Holding myself up with one hand. Klow-ee didn't seem to notice, though.

"You're an alien." She nodded, pacing once more, making my head spin with the back-and-forth. "Of course, you're an alien. Why would I think a mail order bride dating agency would set me up with a normal *gg-iee?*"

Before I could find the energy to speak, Klow-ee spun to face me. Her eyes stretched wide, and her face flushed.

"Does the agency know about this? About...you?"

I bobbed my head, the weight of it pulling me forward. "Of course. They service beings from all over the galaxies to help us find compatible mates."

If her reaction was any indication, that wasn't the answer she wanted to hear. "Mates. What the fuck do you mean, *mates?*"

"My kind searches with our esehhnces to find the one being who can make us happy. True partners to share a life with." Just speaking of mates and knowing how much I hoped to bond with her that way gave me a jolt of need. I crept closer, unable to resist even as she retreated a step.

"Cutlass—"

"Klow-ee, please," I said, pulling on every bit of strength I had. Wanting so badly to calm her in any way I could. Needing to. "I am still me. Still the man who took you to eat out and kiss-sed your sweet lips. The man who stayed up all night to learn everything I could about you. The man who pleasured you with my tongue and cock."

"I know what we did, but..." The anger fell from her face, leaving behind a look that broke something inside of me. An expression of loss. "But you're not human."

Her whispered confession burned, fueling a deep pain inside of me. A fissure of my very esehhnce.

"No, I'm not," I said, trying hard to keep her talking to me. "But I can pretend to be for others. When it's needed, I can act human. Not with you, though. I can't be dishonest with you, my Klow-ee. I don't want to be."

"Dishonest? This is more than just dishonest. It's not as if you lied on—" Her face paled, and she took a step back, fumbling for the vehicle door. "I can't do this. I can't... I have to go."

If there was a human word for the level of pain I felt at her rejection, I didn't know it. But the unending ache was there, deep inside me and throbbing. It was real and all because she was leaving.

"Klow-ee, wait." I reached as if to grab her, my fingers barely brushing her arm as I stumbled slightly on heavy legs, but she recoiled violently.

"No." She shook her head and climbed back into her vehicle, slamming the door and creating a barrier between us. A wall of sorts. One she was not going to let me through. "I need to think. I'll...call you."

And then she was gone.

CHAPTER NINE_

CUTLASS

It took hours to find my way back to the room I shared with Hohddshoun and Maivehricck. I couldn't concentrate on directions and roads, couldn't sense the way back. All I could do, all I could see, was Klow-ee's pained expression. Her anger and fear. Her hate of me.

I had destroyed the fragile bond between my human and me.

When I finally reached the building where we housed, I climbed the stairs with no energy left. This day, this entire weekend, had wrecked me. I needed to recharge so I could work out what to do about my Klow-ee. I needed to rest.

"He's returned," Maivehricck yelled as I opened the door. Both men came to the hallway, Maivehricck looking as surly and angry as ever, while Hohddshoun seemed so much more hopeful. A feeling I did not reciprocate.

"How was it?" Hohddshoun asked. "Is she your mate?"

"I don't know." I pushed past them, needing my bed.

"Why not?" Hohddshoun blocked my way. "What are human females like? Did you claim her? You only have two weeks to set the match and convince her to mate with you. Do you know—"

There was something so satisfying about my fist meeting his face.

"Yes, I claimed her physically. Yes, I think I may have found my mate." I shoved past a staggering Hohddshoun. "She has rejected me, though."

It was Maivehricck who finally stopped me. "Explain."

I didn't want to. I didn't want to think the words, let alone say them. But the three of us had come to this place together, had all signed up to be matched. I was the first, the leader in this process, and they were depending on me for information.

Information I did not want to give them.

"I told her what I was, and she ran. She does not want to be mated to a non-earthling."

His heavy brow dipped. He didn't deal with the humans much. He didn't understand their ways. I didn't understand their ways.

"I need to take these lenses out of my eyes and rest," I said, almost too tired to stay on my feet.

He grunted. "My regrets, friend."

Hohddshoun was still far more optimistic, even after the punch. "It'll work out. Your esehhnce will croon for her and bring you together."

But I was past the point of believing such things. "She doesn't want me."

Maivehricck stared at me, giving me that deep look he had mastered many seasons before. The one that said he saw through every deception and knew your truth. "You have two weeks. Either you convince her, or you lose her. Your choice, really."

But it wasn't. It was Klow-ee's. And I had no idea how to reach her to even attempt to convince her to stay with me. Just the scrawled symbols on my hand that I would have to ask Ampetheia how to read. First, though, I needed a shower and to sleep.

———

The next morning dawned bright and cheerful, a stark contrast to my mood. The scrawls on my hand were gone, the only possible link to Klow-ee having disappeared. And when I stopped by to ask Ampetheia for help, she told me she couldn't give me information on an applicant and kicked me out. I hated that first morning. And the morning after that. And the morning after that. Days passed in an endless stream of sun and misery and waiting, and still no Klow-ee. Still no way to reach her. Still no clue what to do as the end of the two weeks drew near. I could hardly breathe the longer we stayed apart. Klow-ee was gone, and there was nothing I could do. I felt utterly helpless—something I'd never once experienced before—and it was all Hohddshoun's fault.

I was going to kill him for setting me up for this disappointment.

"She may come around," he said, ever the optimist. Maivehricck grunted, though that sound could have meant he agreed or disagreed. He tended to be the dark side to Hohddshoun's light, so I figured he disagreed. As did I.

"She left me the moment her door closed. Ran away from me as if I would harm her. She did not even seem to want to look at me."

"But you think she's your mate."

"Yes, I did." *And I still want her to be mine*, I thought. But those words carried pain with them, something I didn't want to keep piling on myself. So I kept them inside, refusing to admit my failure.

Hohddshoun shrugged as if this was nothing. As if there were options. As if my world hadn't crashed around me the moment Klow-ee ran.

"Then it will work out."

If he'd been standing any closer, I'd have punched him again.

"Come," he said as he headed for the door. "I want to check with the agency on my match. We can ask them about your Klow-ee again."

"Ampetheia won't help."

He shrugged. "So we skip Ampetheia and charm the female at the desk. Or we try to access the information ourselves. Either way, I have a good feeling about today. It's time for a mated pairing."

As much as I wanted to ignore him, anything would be better than sitting around and waiting. I jumped up, unable to resist the temptation of any sort of news regarding her. Perhaps Ampetheia would tell me something this time. If Klow-ee checked in. If she was okay.

If she'd requested placement with another male.

Ampetheia was standing at the front desk when we walked in, almost as if she was waiting for us. As if she knew we were coming. There went the charm-the-other-female idea.

"Ah, two of my three warriors. How are you today? Cutlass, how are things going with Klow-ee? Your time period is almost up, you know."

I growled, looking away even as my heart jumped. Klow-ee must not have requested a new placement if Ampetheia still thought we'd complete the bond. That had to be good news.

Hohddshoun jumped in with an answer when I didn't. "They haven't been able to reconnect yet, but it'll work out."

Ampetheia's happy expression dropped. "I see. So then, what can I do for you two today?"

Hohddshoun gave her a smile, the one he'd been practicing. "I was hoping my match had been found."

"We can certainly check," Ampetheia said, her glittering eyes darting from Hohddshoun to me and back again. "Why don't you come with me?"

We followed the female to the back office where she'd told me about Klow-ee the first time. Where she'd explained customs and woo, made sure my translation core was functional for the language on this planet, and walked me through what would likely happen. Of course, my Klow-ee hadn't responded as expected, so those lessons had been a waste. So much time to prepare myself for my human. So many long days ago since I'd had a chance to speak with her. Too many.

Ampetheia was right... My time was up.

"I'm surprised to hear about you and Klow-ee," Ampetheia said, focusing that hunter's gaze on me as she settled behind her computer. "That match should have been ideal."

I sighed, glaring at Hohddshoun. "Apparently not."

"Perhaps she'll come around," Hohddshoun said, still trying to bolster my emotions. An impossible task.

I had long grown tired of everything Hohddshoun tried. "If you say that again, perhaps I'll gut you and serve your offal for breakfast."

"Behave, boys," Ampetheia said as she typed away, frowning. "I'm sorry, Hohddshoun—off, that's a mouthful. Your name won't translate. How about we go with...Hudson? Sounds similar enough."

My soft growl was ignored as Hudson accepted his new name.

"And my match?" he asked, ever the focused hunter.

"Your match isn't ready. Not quite yet, but we're close. If I had more time..." Ampethei sighed and shrugged her sharp shoulders. "There are just too many applicants and not enough of me. Plus, they're all coming here and expecting me to find them a place to live as well as a mate."

I understood that need. Hohddshoun—or Hudson now—Maivehricck, and I had come to Earth without a place to call home either other than the ship we couldn't bring into the atmosphere. Humans tended to fear such things, so we'd left it hovering near earth's single moon and utilized a portal Ampetheia set up for us. That didn't mean we could go back and forth, though. Once on earth, we needed to stay put so our skin could adjust to the atmosphere and fade to a human-like color. We had spent three nights tucked into one of the extra offices at the dating agency, stealing rest where we could.

Luckily for us, Maivehricck had managed to find work that allowed the three of us to rent a room by our fourth night on the planet. But the other beings...all coming and hoping to find a match like I had found with Klow-ee. They might not be so lucky.

Ampetheia shook her head, confirming my own thoughts with her words. "The next group may end up sleeping on the street, which will cause real problems should they change forms in the presence of a human. I need a big *were-howss* to store them all, then I could concentrate on matching faster."

"I don't know what this *were-howss* is," Hudson said, sounding fierce and ready to go out and kill whatever stood in his way. "But I will find you one. I will bring it to you so you can match me to my mate."

"You're cute," Ampetheia said while baring her teeth in that not-scary way she did. "A warehouse is a big building here on Earth, and I'm having trouble finding one that I can turn into rentable space. But I will, and then I promise I will focus on matching you, Hudson."

He left without another word, probably too disappointed to say much more. As optimistic and happy as the guy tended to be, he'd placed all his hopes on finding a mate through the agency. He'd even stayed positive when I matched first. Obviously, his patience had been wearing thin.

But before I could deal with raising his spirits, there was something I needed. "My Klow-ee, she didn't accept that I was not human."

Ampetheia's eyes went wide, and she scowled. "Why didn't you tell me that straightaway? That changes everything. She'll be cut from the program immediately." She shook her head and sighed. "I apologize, Cutlass. Her letter indicated an open mind and an acceptance of—"

I cut her off with a growl. "She is my match, and I care for her. She wrote something on my hand, a way to reach her, but it came off when I showered. I haven't heard from her in almost two weeks, and I worry. I want to find her. I need to know where she lives."

Ampetheia sat back, looking almost sad. "As I've told you, I can't share that info if she didn't give it to you. That wouldn't be right."

I slammed my fist on the desk. "What's not right is that we lied to her about what I am. That hurt her. Now I want to make sure she's safe and cared for. If she refuses me again, I'll leave her be, but I have to try one last time. Give me some way to contact her, Ampetheia. I have only hours left of our two-week period, and if you don't help me find her, I will never know if she is truly the female for me."

"You have found your true mate," she said. A statement, not a question. And an accurate one.

"Maybe. I think so, at least. I can't know without seeing her again, but it certainly feels that way. But that doesn't matter. I want her safe and cared for, whether she chooses to accept me or not. I need to know she's okay with everything and has a way to reach me should she ever need to." I swallowed hard, focusing on my thoughts of Klow-ee, on the aching need inside of me to find her. "I need her to be happy, even if it's without me."

Ampetheia sat back in her chair and watched me for a long time. The invasiveness of her stare grated, but I held my ground. Needing her to understand how I felt. Wanting her to know my true desires. And maybe she did.

"I sincerely hope things work out for the two of you." She scribbled something down and handed me a slip of paper. "The address on her paperwork is different than the one on her identification. When I asked, she said she'd just moved. My guess is this is the correct one."

The paper had a bunch of lines and circles I couldn't understand, but I'd find someone who did. This time, I'd make sure not to lose out on my lead.

"Thank you, Ampetheia." I was already halfway out the door when Ampetheia called after me.

"Good luck, Cutlass."

I grunted and kept moving. Luck would have nothing to do with this hunt.

CHLOE

"Yo, where's my patty melt?"

I sighed, closing my eyes and sending up about the fifteenth prayer of the afternoon. *God save that asshole at the counter if he doesn't shut up.* I probably should have played nice—offered him a free pop or something for his not-all-that-long wait—but I wasn't in the mood.

"Hold your horses, mister. It's coming."

There went my tip.

It'd been a long couple of weeks of working, crying, and regretting. I never should have left Cutlass the way I did. I never should have judged him for lying to me when I'd been lying to him just as much. Okay, maybe not just as much—I was human, after all—but still. It wasn't as if I was upfront about anything. Still, I felt like an ass. I let my fear of the unknown get the better of me and didn't give him a chance to explain. And I wanted to give him that chance, wanted to let him teach me about himself and see if we could maybe build something together, species be damned.

I wanted to talk to him.

Too bad I killed my phone the day after I left him in that parking lot and therefore had no way to contact him or to know if he was trying to reach me. And with no money to replace the thing, I was completely stuck. I couldn't even reach Amelia to ask for help. I had thought about simply walking over to the agency, but I had a feeling they wouldn't want to help me. Not after I backed out of the match without a word. So I worked, and I cried when I got home every night, and I wondered where my alien man was and if he was thinking of me.

And I didn't put up with customers' bullshit for a measly dollar tip.

Standing at the pickup window, the scent of fried onions and ground beef positively smothering me, I knew I needed to make a change. If I wanted Cutlass, I needed to go after him. I'd been the one who ran, I should be the one who came crawling back. Worries be damned, I needed to go to the agency and see if I could get Cutlass' information from the scary woman who'd matched us. I missed him, and I could only hope he'd missed me as well.

When the patty melt finally came up, I stalked to Mr. Short-Squat-And-Cranky at the counter and tossed the plate in front of him.

"Hey," he yelled, looking all how-dare-you at me.

"Try some manners, jerkface."

Before the guy could spit in my face or anything else he was probably planning, Kelly, my coworker and another girl who lived in the same so-called apartment building I did, came strolling in. And the bitch was smiling.

God, I so wanted to hate her at that moment, but the fact we had to wear this shitshow of perverted fifties housewife waitress dresses with socks, shoes, and a frilly fucking apron seemed like punishment enough. Though, at least hers looked clean.

"Hey, grumpy," she said, sounding like some sort of smoked-up Snow White.

"Shut up." I sighed and walked to the back, pulling my apron off on the way. Another day, another couple of dollars that wouldn't be enough to pay the rent or fix the car. I was screwed in so many ways, none of them good. But I was going to attempt to fix at least one.

"Taking off already?" Kelly asked as I passed her.

"Yeah. Shift's done, and I have an errand to run."

"Okay. Be careful, though. There was some guy pacing outside the building when I left."

"Pacing?"

"Yeah. Tall and handsome as fuck, but he was mumbling under his breath about something to do with a claw. And he kept staring at the building."

Claw. That sounded...odd. And possibly like how Cutlass said my name. Klow-ee.

What if...

"Thanks, Kelly. See you later." I hurried out the door and turned toward home. I knew I shouldn't get my hopes up, but it was hard to fight them. It might not be him, though. How would Cutlass find me, and why would he even try? I was the asshole who left him. The one who ran because of something as stupid as what he was. If anything, he should have left me.

But as I turned the corner, I recognized that shock of dark hair. The broad shoulders. The stride of the man who'd stolen my heart in a weekend, human or not.

Cutlass.

I must have said the word aloud because he spun, staring. Not moving. He was there, really and truly right in front of my place. He'd come back for me. He'd found me. And I needed to get to him right that second.

This time, I didn't just think his name. I yelled it. "Cutlass!"

And he ran.

CHAPTER TEN_

CUTLASS

Klow-ee.

The word sounded like a wail in my head, a primal scream I couldn't ignore. She was there, all wide eyes and soft skin. Staring as if she was happy to see me. As if she'd hoped I would be there. And maybe she had. All I knew was I didn't want to wait to find out, so I ran.

I ran to Klow-ee with my esehhnce crooning loudly only for her...my mate.

She leaped straight into my arms when I finally reached her. A moment of complete and utter abandon and reconnection. I'd never felt such relief, never wanted a female more. I had never experienced desire until I had my chosen mate in my grasp.

I pulled her smaller body against mine, relishing her weight on me. Her heat. So much warmth from one little human. I'd missed that about her, missed everything. And when her arms came up around my neck to hold me even closer, I was finally able to breathe again. This was what I'd wanted, what I'd hoped for. My esehhnce knew Klow-ee was the only female for me. I simply had to convince her of that.

"I missed you," I said, nuzzling into her neck and breathing her in. Almost shaking with the need to touch and claim.

"Cutlass, I'm so sorry."

My name on her lips sent all my blood to my cock. My mate was in my arms once more, and I wanted to bed her immediately. Needed to show her how much she meant to me and how much I desired her. I wanted everything, and I would do whatever it took to get it. Hands grabbing flesh, esehhnce crooning, and cock slick with my seed, I let my mating rumble loose. Let her hear and feel that vibration from my chest.

When she whimpered slightly and rocked herself against my hard cock, I swooped down and pressed my lips to hers, unable to resist the sweetness of her mouth for a second. I also thrust against her perfect cunt. I wanted to reclaim that as well—with both my mouth and my cock. Wanted that so badly, it hurt. Klow-ee was talking in between hurried kiss-ses, though, issuing words I didn't need to hear. *Sorry...so stupid...got scared...never again.* I slid my tongue against hers to quiet her, to end her apologies. Those words wouldn't matter, not if she accepted me. Not if she claimed me back. My Klow-ee. My mate.

I had to ask her. Had to make sure she understood. Because once I claimed her for real, there would be no going back. If I let that bond solidify, she'd never be free of me. And while that thought appealed to me greatly, Klow-ee might not be ready. She might not desire me the way I did her. And as much as that would hurt, I'd honor her choice. I'd have to.

I pulled away reluctantly, letting her legs drop to the ground, still clinging to her arms. "We need to talk."

Her lips turned down, her smile falling. "Those are the worst words in the Een-gllisch language."

That...couldn't be. "Why?"

"Because they usually lead to bad things. Like breakups."

"No. No bad things." I pulled her closer again and pressed my lips to her nose. "Only good from now on, yes?"

"Yes. Totally." She laughed and tossed her head back, looking up at me with such joy on her face. "We do need to talk, though. Would you like to come inside?"

Ah, those filthy images again from the translator. My favorites.

"I want to come inside you very much." I growled and slid my hands down to grab her round, firm backside. "But we should probably get off the street first."

She stared at me for a moment, her eyes wide, and then she laughed. Loudly. "At some point, you're going to have to tell me where you learned the Een-gllisch language."

"I haven't." I followed her inside, pushing the door open and letting her pass before me. Keeping her in my sights so I didn't lose her again. "At birth, all Reithhar have a translation module implanted so they can travel as needed. The agency sent the necessary coding to the module so I could speak and understand Een-gllisch, though it's obviously not always correct."

"No, it's not. But at least it's entertaining." She came to a huge door in a hard, stone wall. A pink notice was mounted to it, and her face crumpled when she saw it. "Shit."

"What is it?" I asked, unable to read the symbols. The translation module showed me pictures of excrement from her spoken word. That couldn't be right.

"*Ee-vickschion noe-tiss.*" She shrugged, her eyes watery and sad when they met mine. "At least something good happened today, right? I mean, I got *ee-vicktted,* but you came back."

"What is *ee-vickschion?*"

"The owners of the building are kicking me out. I haven't been able to pay my rent on time for months, though I never missed a payment completely. Looks like they stopped giving me time to make it up."

"They will make you leave?"

"Yes. They will." She paused, her hand on the door, her head hanging. Still blocking the way inside. "I wasn't honest with you, Cutlass. In my letter. I said I was some fancy, successful photographer, but I lied. I'm just a waitress at a crappy *koe-nee ie-lahnd* down the street."

"Klow-ee, you didn't lie to me," I murmured, pulling her closer. "I never read your letter."

She jerked back, yanking herself from my hold. "What?"

Guess she wasn't ready for that bit of information. "I can speak your Een-gllisch, but I can't read it. The agency handled that aspect. They wrote almost all of my letter because my native language would be too hard to understand."

"So...you never read my letter?"

"No."

"You don't care that our match was made based on lies?"

"Our match was made based on Ampetheia's feelings, not our letters. She's a Freknal."

"What's a Freknal?"

I let the pictures play out in my head, searching for the right one. The right word. "I believe you say *emm-pahthh*? She senses emotional ties between people. The letters keep her from being found out by you humans because you're not accustomed to that sort of being."

Klow-ee stared at me for a long, silent moment. I wanted her to react, to answer so we could end this conversation. Then, I could push her inside and throw her down on the floor. I wanted to rut against her like an animal. Two weeks without my mating bond being completed was far too long. I needed her. Immediately.

But she wasn't finished yet. "My mind is blown."

That definitely didn't translate. "I don't understand."

"It's okay. I'm just feeling dumb. First the *ee-vickschion*, now the whole 'the letters didn't matter' thing. I'd stayed away because I thought you'd be mad that I lied. I mean, you didn't call..." Her eyes went wider, and her mouth fell open. "You couldn't read my number. Is that why you never called?"

"The scribbles on my hand?" I grunted when she nodded. "No, I didn't know what that was, and they disappeared after I showered. I fought with Ampetheia to give me your information, but she wouldn't. Not until today."

She sagged against the door. "Thank God she finally did."

Purring, I pulled her against me and pressed my hard cock into her hip. Curling over her and letting my hands wander as I surrendered to my need to touch her. "I ran here as soon as I found a human to tell me where to go. I'm sorry it took so long to find you."

Klow-ee moaned, her little, blunt teeth pressing into my shoulder as she rocked against me. "I am such an idiot."

Her bite caused my cock to jump, and I was done. Done waiting, done talking, done with everything except claiming her as mine. I pressed my hand against where her door locked and let my Reithhkoneccs go to work. The lock popped quietly within a breath. Perfect.

I pushed her through with a growl, pressing her back against the wall as the door closed behind us. "Don't call yourself names, my Klow-ee. I won't have anyone be cruel to you, not even yourself."

Her breaths came fast and hard, and her eyelids drooped in the most inviting way. "Your Klow-ee?"

My rumbling growl turned deeper, and I couldn't help but stroke her pretty face. "If you'll have me, then yes. I want you as my mate. As my partner in life. I will care for you and protect you always, give you every bit of pleasure you desire. I will do anything for you."

"And what do I need to do to accept?"

I pressed my lips to hers, letting our tongues tangle for the briefest of moments. Needing another taste of her before I answered in the simplest of ways.

"Say yes."

But she didn't. She pushed me away, pulled herself right out of my arms and strolled across the room as if I hadn't just laid my heart bare in front of her. As if she wasn't holding my very life in her hands.

"Klow-ee?" I leaned against the wall, practically holding on to it to stay still. Too afraid of her rejection to make a move. Earth girls were so hard to figure out.

She turned, placing her finger to her lips and giving me a smile. That had to be a good sign. She wouldn't bare her teeth so nicely if she were going to refuse me. Would she?

"I'm thinking," she said, still walking. Still looking at me with something akin to lust in her eyes. Thinking was good, I figured. It meant she was considering. Pondering. Possibly accepting. I refused to think of the other outcome.

As she walked and thought, she also stripped. Her dress fell to the floor first, followed by her shoes as she kicked them off. Then her socks. She was walking and thinking in nothing but white fabric covering her breasts and cunt, and I was hard as stone watching her. Those curves, that long body. All that soft skin. It was mine. Every inch. And I wanted to touch it, taste it, explore it.

My hand slid to my cock almost of its own will. Pressing hard to relieve the ache as I growled a low, "Klow-ee."

She hooked her fingers in the fabric along her hips, and I growled once more. Unable to control the sound of need. That sound made her skin prickle with bumps, made the flush grow from her chest outward.

She liked it when I growled like a beast. My mate took pleasure from seeing that side of me. I would need to remember that fact.

"Cutlass." She turned her back to me and looked over her shoulder, giving me a flirty wink as she put one knee on her bed. "Yes."

There was no delay, no pause. She said yes, and I was on her, pushing her down on the mattress. My chest to her back, my cock against her ass. I surrounded her with my body—my arms around her chest and pulling her tight, my legs on either side of hers, my teeth holding on to the muscle curving from her neck to her shoulder. I was all over her, and I loved it.

And if the scent of her arousal permeating the air around us was any indication, my Klow-ee did as well.

"You want to fuck me from behind, Cutlass?"

It took me a second to understand her words, to flash through the information the translator provided, but when I did, they hit me hard. It was as if a shot of lust had been injected into me. I rutted against her without thought, searching for some sort of relief from the ache in my cock, seeking something only she could give me at that moment.

"Yes, Klow-ee." I fumbled with my clothes, stripping quickly while still trying to hold her down. To pin her. I had to be in control for the claiming, had to be the one leading. Afterward, because there would be many afterwards, she could crawl back on top and have her way with my cock. I looked forward to it, in fact. But not this time.

"Like this," I grumbled as I yanked the fabric from her hips. "Need you like this."

"Doggie style," she said, pulling the fabric around her breasts off. "It's called doggie style."

She rolled up onto her hands and knees. Bent for me. Her plump backside in the air and her head against the mattress. That pink cunt completely on display only for me. A lovely visage from where I knelt behind her.

"Klow-ee," I whispered, caught between wanting to mount her and wanting her to accept me. Needing to make sure one last time that she understood. That she knew. "I can't handle it if you run again. You've accepted me as your mate. I...I wouldn't let you go this time. I'd have to hunt you. I would never hurt you, but I'd track you forever if you disappeared. I care too much not to."

She shivered, but her eyes stayed locked on mine. "I'm not seeing a problem here."

"Klow-ee—"

"I won't try to run again." She grabbed my hand and gave it a squeeze before dropping it to her hip. "I promise, Cutlass. I want you as much as you want me. I promise we'll talk things out as they come up, but right now, I need you inside me. Please."

The mating rumble practically exploded from my chest. I grabbed my leaking cock and lined myself up, never looking away from her beautiful face. Ready to give her everything. To slide inside that tight heat and make her shake, make her quiver and clench on my cock. To wrap my arms around her and hold her tight, never letting go as I brought her pleasure over and over again. I was ready to make her mine.

To claim her as my mate.

CHLOE

"My Klow-ee. My mate." Cutlass had a reverent tone to his voice, a deep and wistful sort of need. One that spoke to me.

"Cutlass," I whispered. "Take your mate."

He pushed his way inside. I say pushed because it was no sliding or nudging. It was one thrust, one great, growly, full-body move forward, and then he was there. So deep in there. And oh my, but he felt good.

I cried out, clinging to the sheets, closing my eyes against the stretch and the burn as my nerves fired off a sky full of fireworks. "Holy fuck."

He dragged his cock almost all the way out and pushed back in, still keeping solid pressure on my body. Holding me down, in a way. I'd never been the biggest fan of this position, but with Cutlass? Yeah. Doggie style just might be my new best friend.

His thrusts moved me up the mattress, and the sheets tangled beneath me. Not that I could give a rat's ass about that. Because his fervor, his complete lack of control, was making him rub all up and down my body, hitting me in all those spots that made my toes curl and the lights go out.

Automatic G-spot finder...every girl needed one.

I came for the first time on an inward thrust that made Cutlass grunt and shake. But my guy, my alien, wasn't done yet. Not by a long shot. He continued at a steady pace, pushing in and out with a smoothness that had me climbing toward another release before the first one was even finished. Over and over, he kept up that ridiculous in and out. Working me up, making me crash, building it again. Three orgasms. Six. Until I collapsed on the mattress, a sweaty, almost sobbing mess underneath him. My skin too tight and my pussy too sensitive. And still, he kept going.

Fucking aliens had stamina. I was all in.

When he finally did come, when he practically knocked me into the headboard with a single, harsh thrust, it was with a roar that nearly shook the windows. *Guess the neighbor knows my dry spell's over.*

He fell on top of me, both of us exhausted and clinging to the other. His weight almost soothing to my tired muscles.

"Well, that was different," I said, my words coming out mumbled as the sheets pooled around my face.

Cutlass chuckled and kissed my shoulder before rolling us both to our sides so we could face each other. And so I wasn't strangled by bed linens.

"Good different or bad?" he asked as he ran his hands over my back.

"Good. Very, very good." I let out a moan at his massage-like rubdown. "Though you might not want to yell so loud next time. These walls aren't exactly soundproof."

He looked around as if seeing the loft for the first time, which perhaps he was considering how our entry happened. "Was this once a home for much taller creatures?"

It took me a second to understand where that question was coming from. "Oh, the ceilings? No. This wasn't a home at all. It was a warehouse. Someone turned the big, open spaces into apartments, and here I am. At least, for a little bit longer."

His eyes lit up as he looked around once more. "*Were-howss?*"

"Yeah. Why?"

The man jumped out of bed and ran for his clothes. "I have an idea."

CHLOE

"Shit, Cutlass." I came awake with a gasp. My gorgeous alien boyfriend had his shoulders holding my thighs apart, his yellow eyes watching me, and his tongue flicking madly over my clit. Typical weekday, it seemed. Alien alarm clocks were the absolute best.

I grabbed hold of his mane—he'd been growing it out, and we were at the point where you couldn't call that shit hair—and held on tight. We'd been living together for two months, and I knew how this morning would go. But I didn't have time for the entire wake-Chloe-up-with-lots-of-hot-sex thing. I almost felt bad stopping him.

Okay, I felt really bad. Mostly for myself because the man was a master at giving me the Os.

"We don't have time," I said, groaning through the words because oh, my God, his cock was resting on my calf and I could feel the wetness running down from how excited he was. Fuck, that bit of precome drove me wild.

As if he knew—and let's face it, he did because I was a total hussy for him—he climbed up my body and pressed inside me.

"Shush. I'll claim my mate today so all the new non-earthling males in the building know you're mine."

His hips rocked against mine, every thrust sending sparks shooting up my spine. In a good way. I grabbed his shoulders and wrapped my legs around his hips. Hanging on for dear life.

"That's sort of like pissing on my leg, you know."

He grunted, leaning down to bite my ear as he pulled one leg higher. Oh hell, that angle was the best.

"I have no idea what you mean, but I don't care. Should I?" He slid his fingers between us, teasing my clit. The bastard.

"No," I gasped. "Just keep going."

"Whatever my mate wants."

Fast, hard fucking and a doozy of an orgasm—sometimes that was all it took to make a morning go from good to best-ever. I knew that fact well. Cutlass made sure every morning was the best-ever before I left for work. Which reminded me...

"I need to shower," I said, still recovering from the three orgasms he'd given me in about four minutes. The man had serious skills.

Cutlass grunted his acceptance and rolled out of bed with me, refusing to stop touching. A weird habit I was oddly in love with. Well, that and him. Because falling in love with my alien mail order boyfriend turned out to be way easy.

"When will the others get here?"

I led the way into the bathroom the agency had remodeled for us. A real, working bathroom. Amazing. "Agency said ten."

He passed by his colored contacts and headed for the shower. I'd stopped caring about the neon yellow eyes the man sported. In fact, they'd sort of grown on me.

"We should get you clean," he said as he pushed me into the shower. "I can't have you meeting the first non-earthlings to move in to the building all..." he growled and smiled, "...dirty."

I rolled my eyes. "Please. You'll probably jack off on my leg so I smell like your spunk before they get here."

His eyes went wide. "You'd let me?"

"No." I jumped in the shower, closing the new glass doors behind me, blocking him. "Now, go out there. I need to get ready for work.

Work. Another something that had changed. I no longer slung hot dogs and fries at a dumpy Coney Island. I ran the building that used to be owned by the dickwad who evicted me. The agency bought it when

Cutlass told them about it, and they put a bunch of time and money into it to make the apartments more livable for their non-earthling clients. The past two months had been nice, what with Cutlass, me, and his two friends being the only residents here, but it was moving day. Time to get new neighbors. Nonhuman ones.

Plus it was match day for Hudson, Cutlass' friend and one of the aliens who'd traveled to Earth with him. I liked the two of them, but Hudson was a happier sort of guy than Maivehricck, though I called him Maverick. All those extra consonants didn't roll off my tongue. Hudson seemed more open to the whole match process. Maverick seemed... grumpy. A lot.

"Do you think Hudson's going to fall all over himself when he meets the woman Ampetheia found for him?" I hollered over the roar of the water. The hot water. Such a concept.

"Probably." Cutlass opened the doors and joined me under the spray, as I knew he would eventually. "He's more excited than I've ever seen him."

"Here's to hoping she accepts him." That was another change I tried to talk the agency into—making sure the humans all knew what they were getting from the get-go. Figuring out that my best friend was married to an alien and that she'd known I was being set up with one had hurt. A lot. Almost more than finding out about Cutlass actually *being* an alien. That fight with Amelia had lasted longer than any other we'd had, but in the end, she was still my BFF. Plus, we had a lot more in common now, what with the non-earthling men in our lives exhausting us every day and night with their overindulgent sexual escapades.

My God, life was good.

But no matter how much Amelia and I both tried to explain to Ampetheia that the humans should be told their match's true history before they met them, she wouldn't budge. Something about the surprise factor. Whatever. That surprise had almost lost me Cutlass and cut deep gouges into my strongest and oldest friendship. I could only hope no other match created such turmoil.

Cutlass, in his perpetually horny state, completely distracted me from thoughts of anyone other than him. He ignored the schedule he knew I needed to keep, as well as the way I stiffened when he wrapped his arms around me. Instead, he took the soap from my hand and pressed his cock against my ass.

Perv.

"We don't have time," I said, trying to convince myself as well.

He bit my neck, rocking his hips. Convincing me without words. Who needed them, anyway? I spread my legs and gave him room because—again—I was a total hussy for him. And he knew it.

"Klow-ee?"

"Yes?"

"I want to eat you out for breakfast." His rumbly voice did things to me, as did his naughty words.

"You know that's not what it's called."

He dropped to his knees and tossed one of my legs over his shoulder. "Of course, it is."

He didn't give me a chance to say no. Just slid his tongue against me and found my clit. I grabbed the top of the doors and pressed my other hand against the wall, letting him do what he did best. The other aliens could wait to be let in. Ampetheia would understand. My mate needed me, craved my touch and taste to help make it through the day. She wouldn't want him to lose his control and go all...alien in front of the humans, right?

Or at least that would be the excuse if I got in trouble.

"Okay," I gasped as he slid two fingers inside me. "Maybe a few minutes."

I would have been insulted by his chuckle if I hadn't already been so close to coming. Did I say the man had skills? Yeah, understatement.

Alien good mornings truly were the best sort of good mornings. And I had years' worth of them to look forward to.

Hudson knew from the moment he saw the flyer in a space station bathroom that a mail order bride from Earth was for him. He wanted a mate, someone to cherish, someone to spoil, and finding her in another species wasn't a big deal in his mind. Convincing his two shipmates to go along was the hardest part, and even then, he knew everything would work out for them.

Macy had a plan. Go to school, become a doctor, and keep her twin sister healthy. If men fell to the side along the way, she could catch up on the whole dating thing later. But when said twin sister decided to apply for a mail order bride program as Macy, things got a little complicated. Suddenly there was a hot guy with rock-star charm looking at her as if she was the greatest thing on Earth, and she had no idea how to deal with that.

One ad in a space station, one sister who should know better, and a positive attitude that's almost impossible to break.

CHAPTER ONE_

MACY

Application 325E
Lead Generator: Facebook Ad
Species: Human
Planet: Earth
Breeding Rank: Receptacle
Intake Office: Detroit, Michigan, United States
Original Content: There's nothing I like more than to curl up with a good book and a glass of wine, but having a man in the picture to snuggle with would make it that much better.
Translation: Human female seeks warm and quiet male to bring to her mating bed. Instructional documents included.

"You did *what?*"

"Hear me out." Stacy—my sister and also, apparently, my pimp—put her hands up and tilted her head in a way that said she was going to attempt to argue her way out of the doghouse. She'd taken on that same exact position every time she'd done something stupid since we were kids, but I wasn't having it this time. Nope. It was one thing to steal my dolls and cut off all their hair or ride my bike into the creek and leave it there to sink; it was completely another to sign me up for…for…*this*.

"I don't want to hear you out," I said, trying to keep my voice hard and what I hoped was deadly. Not that I'd kill her, but I wanted her to be afraid. To be very afraid. "I want to hear you say 'I'll fix it, Macy. I'll get you out of this mess, Macy. I'm sorry I was intrusive and unbelievably arrogant, Macy.'"

"Well, now you're just being rude."

The laugh that burst out of me sounded harsh even to my own ears. "I'm rude? I didn't go against your will and sign you up for some sort of perverted, modern-day mail order bride program."

"It's not perverted." The eye roll was both implied and given, after a pause where my guess was she'd tried to fight the urge. We'd discussed her eye-rolling numerous times. Discussions that usually led to me screaming and her…well, rolling her eyes.

But this time was different. This time, she'd truly overstepped. If I could feel more rage, I figured I'd probably die from it. Or maybe turn all black-eyed witch like Willow in that Buffy show. Though she'd been a lesbian at the time and had gone all *destroy the world* because her girlfriend had been killed right in front of her. I wasn't gay, hadn't had a boyfriend in—nope, totally not thinking about that length of time—and was only fighting with my sister. Bad analogy.

I took a deep breath, trying really hard to stay calm and rational. "Stacy, I don't want to be part of a mail order bride program. I didn't even know they still existed."

"Oh, sure." She tugged her long, dark hair into a ponytail that almost matched my own. "Though usually, they're for foreign brides, and there's a big fee on the receiver's end. This is totally something else, though."

It was *something else,* all right. "Great, so I should expect to be in a catalog for lonely men who want to write me letters."

"Catalog? Ew, no. It's not the fifties, Mace." Another eye-roll. "You'll probably be up on some website. Don't worry, though, I used a great picture of me for you. No one can tell us apart anyway."

Well, didn't *that* make everything better? I rubbed my forehead and paced the length of the room as I tried to figure out how to get through to her. Stacy was my twin, an almost exact duplicate of me genetics-wise, so how could we be so opposite? How could she know so little about me? How could she think this was something I'd be okay with?

"Stacy, let's try this again. I don't want to be a mail order bride. I don't want to join some dating agency program to find me a man. I don't even want a man. I want to finish med school, pass the second part of the USMLE, and pick a specialty. I want to get a solid match at a good hospital, work toward a good job, and pay off the ridiculous amount of debt I've incurred educating myself these last six years."

Stacy sat on my couch—rolling her big, dark eyes again for good measure—and started to file her nails as if she had no problems in the world.

"No, you don't."

If I wasn't busting my ass so hard to be a healer, I might have actually killed her. "Yes, I do. It's all I've ever wanted."

"No, it's all you ever wanted after Daddy put the idea in your head. Before he started pushing you as the smart one and the one who'd follow in his doctorly footsteps—"

"Doctorly isn't a word."

Ooh, she gave good glare. "Before he said you were going to be a doctor, you wanted to be a firefighter."

"Jesus, Stace. What kid didn't?"

"And then you wanted to be a dancer, but you sucked at it. Then it was a baker. Then a veterinarian."

"Humans, animals. Same difference." *Sort of.* I shrugged, but it was halfhearted. I really had wanted to be a vet when I was in middle school.

And Stacy knew it.

"But then dear old Daddy got into your head, and you became a weird little version of him. A mini-Daddy, stethoscope and all."

Not true. What made me want to be a doctor was almost losing my twin sister to cancer. Not that she needed that particular noose around her neck. "I'm not as bad as Dad was."

"Please," she scoffed. "Throughout high school, becoming a doctor was all you could think or talk about. It was all you actually cared about."

That and keeping an eye on her to make sure she was okay. I don't think any of us ever got over the year she was sick. Any of us except Stacy.

"You're wrong," I said, still stuck on memories of her in a hospital bed. I was too young to stay with her, and my parents didn't understand how much I worried. We didn't have cell phones then, so there was no way to send a text or a quick message. My parents would sometimes go days without taking me to the hospital to see her, would skip over her name at the dinner table and brush aside my questions. On those nights, I'd cry, thinking my sister was dead and they didn't tell me. I still got a little anxiety when we went too long without talking.

But that was a long time ago, and I needed to focus before she steamrolled me into doing something I didn't want to do. "I cared about a lot of things beyond academics in high school. I liked being in band and cared about that."

Stacy snorted. "Yeah, and it's a good thing you did. Otherwise, you'd still be the proud owner of a very sad little V-card. Though there was that whole throwing up thing with him."

The way she scrunched her face and looked at me as if that situation had been my fault? Well, that was just mean. She was the one who'd given me the bottle of whiskey to drink before *the big event,* as she'd named it. That was such a bad idea. "It wasn't pretty, but my sex life—"

"Don't exaggerate. One summer with a bass drummer does not a sex life make."

"He played the quads."

The nail file went flying past my head. Had she thrown that at me? The bitch.

"Are you hearing yourself?" she screeched before I could comment on the flying-file-of-death thing. "You're nothing but a walking, talking studying machine. There is more to life than dead bodies and the possibility of being able to study live ones one day. You are wasting so much time not living."

"I'm living." But was I? My argument sounded weak, and I didn't have the confidence in the statement to make it stronger. And once again, Stacy knew it.

"Really? Because I haven't seen any evidence of that in years. I thought maybe once you got to college you'd loosen up, but you just doubled down on the *all I can do is study* thing. Four years of no parties, no men, and no...anything fun was enough, but no, you had to sign up for medical school. Are you going to spend another four years studying before you begin some horrific, all-consuming lifestyle known as residency?" She shook her head and gave me a pitying sort of look that made my skin itch. "Aren't you lonely, sis?"

Oof. And wasn't that a question I didn't want to think about? Of course, I was lonely. Long hours in classes, labs, and libraries meant there was very little time for anything else. I kept clinging to the hope that once I started my residency, I'd get out more. Find a group of like-minded people to grow close with like on *Grey's Anatomy*—without all the death of friends and killing of fiancés and stuff. I never would forgive Izzie for the LVAD stunt. Poor Denny.

He wasn't real, Macy. Shit, back to the conversation at hand.

"I'm not lonely," I said, but my voice betrayed my lie, so I sighed and tried again. "I'm not...*excessively* lonely."

But my twin would never believe that crap. "I want you to be happy."

"I am happy."

"No, you're focused on succeeding. That doesn't mean you're happy."

"That also doesn't mean I need to sign up to be a mail order bride."

"You didn't...I signed you up."

"Stace—"

"It's going to be great," she said as she jumped up with a huge grin plastered on her face. She grabbed my arms and pulled me closer, almost touching noses. Whispering in the way we used to as kids when we didn't want the parentals to know what we were planning. "They have a superhigh success rate. They match you to a man based on a letter you write, and then set up these immersive dates so you can get to know each other."

"What do you mean, immersive?"

She waved me off. "Don't worry about that now. Just trust me. I know you, and I know this is just what you need to break out of your slump. You need a little adventure before you have to focus on your residency, right?"

She had a point. I had no grandiose ideas of what residency would be like, no matter how much *Grey's* I'd watched over the years. The hours would be brutal, the schedule unforgiving, and the work near impossible. These would be my hell years. Having a man to lean on during that time, maybe to share the experience with, wouldn't be all bad, I guessed.

But that didn't mean I'd forgiven her. I'd just...come around. A bit. Only to the dating part.

"Fine. So when do I write this letter?"

Stacy's dark eyes went wide. "Oh, right. See, you were so busy with finals and I didn't want you to miss out, so I sort of...already did that for you."

I blinked. Again. Staring at my sister as if I didn't know her. "You wrote my letter?"

"Yeah." She bit her lip for a single second of doubt but then, in typical Stacy style, skipped over all the craziness her admission caused and smiled through the whole shitty thing. "See? It's going to be great. I've taken care of everything."

"But...*you* wrote my letter. You'll be the one matched."

"Oh, no. I wrote it as you."

"Stacy, I know we look exactly alike, but that doesn't mean we are. How could you just write it as me? How would you know what I want in a man?"

Stacy waved me off and headed to the bathroom. "Please. One, I know you better than you know yourself. And two, I read your journal."

It took a whole ten seconds for those final words to sink in. "You what?"

CHAPTER TWO_

HUDSON

Application 5748SL
Lead Generator: Advertisement at Space Station PF456-G2
Species: Reithhar
Residence: Former planet Xouthhgros, Former planet BHG489
Breeding Rank: Inseminator
Match Requirements by Species: Breeding Compatibility, single-minded focus once matched, extremely sexual beings
Intake Office: Space Station PF456-G2
Original Content: Reithhar Master Hunter from planet Xouthhgros looking for female mate to care for and cherish.
Translation: Rugged but charming man with a great love of the outdoors looks to get wild in the bush.

Practicing human emotional responses was hard work, much harder than the construction Maverick and I had been doing. Looking in the mirror I'd just installed, I cocked my head, baring my teeth in what humans called a *schmy-ell*. Yeah, that looked right. Almost human quality, really.

"You need to quit making that face," Maverick said, growling his words.

"Why? The humans are said to like this." I bared my teeth again, still happy with the expression. The lenses covering my yellow eyes looked convincingly brown, and my lips were finally able to bend into the expression humans preferred. I could easily pass as an earthling, which was exactly what I wanted. I just needed Ampetheia, owner of the Intergalactic Dating Agency in Detroit, to find my match so I could test my humanness.

"We're not around humans. Quit making that ridiculous face and work."

"You should try it."

"Work? I do. Every day. And then I come here and work more for Klow-ee."

"Not that." I wiped down the edges of the mirror. This *drii-waarll* humans used in their home building was messy. And weak. I'd already broken six sections. I would need to search out videos on the human internet to explain why they used such products. "You should *schmy-ell*. It's a happy look, and one humans prefer."

The expression on his face was not even close to a happy look. "Over my dead body."

"That can be arranged." Klow-ee, mated human female to Cutlass and our current crew leader, came racing into the room, barely dodging the buckets of drywall mud, tools, and paint cans we'd set up. "What are you doing, Hudson?"

I bared my teeth. "Learning to *schmy-ell*."

She blinked, her eyes focused on my mouth. "Yeah, okay. But it's smile. No pause."

I grunted softly. Smile, not *schmy-ell*. Noted.

Luckily, Klow-ee was always willing to help me with my need for information on humans and Earth. The communication core all Reithhars had installed at birth processed many languages from across the galaxies. It worked on most of the *Een-gllisch* language the humans around us spoke, but it wasn't always accurate. And translating via picture, as our cores did, could be downright confusing. A smile looked aggressive to a Reithhar Hunter like me, but humans saw the expression as a good thing. Very confusing, but fascinating at the same time.

"I'll try harder," I said, already itching for the device humans called a *tahhb-lit*. That's where the internet lived and where I could watch videos of anything and everything. Including humans smiling and speaking. I would study more.

"Okay. Fine," Klow-ee said, tapping on the screen of her own *tahhb-lit*. I doubted if she was watching videos, though. Her screens always looked like lines of words. "Look, I know you guys have been working all morning, but I really need you to get this place done. Like today. Now. Now would be good."

"We're working as fast as we can." Maverick shot a look my way. "Some of us. Others are attempting to learn human facial expressions."

Klow-ee smiled. "Aw, Hudson. Don't worry. I'm sure you'll be matched soon." Her face went more stiff and stern. More work Klow-ee than friend Klow-ee. "But until then, we work. We've got four days to have this place done. Where do we stand?"

How could humans be so oblivious? "We stand in the *you-net*, on the hard floor you asked us to install last week."

She blinked before making the breathy sound she sometimes did. Cutlass said that was the sound of her being annoyed, though why she was annoyed that I answered her question, I had no idea. Humans rarely made sense no matter how hard I tried to understand them, but I loved trying anyhow.

Klow-ee rubbed at a wrinkled patch of skin between her eyes. She did that a lot when working in the *were-howss* where we all lived. "Maverick, what's the situation?"

Guess I'd answered wrong.

My Reithhar brother didn't hesitate to answer her question. "Two days to finish."

"Perfect. Then we can move up to the next level. Ms. Ampetheia will be thrilled if we get these last units done early."

Units, not *you-nets*. I noted the difference, hoping next time I'd get the word right.

But what really stuck with me was that Ampetheia would like it if we finished early. I would do just about anything to make that female happy. I'd been waiting weeks for her to match me to my female mate, and I didn't want to make her mad when I was so close. Not that I knew if I was close, but she'd said she would devote her time to finding me a mate when she had a *were-howss* building to house the coming aliens who would be her future clients. The building had been secured thanks to Klow-ee and Cutlass, and Maverick and I had spent many Earth days fixing it so the non-earthlings would be comfortable. It was time for Ampetheia to deliver on her promise.

And still, I waited.

"Where is Cutlass?" Maverick asked as he dragged a rag down the wall he'd been sanding. He hated dust and grit almost as much as I hated the too-bright glow of some earthling interiors. For me, that light was painful. As a Reithhar Hunter and pilot, my eyes were sensitive. Too sensitive for planet Earth at times. For Maverick, as a Master Mechanic, his life was more about making sure grit didn't get into something that it could wear down and break. Maverick truly hated grit.

Klow-ee, on the other hand, didn't seem to notice how much debris floated in the air around us. "He's dealing with the painters on the first floor. You Reithhar have a great eye for color."

Maverick huffed. "Our eyes see much more than yours, human."

True, and yet a dangerous statement to make. I turned slowly, keeping my eye on the human in the room. She may have been little, but she was deadly in her own ways. Maverick's bad mood would get him in trouble with Cutlass if he kept it up. Klow-ee wasn't going to like Maverick implying humans were inferior to Reithhars; she was sensitive about her limitations as a human. She could tell Cutlass what he said, which could cause a fight.

But it wasn't Cutlass I really worried about. It was Klow-ee herself. She had a temper.

"Yeah. I get that," Klow-ee said, her voice carrying that tone that said she was ready to go all warrior on Maverick. Again. It seemed to be their favorite sport. "You guys are big, tough, spaceship-driving aliens. Badasses of the universe. And then there's poor little old me, the simple, soft human with bad eyes and worse ears. Is that what you're trying to say?"

"Yes." Maverick was not smart when he was irritated.

I threw a metal tool at the idiot before trying out my smile on Klow-ee. "Ignore him. I always do."

Klow-ee looked from him to me and back again before lifting that chin of hers. Such a brave little thing Cutlass' mate turned out to be.

"Let me know when you finish in here so we can move on to the next floor. And nice smile, Hudson. Good work."

As soon as she was gone, I threw another tool at Maverick. "Cutlass is going to kill you if you keep acting that way around his mate. Or she might. I wouldn't ignore her threat."

"He can try. He won't succeed. And she has no chance."

"*I'd* succeed if you upset my mate that way." And I would. Being mated was a desire I'd had for many turns around the galaxy. I was much older than the Reithhar with me on Earth, though I didn't look it. Not to humans. Still, that extra time wore on me. I was ready to be matched, to find my mate, and to cherish her. She would be my entire world, and I would make sure she was well cared for and fed.

I just had to wait for Ampetheia to find her for me. We would not have the dark period like Klow-ee and Cutlass had, where they were apart for what had seemed many days. We would match and be mated quickly. Everything would be fine once Ampetheia found her. I was sure of it.

———

Almost two Earth weeks later—two long, Earth weeks of working, learning, and going to bed hoping my match would be found the next morning—I finally received the call I'd been waiting for. Ampetheia had matched me. It was the day the other non-earthlings were to start moving into the *were-howss,* but I didn't care. I had a match to accept. If Klow-ee hadn't reminded me to put in my lenses, I would have run out of the building with my yellow Reithhar eyes glowing and scared half the neighborhood. That little human was handy to have around.

Still, those lenses took time to put in.

I burst through the doors to the Intergalactic Dating Agency exactly twelve minutes after hanging up the phone. "Hohddshoun, Reithhar Warrior Master Hunter of the planet Xouthhgros and Navigational Commander for the former BHG489-2140 Colony. I'm here for my match."

"My stars, did you run here?" Ampetheia asked, looking a little surprised by my entrance.

"Yes. Of course." I never understood the custom of asking such obvious questions. "Who is she? When can I meet her?"

The orange-eyed Freknal female could only blink. At first. "Why don't you come along with me?"

Two minutes and a long walk down the hallway later, I sat at her desk looking over the file on my mate.

"I'm sorry it's taken so long," she said as she took the seat across from me. "I've been staring at this paperwork for days now."

"And you didn't call right away?" I ran a finger over the scratchy symbols. Klow-ee was teaching us to read her *Een-gllisch*, but it was a long process. There were only a few of her words I recognized. I had learned eighteen different languages while on the colony; the fact that I hadn't learned the human one for where I ended up frustrated me.

"No. There was something off about this application. There still is."

That sounded ominous and not at all how I wanted my mating to start. "Off?"

She waved a hand in front of her very orange eyes. "It's as if I'm seeing double. Sort of like a mirror image of the girl. If the link to you weren't so strong at times, I would have tossed the application right away. I don't match without being certain."

"You have doubts?" I knew better than to question the advice of a Freknal in terms of matings, but I had to be sure. Freknal creatures were known for their abilities to see connections and feelings nothing else in the universe could. That was why I'd sought her dating agency—a Freknal would pick correctly the first time out. Except, it seemed, when it came to me.

"Minor ones," Ampetheia said as she pushed the papers closer to me. "I'll figure out why the visions are so...odd. But for now, I'm sure she's your match."

Relief was a sweet balm on my old soul. I had waited a long time to hear those words. She found my match. My mate. I knew there was a chance I wouldn't croon for the human. That my esehhnce—the deepest, most instinct-driven part of me—would not accept her to be my mating partner. But I felt that was unlikely and therefore not to be worried about. If the Freknal said we'd match, then we would. I had faith in her abilities. I'd seen her kind work their magic before.

Worse, though, was that I also knew there was a chance the female wouldn't accept me because I wasn't human. Klow-ee almost didn't accept Cutlass at first. Ampetheia was upfront during the application process that some humans couldn't get past us not being from their planet. That was why we couldn't tell them. Not until we'd spent two weeks taking them on what humans called *dae-tss* and giving them time to get to know us. Not until we'd impressed them enough for the human to want us in their lives and their beds.

Especially their beds.

My cock grew hard thinking about the possibilities of a warm, soft human female underneath me. They weren't weak, not by any stretch, but they were very different from our kind. Most didn't have the hard muscles and size of the Reithhar, which meant a very different experience during bedgames than what we were accustomed to.

I looked forward to it. A lot. Especially when I was alone in the shower with my hand on my cock. I had to keep my stamina up so I could pleasure my mate, and those showers gave me good practice opportunities.

My mate would accept my non-earthling status; she had to. Klow-ee had eventually accepted Cutlass, and they were happy and mating every chance they could. I deserved the same. Besides, nothing was going to stand in the way of finding the female meant to be mine. Nothing at all. I'd traveled across solar systems to get to Earth; I'd given up my job, my home, and my life to be here so I could find her. My hunter senses had brought me to this place, to this Freknal, so I could find a mate. This *would* work; I'd make sure of it.

"When do I meet her?"

CHAPTER THREE

MACY

A few weeks after the blowup with Stacy, there was a voice message on my cell phone. One from a number I didn't recognize.

"Miss Macy, my name is Ampetheia from the IG Dating Agency. I'd like to speak with you regarding a possible match with your application. The gentleman is eager to meet you, so please call me back straightaway. My number is..."

My attention faded as the woman rattled off a series of numbers. I'd been matched. I truthfully hadn't thought it would happen, what with Stacy writing my letter and all. And yet there I was, standing in the parking lot at Wayne State University after having spent the last ten hours in the library, listening to a woman tell me she'd found me a match.

No, not match. Husband.

I dropped to the curb, landing hard on my ass, which only jostled my already addled brain. Husband. That's what this agency did. It found wives and husbands for their clients. This was no Tinder app, no dating profile on Match or OK Cupid. This was a full-on, committed relationship from the onset.

What had Stacy been thinking?

I could have asked her right then, because she called as if on cue. Typical. The girl called me six hundred times a day, it seemed. My fault, really—I never refused her calls, too worried about the cancer coming back and losing her incessant calls forever to let the intrusions bother me. Much. My long, silence-filled study session must have driven her crazy. Stacy could not live with text replies only.

"I can't talk right now," I said as soon as I swiped to answer.

"Are you still studying? Jesus, woman. Get your ass out of that library and have a life."

"Yeah, I'm trying. Got to go, though. I'll call you back in a few."

"You'd better."

When the line went silent, I held on to the phone and...did nothing. That voice mail from Ampetheia repeated in my mind. This was a chance at something. I didn't know what, exactly, but it was something more than a quiet library, a smelly lab, and an overbearing sister. This was the possibility of something that was just for me. Something I would never think about doing, normally.

But as I stared at the phone, the idea of having some sort of wild, sex-filled weekend with a stranger didn't scare me nearly as much as it probably should have. I needed a vacation from my life, and this was just what the doctor—or sister, in my case—ordered. Maybe it was the fact that I'd turned my brain to mush with an extended study session, but at that moment, a pre-arranged hookup with some letter-writing stranger seemed like such a good idea.

My fingers flew over the screen as I replayed the message to grab the number, and then I was dialing.

"IG Dating Agency. How can I help you?"

Time to put up or shut up. I took a deep breath, closed my eyes, and let go of the inhibitions I'd been carrying around for too long.

"Hi, my name's Macy, and someone called me about a man. A match." Another deep breath. "My match has been found."

"Oh, congratulations. Let me transfer you to Ms. Ampetheia so she can give you all the details."

Their hold music sucked, but I wouldn't let that mar my positive mood. This would be fine. Great even. Potentially perfect. I just had to meet a complete stranger in some sort of immersive situation and not throw up on him. Easy, right?

Another woman picked up the phone just as a rocking saxophone began to play what should have been a guitar solo. "Ah, Miss Macy. It's wonderful to speak with you. I'm very much looking forward to fulfilling your match. I think he's going to be perfect for you."

I was totally going to throw up on him. "Great. I'm excited to meet him."

"Excellent. Your letter gave us some lovely insights into you, and I'm sure you're going to fall completely for the man I picked. Let's just get you set up then, so you and he can become more than letter-writing pen pals."

Even my exhaustion couldn't let those words slip past. Letter? Oh, right. I'd been matched to a guy who was perfect for me from the letter I'd sent in with my application. Cool, awesome, great. Except for the *I didn't write the letter* thing.

Throwing up on him was no longer my biggest fear.

HUDSON

The hotel was teeming with humans when I walked inside. The space was so crowded that the scents nearly overwhelmed me and the noise caused my ears to ache. Still, I hurried through the chaos toward my destination. My match was waiting for me.

As I weaved my way through the throngs of humans, I couldn't help but look each female over, wondering if she would resemble my match. There were so many different skin colors on Earth, so many shades of fur and eyes. A veritable rainbow of options. Back on Xouthhgros, my own skin would have been a deep green and my eyes a duller yellow. When we lived in the colony on BHG489, my skin dulled, fading almost to a gray. But on Earth, whatever made up the atmosphere caused our skin to brighten. Cutlass was the lightest, while Maverick held on to a darker tone. I sat somewhere in between. We seemed to fit right in, which was good because Earth was the only place with a Freknal helping match mates.

More humans caught my eye as I worked my way through the crowd. Were any of them my match? I doubted—she was already supposed to be in the room where we would meet for our one night alone. But what if... Would her skin be dark like the women in the far corner? Would she have hair the color of fire like the woman behind the desk? Would she be painted like the one with colorful splashes all up and down her arms? I had no idea, but the possibilities seemed endless and I wanted to know. In fact, I couldn't wait to find out.

A quick trip in the floating box humans called an *ellah-vaddohr* and I was on the right floor. Klow-ee had taught me English numbers—apparently, Cutlass had struggled with them during his immersive date—so locating the room wasn't difficult. It took mere seconds for me to reach the right place. And then I stood outside the door, readying myself. Knowing this was it. The moment I'd meet the female I'd matched with. The start of a new life for me on Earth.

I wanted to sniff her out, but the smells from other humans and past guests were too strong. My ears ached from all the noise as well. This hotel was not the place I would have picked, not for a hunter like me. I'd prefer someplace quiet and far away from others so I could properly learn the characteristics of my match. Her scent, the sounds of her body, the feel of her. But I wasn't given the option, so this was where we would spend our time. One day—not the normal two like Cutlass and Klow-ee had. My mate had something called *skuule* that made it impossible for her to stay longer.

I needed to quit stalling.

I took a deep breath, bared my teeth in a smile to ease any worries she might have, and opened the door. To nothing. The room was empty. No female, no match, no new start waiting for me as I'd been promised.

If it were possible for the lights to dim, they would have. Everything around me seemed to grow darker, including my mood. I had waited so long, had traveled so far, only to be denied the one thing I truly wanted.

If I didn't have such a strong control over my body's instinctual responses due to my many years spent mastering my stalking skills, I would have destroyed everything around me. Instead, I turned to the one thing I knew to do.

"Everything will work out," I whispered to the empty room, a mantra of sorts. And then I pulled my Reithhar instincts forward, and I hunted.

I hunted through the room, scenting and investigating every nook and corner. The strong scent of the chemicals humans cleaned with hovered in the air and muffled every other scent. The tracks in the carpet from a vacuum were solid and the bed linens crisp and perfectly in place. No sign of another human having been in the room since the cleaning person. My match hadn't come and left; she'd never shown up.

Had I gotten the time wrong? Had Ampetheia sent me to the wrong place? Or had my match backed out of our arrangement before she'd even met me? I would need to find Ampetheia and have her figure out what happened. My match may have forgotten, or she may have been injured on the way to the hotel.

That thought was one that sent ice skittering down my spine. She might need my help. I couldn't sit and wait for her to arrive; I'd need to hunt her. To track her. That was my talent. But I had nothing of hers, had never met her, and had no way to know how to find her.

And it seemed as if I never would.

Ampetheia had promised the match would be good, but she'd doubted something. Apparently, her doubts had won this event. I waited for close to an hour for my match to prove me wrong and show up, but to no avail. There was no female coming for me, no match to take on a *daette*, no esehhnce to croon. I had nothing, but I was going to make sure Ampetheia found a way to fix that. Everything would work out. We hadn't traveled across galaxies to end up with nothing. Well, maybe Maverick had, but he was a cranky bastard long before our colony exploded. I was ready for a match.

Wanting to confront Ampetheia in person, I stormed across the room and threw open the door. The empty hallway wasn't empty, though. A short, dark-haired woman stood right outside the door. She had the biggest eyes I'd ever seen behind some sort of framed lenses. And she looked positively frightened.

"I...I'm sorry. Is this..." She looked at the numbers beside the door. "I think I'm supposed to be here."

"You are my match?" Those words came out harsher than I'd expected.

The girl flinched at my tone, which only made me feel like more of an idiot. Of course, she was the match the agency had picked for me. Why else would she be standing outside the door?

"Match...uh, yeah. I'm Macy. You must be Hudson." She held out her hand, a human greeting I had yet to truly understand. Still, I grabbed the proffered body part and shook it as I'd been taught. The touch of her skin against mine soothed me in a way nothing else could have. The scent of her teased, and the warmth of her flesh surrounded by mine intrigued. My cock grew hard for her, and my mouth watered. Already, I felt a pull. This would be a good match, a strong one. I couldn't wait to bury my face in her cunt and make her mine.

I'd been right; things would work out.

"I'm sorry I'm late," she said, looking far more nervous than I would have expected. "I got hung up in the *lahhb.*"

I didn't know what a *lahhb* was, but I didn't care. My match was here. Standing before me finally. And she was so damned beautiful. Short, even by human standards, but with a presence about her that took up more space. She had big, hunter eyes but small, tidy ears. Prey ears. She would be at risk of being sneaked up upon with her hearing so restricted, but I'd make sure she was safe. I'd teach her to be a predator instead of prey. I'd protect her, too.

Though, perhaps I wouldn't need to. Because when I finally took a deep breath, when I pulled her scent into myself to analyze, my opinion of my match shifted.

She smelled of dead things.

"Uh, should I...come in?" My match raised her shoulders in what could only be some sort of discomfort. I nearly kicked myself for getting lost in my senses and not paying attention to her needs.

"Yes. Of course. I just arrived myself." A lie, but a necessary one. Besides, I hadn't been waiting for her that long.

The female, Macy, slipped past me, which only brought more of her scent to my attention. So very interesting, this scent of death overlaying her natural, human smell. Was she a hunter on her planet? Or something else? A chemical smell also seemed to emanate from her, but there could be many reasons for that. Humans seemed to like their chemicals. I was more intrigued by the dead things.

Macy looked over the room with a little bit of a hunch to her shoulders, her steps quick and her hands fidgeting with her bag as she paced the width of it. She was afraid. Something I hadn't truly been prepared for. My kind was brave and fought hard, but humans were not as predatory. I'd need to be careful with her, gentle. Quiet, even. At least until I figured out what she'd killed to gain that scent.

"So," Macy said as she reached the opposite wall of the room. The farthest spot away from me she could go, I noticed with interest. She resembled a caged animal, something I found almost fascinating. Humans always seemed to amaze me with their mix of instincts and unusual customs. "Do you do this often?"

Not a question I was expecting. "Rent hotel rooms?"

"No. Well, maybe. I meant do you apply to mail order bride programs a lot. But travel is a good topic. Do you travel much?"

I bit back a smile, leaning against the wall opposite the female so as not to intimidate her. "No and yes."

She tilted her head, her soft, shiny hair falling in gentle waves almost to her waist. I wanted to feel it, wrap my hands in it, and hold her while I mated her mouth. That was not something my kind used during bedgames, but it was a human mating custom I wanted to try. I'd seen Klow-ee and Cutlass mouth mate enough to know the basics. I'd figure out the rest.

But my Macy was not yet ready for that, it seemed. "No *and* yes?"

She tossed her hair over her shoulder, and the scent of death grew stronger. I couldn't resist another second. I pushed off the wall, stalking closer in a slow, wide arc.

"No, I do not apply to mail order bride programs often. This is my first and hopefully last time. And yes, I have traveled. Quite a bit, in fact."

Her breath caught as I finally inched close enough for her to notice. She stood stock-still, those wide eyes on mine, her entire body flattening against the wall.

"Where—" she froze, her throat pulsing once as she swallowed "—where are you from?"

A question I technically couldn't answer.

"It doesn't matter. You should not be afraid of me, little one," I said, keeping my voice calm and quiet. "I won't hurt you."

My brave mate tried so hard to look fierce. "I'm not afraid."

"Your body tells me otherwise." I inched closer, close enough to touch. Close enough to feel the heat rolling off her. Close enough to have to hold myself back from touching her. "Your heart is racing. Why?"

She stared at me for a long moment before finally whispering, "Because you're so...huge."

"And that scares you?"

"No. I'm not... Okay, a little." She did that shoulder lift again. "I'm nervous. This is all new to me."

I hummed and took a step back, giving her the space she needed. "I don't want you to be afraid."

"I'm just really out of my comfort zone. I haven't dated much because of *skuule*, and then I was planning on running home to get ready for this weekend but I got stuck at the *lahhbs* because my partner couldn't figure out—"

Her wide eyes went even wider, and she seemed almost to sink into herself.

"What?" I asked, enthralled by every gesture. Unable to look away for a second. I was already learning so much just by watching her. If humans intrigued me, Macy fascinated. I couldn't look away from her for a moment. I could barely wait to touch. To taste. To devour.

To get to the point where everything was worked out and she was truly mine.

"I didn't get a chance to shower after *lahhb*," she said, almost whispering the words. "I must stink."

"Stink? No." I gave her my best smile, and she seemed to relax. "You smell of dead things."

"Oh, *gee-suss*." Macy grabbed her bag from where she'd dropped it and hurried toward the bathroom. "I am so sorry. Give me ten minutes to shower, and we can start again."

"You don't need to cleanse yourself, Macy. The smell of death doesn't bother me."

She spun, holding her bag to her chest. "How would... Oh hell, never mind. Ten minutes. I'll be back."

CHAPTER FOUR_

MACY

"Stupid, stupid, stupid." I jumped into the shower, nearly squealing at the freezing water spraying me down. Cold showers hadn't exactly been on my wild, sex-filled weekend plans. It wasn't even a full weekend—one afternoon, one evening, and one morning. That was it. Less than twenty-four hours to do...anything. School sucked hardcore sometimes.

As the water warmed to a temperature above freezing, I unwrapped the tiny, complimentary bar of soap and lathered up. Please let the generic soap they supplied be enough to handle the stench of the anatomy lab. My mind spun in circles as I moved on to scrubbing my hair. What had I been thinking? Well, I knew what I'd been thinking. I hadn't wanted Hudson to think I'd blown him off, so I'd rushed to the hotel. Stinking of putrid flesh and embalming fluid. Lovely first impression I must have made.

My phone rang from my bag, and I hissed a quiet curse. I gave myself about ten seconds to consider not answering it, but I knew it was Stacy. She'd never stop calling if I didn't tell her I was at the hotel and my match wasn't a serial killer. So I stepped out of the shower as carefully as I could...and slipped, of course. I practically slammed headfirst into the sink, but I answered the damned thing.

I deserved the Sister of the Year award.

"What?" I hissed, hoping Hudson couldn't hear me over the sound of the running water.

"Did you make it?"

"Yes, of course." I sighed and grabbed a towel, hoping to keep the water I was dripping on the floor to a minimum. Hoping—and failing. "I need to go. I'm in the shower."

"Ooh, already? You don't waste any time."

"I'm alone. And smelly. I have to go."

"Wait...what's he look like?"

How to answer that question... Hell, there was only one way. "Like Adam Levine worked out for about a million hours. Taller, bigger, thicker, but still just as hot as that hand-over-the-crotch photo shoot."

"Jesus," she hissed. "You'd better get on that. Call me later."

Dropping the phone back in the bag, I took a deep breath and held it. Call her later? I was on an immersive date. Hopefully, there would be no calling. A pipe dream considering Stacy's habits, but one I wasn't ready to give up. A full day without the constant ringing seemed blissful, even without the man.

Speaking of the man...

I showered in record time, making sure to scrub every inch that could possibly carry the scent of the lab and even a few that couldn't. Hell, no one would be able to blame me if I ended up in bed with the guy. For one, there was only one bed. Two, this was my vacation-from-my-life weekend. My shot to let loose and get a little wild. With a stranger. Without puking on him.

But the biggest reason why no one would ever blame me for getting freaky with that man was that he was gorgeous. Like rock star, movie star, pop-culture phenomena hot. What the hell was he doing signing up with a dating agency? He must have had women throwing themselves at him. Why hadn't he caught one yet?

And what the hell was I supposed to do with a man who looked like that?

With a towel wrapped around my chest, I wiped the steam from the mirror and gave myself a once-over. I was *not* hot-guy-girlfriend material. That opinion wasn't because of any sort of low self-esteem—I happened to think I was pretty cute, really. Big eyes, long hair—both dark—and a body created by not having enough time to really eat for six years...I was probably a seven-point-five. With makeup. And a great bra.

No, not being a superstar's type was less about my opinion of my looks and more of a simple truth. I didn't have the boobs, the ass, or the face for someone handsome enough to be in the limelight. But what I did have was an awesome brain, a good body, and a look guys tended to notice. I hadn't ever used any of those things to my advantage, but I could fake it for a weekend. Sure, Hudson would probably walk away once I told him what my life was going to be like for the next five years as I finished med school and started my residency. Hell, I would probably run if the situation were reversed. But for once, I was going to have a little fun. Everyone needed a vacation from real life now and again.

And mine was about to start.

I slapped on some makeup, pulled on a fresh outfit, and headed back to the room, ready to throw myself into a weekend of distractions. Hudson sat in a chair on the other side of the bed, staring at the door I'd walked through as if waiting for me. A fact that made my skin flush and my smile come unbidden.

Rock-star hot, for real. "Hi."

"Hi," he answered, sounding way calmer than I felt. "Feel better?"

"Yes, absolutely. At least I don't smell anymore."

"I didn't mind it when you did." He rose to his feet, closing the gap between us in three easy steps that made my heart speed up like crazy. But hey, what was a little tachycardia among friends? Or strangers. *Crap, concentrate, Macy!*

"So..." I started, still trying to keep from needing defibrillator paddles just to stand close to the guy. "Did you want to do something? Together?" One eyebrow went up on that ridiculous face. Just one. Like the number of beds in the room to do *something* on. "Not like *that* something. But...something."

Kill me now.

But Hudson just smiled at me, making those lovely fibrillations spread throughout my body. "May I take you out now?"

"Out?" I leaned closer, unable to resist the draw of that deep, sexy voice. Did he gargle with some sort of liquid aphrodisiac or something? Brush with toothpaste made of pheromones?

"Yes. Out. Outside. We should go on a date." His casual grin was positively lethal, and the way he said date indicated an accent that could easily make me wet. He was such a deadly package.

Deadly to my brain, apparently. "A date?"

I really wanted to smack my own forehead for that one.

Hudson, though, just kept that smile on his face, his gaze intense as he watched me. "I'd like to learn you."

The wording of his statement barely registered as my mind went to the one place it really shouldn't have.

"But my hair is wet."

Yeah, I'd be kicking myself for weeks over that one. Hudson looked completely confused, and rightfully so. I bet he'd never been turned down because of wet hair before.

"My hair" —I pointed at my head, as if that would help the situation — "is wet. I look like a drowned rat."

But even imagined rock stars have charm. That's the whole point of the fantasy, right?

He gently tucked a strand of wet hair behind my ear. "You're beautiful, wet or dry. Everything will work out, Macy. Just come with me."

My brain's pleasure center had to have lit up like Times Square at that one. Hell, my panties may have even gotten a little damp. Not as much as my hair, though. Still, drowned rat with a man who looked like Hudson sounded better than hiding in a hotel room alone.

"Okay. Out it is. Let me just grab my purse."

———

Out for Hudson turned out to be Hart Plaza, where some sort of music festival was going on. Totally fitting for that rock-star image of him in my head.

"Do you do this a lot?" I plucked off a chunk of cotton candy from the bag he'd bought us and brought it to my mouth. Hudson's eyes followed the pink fluff, growing dark and heated as I placed the spun sugar on my tongue. Mydriasis in action. Ha, score one for the dorky scientist.

He blinked and seemed to refocus on my eyes instead of my mouth when I pulled my hand away. "Sorry. Do I do what a lot?"

I would have gone for another bite, but I actually wanted him to answer my question. "Come to these outdoor festivals. Do you do it often?"

"As much as I can." He directed us toward the fountain that looked like an upside down thumbtack where there were fewer people standing around. "I like being outside, and I like watching people. There is so much to learn here, so much that is different from where I was bred. I find your culture fascinating. These sorts of things fulfill both my likes and give me an opportunity to educate myself."

A perfect answer for someone as obsessed with learning as I was.

"I like these things, too. Watching people, especially." I chuckled and shook my head. "When I was little, my twin sister and I used to make up stories about people around us when we were bored."

Hudson's brow furrowed, and I could have sworn his eyes grew even more intense. "What is a *twi-ihn?*"

I opened my mouth to reply then shut it again. Even with his previous comment, I hadn't really thought about the fact that Hudson wasn't from the Detroit area. Heck, he had a bit of an accent, which probably meant he wasn't from the United States.

Why did that fact make him even more appealing?

"A twin is a sibling born of the same pregnancy. Stacy and I are monozygotic, or identical, so we were developed from a single ovum and have identical genomes." I shut my mouth with an audible clack, nearly ready to crawl into a hole. Who the hell talked about a sister in terms of ovum and genomes? Stacy was right—I really did need to get out of the lab more.

"Sorry," I said with a self-deprecating headshake. "It's the medical school. They pound facts into you until you can regurgitate them without actual thought."

I flinched. Talking about regurgitation during a first date probably wasn't the best plan, either.

But Hudson only looked confused, not bored or disgusted. "Why would you be sorry? I've seen the shows about doctors. It seems very difficult and takes a lot of school."

"It does. I love it, but I forget to be normal and not so...doctorly sometimes." I wasn't the biggest fan of the name my sister called me when I was trying to be logical, but it worked in this situation. Doctorly, it was.

He shrugged in a casual sort of way. "Understanding how the nature of husbandry and life cycles work is necessary where I'm from. I understand what pregnancy, ovum, and genomes are. That description made sense."

Heh...well, then. Score one for the hottie. "Cool. Yeah, good."

Hudson grabbed my hand and led me closer to the fountain at a slow, almost leisurely pace. "Were you born first?"

"Yep. By a whole three minutes. Stacy never lets me forget it, either."

"What's she like?"

I hummed, thinking how to put my sister into words that weren't *intrusive* and *overwhelming* and *crazy*. "She's a lot louder than I am. Freer, too. She does exactly what she wants, when she wants, and worries about the aftermath once she's had her fun."

He frowned. "She sounds dangerous."

"That's one way to put it." And also completely responsible for us being together at that moment, so maybe not so bad. Not that I'd admit that fact to him. "What about you? Any siblings?"

His pause was noticeable, and when he spoke, he didn't sound as comfortable or confident as before. "No. It is not common where I am from to have more than one—how to say—cub?"

Cub. Like an animal. Such an odd term to use. "You mean child?"

"Yes, of course. Child." Hudson stressed the D in child, making it sound more like *chil-duh*. The accent didn't give me an idea of where he was from, but I'd never been all that good with accents. Still, it was unusual.

"What was it like, growing up with a twin?"

Less of an accent that time. He learned fast.

"Fun and frustrating in equal measure. We look exactly alike, so people always had a hard time telling us apart. Sometimes, we'd use that to our advantage. Other times, she'd do something stupid and blame me for it. But when it was just us?" I smiled, remembering all the times Stacy and I were in our own little twin world. "It could be amazing. She understood me in a way no one else did."

Memories of Stacy and me played through my mind, leading me to the bad ones. The ones I hated to talk about.

"Why are you sad?" Hudson asked, completely focused on me. His gaze was almost too much, leaving me bare before him in a way I was unaccustomed to.

I lifted a shoulder and broke eye contact, unable to hold that stare. "Nothing. Just...thinking."

"Bad thoughts."

"Everything worked out," I said, trying to smile. This wasn't the day to talk about the year Stacy was sick. "The good far outweighed the bad. We would play secret games together and speak in code, and we were always telling each other stories. We used to go to the park and make up whole lives about the people there."

Hudson's eyes never left mine. His entire body seemed almost filled with energy, as if he wanted so badly to say or do something. As if something about what I'd said excited him. He looked almost like a child about to see Santa Claus.

"Everything always works out," he finally said. That...wasn't what I was expecting. "I like this idea of private stories about strangers. You should tell me one."

He leaned against a low wall, pulling me close as he did. Wrapping his arms around my hips in a move that could have been considered brash if it hadn't been so unbelievably sexy in a weird, almost possessive sort of way. We'd been inching closer as we walked. The pull-and-touch was sort of expected. And definitely enjoyed.

I leaned against him, half afraid I'd feel something hard against my back. Half afraid I wouldn't.

I totally felt it. "I think I'm being coerced."

"I don't know what *coe-wersed* is, but I promise to reward you if you tell me one." His fingers tickling the sides of my legs might as well have been some sort of magic weapon. How could I say no when he made me feel that good? Coerced was an understatement.

"Reward me with what?" I looked up at him over my shoulder, going for a flirty and fun smile. Hoping I didn't cross the line into obvious and desperate. It was a fine line. One I apparently stayed on the correct side of.

Hudson's own smile spread across his face in a way that made my body clench with need. Though it had nothing on his voice as he uttered, "Anything you want."

Yeah. I wasn't winning a fight against all that.

"Okay, fine." Needing a distraction from the arousal the man made bloom inside me, I scoped out the crowd until I spotted a man, a woman, and two kids—who looked nothing alike—all standing together.

"Those two," I said, pointing. "They're both divorced from their first marriages and just getting back into the dating scene. They've been seeing each other for a few months and finally decided to move things forward in their relationship, so they're here with their own kids to introduce them."

Hudson wrapped himself around me, resting his chin on my shoulder in a move that felt oddly—but charmingly—territorial. What was it with him and these ownership moves? And why the hell did I like them so much?

"And how's it going?" he asked.

It took me a second to realize he was asking about the couple and kids across the way. "The kids hate each other."

"Understandable. No one likes to give up their territory." Hudson chuckled and pulled me in closer, pointing to our right this time. "What about them?"

I looked over at the older couple by the fountain. They were holding hands, the woman leaning into the man's side a bit. "Married forty years, still happy, still in love. They're empty nesters now with the kids gone, and they have wild, kinky sex all over the house."

Hudson laughed so loud, people turned to look.

I couldn't hold back my grin. "So you don't know what a twin is but you know kinky?"

"I like to learn, Macy. I especially like to learn about things that capture my interest. Hunting, building, and sex capture my interest quite easily." His voice...it wrapped around me. Teased a bit. His accent flattening into more of a Midwestern pattern.

"You like learning like I like learning," I whispered, unable to hold back a smile.

"Of course. We were matched, remember?" He nodded toward the crowd across the plaza. "What else? What stories are there to tell still?"

But his arms felt too good to focus on anything other than that, and my brain was too frazzled to be creative again. "Your turn. Pick someone and tell me about them."

He hummed, looking around the crowd. "There."

The couple he pointed out was younger, our age perhaps. The two were wrapped around one another, stealing kisses and letting hands wander to places that were probably a little over the PDA line and into exhibitionist territory. I was weirdly jealous of them, to be honest.

"What's their story?" I asked as they locked lips once again. The man's hand slid to her hip and then around to grip her ass. Something that looked awfully nice from where I stood.

Hudson pulled me closer, humming in my ear, his hands sadly not on my ass. "Like us, they're on a date."

"A first date?"

"Yes. A first date. And their chemistry is electric."

I knew that feeling. "They're awfully familiar for a first date."

"They're drawn to one another," he said, his voice dropping into a tone that sounded oddly like purring. "They feel an attraction they can't deny. Just like us."

Yeah, I felt the attraction all right. My match had his arms around me, his erection pressed into my ass, and his lips millimeters from my ear. I was surrounded by him in this very open, very public place. And I liked it. One more bite, and he'd break me for sure.

"So what are their plans?" I asked, teasing him with a slow roll of my hips. I'd assumed it was a safe question. I should have known Hudson wouldn't play anything safe. What rock star did?

"They'll leave soon. Go back to someplace private." He bit my neck, giving it a soft lick when he pulled away. "And they'll not sleep for days. Because he'll be devouring her cunt instead."

Syncope. Otherwise known as fainting, a sudden loss of consciousness, usually caused by a lack of oxygen in the brain. Not usually caused by massive arousal and sexual desires brought on by a man with his lips against your ear. And yet...

"Jesus." I sagged in his arms, my knees weak and rubbery.

Hudson simply held me tighter and nuzzled into my neck once more. "I'd rather you say my name in that breathy voice."

Challenge thrown. I tilted my head back, shivers racking my body at his lips and tongue working over my flesh. The man was going to kill me in the best way, and we were still dressed and in public. I couldn't even imagine what would happen once we got back to the hotel room. The one with only one bed.

Thank you, IG Dating Agency, for that genius planning.

"Macy?" Hudson said, practically growling as he gripped my hips and pulled me tighter.

"Yes?"

He rocked slightly, letting me know exactly how much he felt a connection to me. How much he wanted me. How much he—

"I want to lick your cunt until I make you scream."

Well…at least he was direct.

CHAPTER FIVE_

MACY

He didn't make me come.

Not for a lack of skills or anything. I mean, a guy that hot had to be amazing in bed. Otherwise, he was one big masturbatory fantasy without a happy ending. God would not be so cruel. No, I'd bet he was great in bed. I was looking forward to finding out for myself...but before I could act on his "I want to make you scream my name" declaration, my sister called.

Answering the phone may have been the worst mistake I could have made.

You ever have that friend who always invites herself along to everything? The one who can't take a hint, and therefore ends up at every family birthday party, picnic, and holiday event, even though no one else knows them? Stacy was *that* friend, except she wasn't only a friend to me. She was my sister, my twin, which meant she knew exactly what to say to get me to back down and agree to let her join Hudson and me. On our date. Our first date. After he'd offered to go down on me until I screamed his name. A promise I was certain he could deliver on.

But, no. I answered the phone, which meant Stacy was gate-crashing our date. Hudson was going to run away screaming when he realized the level of crazy that came with my family.

Speaking of crazy...

"This is so cool. I've never been to one of these festivals. Macy goes to school down here, but I try to avoid the city. Everyone says it's too dangerous." Stacy practically skipped across the plaza, looking around in wonder as if she were some sort of tourist. As if we hadn't grown up twenty minutes away from the very plaza we stood in.

I, on the other hand, gripped Hudson's hand and did my best not to drown in guilt and sexual tension. He'd wanted to make me come, and I'd invited my twin sister along. That wasn't weird, right? Shit. It was totally weird. Though, technically, she invited herself. I just wasn't able to tell her no. And so the two of us suffered. Horribly.

"So, Hudson," Stacy said as she turned to face us, an evil glint in her eye that told me she was about to play dirty. "How is everything going with my sister? Has she bored you to tears yet with her talk of the lab and all the gross things she does there?"

My face burned. I tried to pull my hand away from Hudson, but he held fast. Focusing on me even as he absorbed Stacy's question. He didn't let me move a single step from his side. Not even an inch.

He did answer her, though. "It was going well—and no tears."

I almost choked at his response. He was so dry with her, so bare-boned. I knew Stacy well enough to know that she would have no clue how to take that. He'd offered her nothing to work with, and that might have been the best gift he could have given me. Other than the licking me until I screamed thing. That probably would have made an even better present.

Stacy, meanwhile, seemed gobsmacked by his answer. I could see it on her face as she tried to engage him again. "You're really going to have to work to get her out of the house, unless, of course, you happen to have moldy old books and dead bodies lined up somewhere. Got any awesome plans for her?"

Hudson pulled me closer, one hand sliding to my waist, the other reaching down to grab hold of my ass just as the guy from his story couple had done. It was a telling move, one that screamed ownership and protection. Physical intimacy, even. My hands found their way to his chest—his hard, muscular chest that filled out his fitted T-shirt perfectly. Jesus, the man put those hot, oily body builders to shame.

And then he opened his mouth, and I'm pretty sure my panties melted.

"Yes. I plan to take her back to the hotel room and make her come on my tongue."

HUDSON

Knowing humans thought of Macy and her sister as identical only proved to me how poor their eyesight had to be. There were slight variances that were easy to notice. A different curve to their ears, a small change in the shape of their eyes. And the lips—Macy's lips looked nothing like Stacy's. How did humans not notice such things?

Though at that point, I should have been paying more attention to Stacy's expression. Macy's sister looked at me as a great predator that had finally been taken down would look at their foe. In surprise and shock that they'd been bested. I hadn't spent most of my life mastering the skill of the hunt to fail because of a small, human girl.

"Excuse me?" she said with a tone to her voice that I immediately understood meant she was cross with me.

Interesting.

I raised and lowered my shoulders in a move that humans seemed to use to denote a casual attitude. "Your sister and I will get along just great once you leave us alone to continue our date."

The little human who looked so much like my match huffed and put her hands on her hips. The move made her appear larger and reminded me of some of the flying prey I once hunted on Xouthhgros. It was a show, one to fool a lesser hunter. One that did not fool me.

"Is he always so rude?" she asked Macy.

But my female was not fooled either. She pushed herself closer to me, curling into my hold as if seeking comfort or protection. Both things I would happily offer her.

"He's not rude," Macy said.

"But you invited me." Stacy dropped her arms and cocked her head, focusing solely on her sister.

"No, I didn't," Macy said. "You invited yourself."

"You didn't tell me no."

Macy peered up at me for a moment before sighing. "You're right, I didn't. And that was my fault. But really, Stacy, who invites themself along on someone's first date? Why would you think that was a good idea?"

The wily one started to breathe heavy and drop water from her eyes. A fascinating trick, really. "I just wanted to check in on you."

"And now you have," I said, giving Macy an extra squeeze. "Your sister is safe with me."

Stacy stared hard at her sister, but my match said nothing more. Instead, Macy curled into my chest and allowed me to support her, to hold her. To prove she was mine.

"Fine," Stacy eventually spat as she turned to leave us. "I'll just...go."

Macy sighed. "Wait. Let us walk you to your car."

I grunted my disapproval, but Macy patted my chest and gripped my hand in hers. That reassurance was enough for me to agree to follow the sister to her car. The sooner we got rid of the sister, the sooner I could get Macy back to the hotel. I needed to prove to her how good of a man I could be so she would agree to be my mate. There was no denying I would croon for her—it was only a matter a time.

The walk over to a garage in Greektown was long, but it brought us closer to our hotel. I considered that a positive. The closer we were to the hotel, the sooner I could get Macy back into the room and strip her down. I wanted to tease her, to enjoy the taste of her cunt on my tongue, and to feel her come around my cock. I wasn't sure if any of that was a possibility, but being alone in a room together seemed the best place to at least attempt to entice her into the bed.

Stacy didn't say anything as we escorted her to her parking place. That wouldn't have bothered me, except it appeared to bother Macy. She looked miserable, which only made me more cross with her sister. Why had she interrupted us on our date? And why, if Macy was of her blood, had she tried to embarrass my match? Even though we were not of the same kin, Cutlass and Maverick would never do such things to me. They would come if I needed them, without question, but they would never interrupt without cause. I did not understand human clan connections.

Macy hugged her sister when we got to the car. "I'm sorry. You know you can call and check in at any time."

"Do you mean that?"

"Totally." Macy gritted her teeth, something that made me think her response had not been completely truthful.

"Good." Stacy gave me a bit of a death stare. "And lose the rudeness. We're practically family now, and I'm part of the deal with her."

Biting back a growl was difficult, to say the least. Why was this human so determined to live with her bad mood? She had barely smiled at all, something very unlike the other humans I'd gotten to know. Including my Macy, who stood looking almost afraid as she glanced from Stacy to me and back. That wouldn't do. As much as I'd learned about human culture, being up close to a relationship as intricate and complicated as *twi-ihn* siblings left me speechless and without a plan. But as always, I was confident Macy and I were matched for a reason. So I put on my best smile, held tight to Macy's hand, and pinned Stacy with a look that sent most prey animals scuttling back to their dens.

"It was nice to meet you, Stacy. I look forward to seeing you again."

She blinked, seeming to be unsure of what to say.

"See?" Macy said, drawing Stacy's attention. "We're fine. Go have fun. I'll call you later tonight."

Stacy didn't seem convinced. "Fine. You'd better be nice to her."

"I will." And I would. The second we made it back to the hotel room and I got Macy alone, I was going to be extra nice to her. With my tongue.

Everything would work out as soon as the sister went home.

CHAPTER SIX_

You know what big beds are good for? Sleeping. Know what else? Me neither, because my sister was an evil, evil woman, hell-bent on making my life miserable.

"It's ringing again," Hudson said as he tossed his clothes in a bag. How that man could even look at me after the bullshit night we'd had, I didn't know. Thankfully, he seemed more sad than angry. A fact that actually didn't make me feel any better.

I snagged the phone from where I'd left it only a few minutes before and swiped to answer. "What?"

"Jeesh, sis. Such a cranky greeting."

If I could have crushed the damn thing at that point, I would have. "You have called me every ten minutes. You have interrupted meals and talks and my one immersive date. What more could you possibly have to say to me right now?"

Stacy sat quiet for a few moments before a faint, "Drive safe," came over the line.

I sagged, all anger blown out of me by two soft words. "I will. I'll call when I get home." Sighing, I hung up and slipped the phone into my purse. "I...am so sorry."

"For what?"

"For her. We're really close, and I know she's only doing this because she pushed me to go so far out of my comfort zone by meeting you. It's just…" I didn't even have the words for what her behavior was. Not then. Probably not ever. How did you explain to someone that you called each other a hundred times a day just to make sure the other was alive?

There was no holding back my sigh. "We're really close."

Hudson chuckled softly before bending over me to give me a sweet kiss, one that I wanted to lengthen and dive into, that I wanted to allow to get out of control.

I sucked so hard at losing control, though.

"Don't apologize for your sister," he said against my lips. "She worries about you. And we have time to be alone. This was not the only time you'll see me."

"I know, but…"

He kissed me again, laying me back on the bed and resting on top of me. That kiss became more of what I wanted. Deeper, stronger, rougher…more of everything good and sexy in the world. As we'd done too many times to count, we wrapped ourselves around one another in that big old bed and fell into the lust-fueled haze of making out.

But this time was different. This was it. I could feel the connection, the desire coming from both of us. This time, we'd finish what we started. No interruptions, no stopping, nothing in the way. My sister wouldn't call again, and if she did, I'd totally ignore it.

As Hudson's hand crept under my shirt to cup my breast, I wrapped my legs around his hips and pulled him closer. So hard, so strong. The man made one hell of a sexy blanket.

Hudson pinched my nipple as he bit my bottom lip, rocking his hips into mine for good measure. My entire body begged to scream yes. I wanted more of this. More rubbing, thrusting, teasing. More of him and me together. Even with our clothes on, there was no denying the heat between us. The chemistry. This was our time, and there would be no stopping us from finally getting exactly what we needed.

I arched my back and pressed against where he was hard for me. So hard. He groaned something that sounded more growl than not and rocked his hips into mine, desperate and needy. I wanted him…wanted this…wanted everything he had to give me.

"Hudson," I whispered, ready to surrender. Ready to end this insane roller coaster of need and buildup and crash. Ready—

"Housekeeping." The door to the room flew open, and without knocking, an older lady walked in with towels over her arm.

Team Cockblocks: 492. Team Hudson and Macy: 0

———

Walking out of the hotel with a very unsatisfied Hudson by my side was one of the worst experiences of my life. Not only because I was a shaky, needy mess, but because Hudson was, too. The universe simply did not want to see us get laid. The bastards.

"So you'll call me?" I asked as we reached my car. Ugh, the tone of my voice was another fuck-up on my part. I sounded desperate even to my own ears, which only made me cringe. But Hudson didn't seem to care. He wrapped his arms around me and held me close, pressing his lips to mine for a not-quite-public-approved kiss. Screw anyone watching us, though. I needed his hands on my ass and his tongue brushing mine.

Though I did pull away when I moaned. Loudly. I totally had a thing for the way he grabbed my ass.

Hudson groaned quite a bit softer than I did and rocked me slightly in his arms. Sort of dancing with me, but not. It was cute.

"Of course," he mumbled against the top of my head. "I'll call you right away."

I sighed and curled into his embrace. "Oddly enough, I'm going to miss you."

"I don't think that's odd at all. I'm going to miss you, too, Macy."

"We'll just have to go on another date soon, then." I bit my lip and looked up at him, so fucking happy when he smiled.

"Of course we will." He kissed me again before pulling away enough to rub his nose along mine. "Next time we go out, maybe you can turn your phone off so she can't interrupt us."

My response came before I even gave a thought to it but not before pictures of my sister, completely bald from the chemo and lying in a hospital bed with tubes and wires attached everywhere, popped into my head. "But she might need me."

He frowned, a quick expression he replaced with a smile almost before I completely caught it. And didn't that make me feel worse? As if Stacy's needs were greater than his. But by the way I'd acted this weekend, that's exactly the picture I'd painted. I'd let Stacy run rampant through my immersive date with my potential husband, never putting my foot down and saying I needed time alone with him.

But maybe that was part of the problem. Maybe I was too afraid of being alone with Hudson to turn off the damn phone. Which was silly, right? I mean, it wasn't as if he'd pushed or done anything to scare me. He and I pretty much just cuddled and hung out on one side of the king-sized bed, talking a lot, eating occasionally, and kissing more than I had since my pre-having-sex days. Long, drawn-out make-out sessions that ended with the ringing of my phone every single time, leaving both of us hot, bothered, and unfulfilled. What we did not do was bump uglies. Knock boots. Mattress dance. Take a ride to O-town. Horizontal mambo. Nope, none of that. And as I stood in the parking garage of the hotel Sunday afternoon, I mentally kicked myself for every stopped session. I'd given myself a case of epididymal hypertension, more commonly known as blue balls. If I'd had a scrotum, of course. Which I didn't, but there was a case of a patient born as a—

Where had my brain gone?

"I really do have to go," I whispered, pulling myself from his arms in the most reluctant move ever. "Way too much studying to do."

Hudson sighed and let me go, though his hand lingered on my arm as if to steady me as I sank into my car. Good thing, because I was feeling surprisingly weak. Asthenia, a condition where the body loses strength in part or in whole. That was me. All...asthenia-ish.

And apparently, not ready to go yet. "Hey, Hudson?"

"Yeah?"

"I really am sorry. For everything."

His smile didn't even seem forced. "Don't be. It was a good date."

I shut the car door and hung my head. "No, it wasn't."

He yanked open the door and leaned in, pinning me to my seat. His mouth was fierce on mine, demanding and sure as he kissed me like a man possessed. Like a man in need.

Like a man I wanted to kiss me every day, so long as it was just like this.

When he pulled away, I practically licked my lips for one more taste of him. "What was that for?"

"A reminder." He kissed me again, softer this time, sweeter. His thumb rubbing a small arc along my cheek. "We were matched for a reason, my Macy. And no matter what happens, no matter how many times your phone rings or who walks into the room, at the end of two weeks, I'll still want you as my match."

"How can you be so sure?"

"I'm a hunter. Patience and confidence come with the job."

A hunter...huh. That made sense. "Dead things."

He grinned. "Yes, dead things. I'm used to that smell. Now go study so you can call me later. And drive safely," Hudson said as he stepped away from my car.

"You too." I slid the key in the ignition, and four seconds later, was heading out onto the street. Which hurt. A lot.

Driving away was strangely the most difficult thing I'd ever done. I didn't want to go home and study—I wanted to stay with Hudson. To spend more time with him. To say screw all the hours spent huddled over books, the money on tuition, and the lost opportunities for social anything. I wanted to say screw it all and screw him instead. What was wrong with me? I'd known the guy for twenty-four hours... It wasn't as if I'd actually fallen for him or anything. There'd been no time for that sort of nonsense. I lusted after him, sure. But love? Real feelings? Not possible.

Not really.

HUDSON

The sister needed a mate of her own so she would leave mine alone long enough for me to get her naked.

Still, as I made my way back to the *were-howss*, I could not stop my smile. I had met my mate, the female I would be with forever. And she was perfect. Smart and educated, going so far as wanting to be a healer for her people—an honor where I was from. She was funny and creative. And she was beautiful. Her long dark hair and big brown eyes were imprinted on my brain. I would think of them as I took my cock in hand later. Think of her sweet smiles and the flush of her skin when I made her laugh. I would think only of my Macy.

And I would do anything to see her again. Soon.

When I got back to the *were-howss*, Cutlass and Klow-ee were waiting for me in their unit.

"So," the little human asked. "How'd it go?"

I grinned, unable to hold it back. "Good."

Klow-ee leaned forward as if waiting for something. And then she frowned. "That's it? Good. A cheap pizza is good, a jog through the park is good, hell, a pap *schh-meer* can be good. Meeting your match shouldn't be...just good."

I raised a shoulder, still grinning. "It was good. She wants to be a healer for humans. She's very smart."

"Okay," Klow-ee said, drawing out the word to sound like two. Ooh and kaee.

Cutlass chuckled and pulled Klow-ee back into his lap. "Hudson is happy. That should tell you enough."

But his mate did not look accepting of that. "Hudson is always happy. That's just him."

Klow-ee refocused on me, cocking her head like a bird of prey. "Did you tell her where you're from? That you're an—" she lowered her voice "—alien?"

I never understood why she said that word so quietly. "No. I enjoyed her company, though. She's the right match for me."

"Congratulations," Cutlass said. "Did you mate her?"

Klow-ee smacked him in the chest. "Jeez, Cutlass. Way to be *suu-tull*."

"What is *suu-tull*?" he asked, looking from her to me and back again. I could only shake my head. That word didn't translate.

"Shit. You guys need reprogramming for the language or something." Klow-ee scrunched up her face in an odd, totally human way. "So, since my man here came in like a wrecking ball...did you?"

"Did I what?" I asked as I leaned against the wall by the door.

"Mate her? Have the sex? Get down and dirty in the C with the D?"

I only understood one of those questions. "No. We did mate mouths, though. I can see now why you and Cutlass are always attached at the lips. Her taste is addictive."

They both stared at me as if I was an idiot. And maybe I was because I had wanted very much to bury my face in Macy's cunt, and I had not. Because of a phone that pinged and beeped and danced across the counters far too often. I guess I could have tried harder. Macy could have spoken to her sister as I licked her. Well, she could have listened. I hoped to be good enough to keep her from being able to speak more than my name. And maybe the word more. I liked the word more. But my mate was obviously tied to her sister in a way that was stronger than most sibling relationships. Why, I had no idea, but there was a need for connection between them. I couldn't tear them apart for my own needs and wants.

Cutlass finally broke the heavy silence. "You met the female you want to be your mate and did nothing?"

Before I could answer, Klow-ee smacked him in the chest. "Way to be supportive."

"You're a stronger man than I," Cutlass said as he rubbed the arm of his mate.

Klow-ee smacked him. Again. "Or she's not as much of a *hu-sssee* as I was."

Cutlass looked to me as if I was supposed to understand his mate's words. I didn't, so I only stared back.

A strange beeping sounded through the room, soft but persistent. It reminded me of Macy's phone, but not the same tone. Had the damn thing followed me home? I growled, looking around to pinpoint the annoying noise.

"What was that?" Cutlass asked.

Klow-ee rolled her eyes enough to show the whites along the bottom. "Where's your phone, Hudson?"

"What phone?"

As another ping sounded, the human dove for me. I took a step to the side, trapped against the wall as I was, but Klow-ee didn't relent. She followed me, thrusting her hands into my pockets. I shot Cutlass a helpless look, hoping he'd tear his mate away so I could go back to searching for the noise.

He did not. In fact, I was pretty sure he laughed.

"The phone," Klow-ee said as she patted my ass for the second time. "The little silver thing I gave you. Where is your phone?"

"Oh. That." I pulled the device out from the throat of my boot and handed it to her. She looked from my boot to the phone and then back to me.

"You keep your phone in your shoe?"

"You told me not to lose it. I won't lose it if it's next to my hunting blade."

"I don't think I want to know." She handed me back the phone with a huge smile on her face. "You have a text message."

The translation images for those words didn't make sense. "A what?"

"It's like a letter, but shorter and electronic. It's from someone named Macy."

"That is my mate." I gripped the device, trying hard to understand the lines and arcs. "What does it say?"

Klow-ee peeked over my arm. "It says she's still missing you and wants to know if you'd like to have dinner tonight."

"Yes." I shook the device and raised my voice. "Yes. I would like that very much."

Klow-ee placed her hand on my arm. "You need to send her a text back."

Yes. Of course. I just needed to... Wait, what?

"I don't know how."

Klow-ee glanced at Cutlass before sighing. "Okay. I'll step in and help, but don't ask me to lie to her about your alienness. And don't expect me to be the go-between if you two start to sext."

I watched as her fingers flew over the screen. "What is sext?"

"Sending naughty notes and pictures."

Once again, the human methods of communication baffled me. "Pictures of what?"

"Dick pics." Klow-ee waved in the direction of my cock. "I don't want to see your junk."

I looked at Cutlass, disappointed in my friend for the first time since I'd met him. "She calls your cock junk? And I thought *I* had failed my female."

Cutlass didn't look happy. "My cock is not junk."

"Your mate says it is."

Klow-ee, meanwhile, said nothing as she dealt with the text

messages. Minus pictures. Though I thought I saw a smile curving one side of her mouth.

"My mate knows my cock is good," Cutlass said with a bit of a growl. Klow-ee glanced up at me and blinked a single eye. She was an odd human.

Cutlass seemed to take her non-response as a challenge. "I'll prove my cock is not junk. Right now."

Klow-ee shoved the phone in my hand and gave me a large smile. "Meet her at Xochimilco at seven." She spun to face her mate, cocking a hip. He growled, stalking closer. His gaze intense and focused solely on her. The air filled with the scent of arousal, both hers and Cutlass'. It was time for me to go.

"Thank you, Klow-ee."

"No, thank *you*, Hudson."

Cutlass grabbed her, his hands gripping her ass and his face buried in her neck. Definitely time for me to go. I didn't need to see their mating.

I had my own female now.

CHAPTER SEVEN_

MACY

Eight days, three dates, and a hell of a lot of battery power after we left the hotel, and I was ready. I'd learned a lot about Hudson in the time we'd spent together. I knew he liked his steaks rare, his vegetables nonexistent, and me writhing around on top of him as we dry humped on my couch. I also knew he was a kind, funny man who looked at me as if I was the greatest thing that had ever happened to him and who forgave me every single time my sister interrupted one of our impressive make-out sessions. Which was every time. Still, he seemed to think I was sexy and special and worth waiting for.

Tonight, I was going to do my best to live up to that.

"So it's the big reveal tonight," Stacy said as she lounged on my bed.

"The big reveal?"

"I noticed you matched your bra to your undies. You only do that when you expect someone to see them."

"He's seen my bra and undies."

"But has he been inside them?"

Technically, no. His hands, sure. But otherwise, we'd been fairly chaste. Okay fine, dry humping our brains out wasn't exactly chaste, but that didn't count. Not really. Neither did me giving him a hand job or him making me come with his fingers. Mouths and other places were all that really counted.

And I was more than ready to make some things count.

"Why are you here anyway?" I asked as I tried once again to get my hair to behave. "I thought you were going out with Chad tonight?"

"Chad's on time-out."

Not surprising. My sister's pseudoboyfriend was an asshole of the utmost persuasion. Why she bothered with him after all these years, I had no idea. Guess that whole first-love thing tended to stick a bit, even when it shouldn't. "What for this time?"

"Being Chad. Again."

Which probably meant she'd caught him flirting, texting, Facebook messaging, Instagram DMing, Snapchatting or otherwise having sexual conversations with women who weren't her. Bastard.

But this topic was neither new nor unexpected. I needed to tread carefully. "Maybe you should dump him."

"Maybe I should find myself a nice mail order husband like you've got with Hudson." Stacy's words came out with venom behind them, but I knew she didn't mean them that way. Not really. Her heart had been broken a million times by Chad. She couldn't help but lash out when that was brought back to her attention. So I ignored the heat and the hurt behind those words, and I concentrated on straightening my hair.

"He's not my husband."

She huffed a disbelieving sigh. "You two are practically attached at the hip. He might as well be."

"I have a few more days to decide if we're locking things down. Don't rush me on what is already a really rushed schedule."

She appeared in the mirror behind me, looking over my shoulder and meeting my gaze. "I can't believe it worked."

There was such sadness in her voice, such longing. That pain ate at me, but I knew if I pushed her to walk away from Chad and do something to find someone new, she'd lash out again. We'd had the Chad discussion a hundred times, especially how dangerous it was to be sexually involved with someone who wasn't monogamous. Those discussions led to things like screaming matches and slide shows of disease-riddled genitals, neither of which I was up for at the moment.

So I ignored the elephant in the room. "I can't believe you signed me up for it."

She nodded, still looking like a woman on the defensive. "Just think, if I'd signed myself up, I could be the one about to marry that hunky foreigner."

Intermittent explosive disorder. Personality eruptions which occur suddenly. Often preceded or accompanied by rage, irritability, tremors, chest tightness, and palpitations. Sounded about right.

"That hunky foreigner has a name," I said, trying to control my voice as I resisted the urge to smack her with my hairbrush. Stacy stared, almost challenging me. But unlike every other time in our life, I wasn't backing down. Not on this. Not on Hudson. He was mine...period. She could find her own hunky foreigner with or without a name.

A knock at the door interrupted our weighty silence, though it didn't stop the anger pulsing through me. I knew she didn't mean it—at least, I was pretty sure—but Stacy's words still stung. I liked Hudson...a lot. I didn't want to think about what would have happened if I'd written my own letter or Stacy had joined the program as herself instead. I couldn't.

"I'll get that," Stacy said just before she disappeared into the hallway. She suddenly sounded so happy. So...peppy. She was about to cause trouble. But I had a feeling Hudson could handle her just fine.

I rolled my eyes and finished my hair, eventually following behind her. I knew it was Hudson before I reached the living room, could almost feel him in my place. But it was Stacy's syrupy sweet come-on voice that stole my focus.

"Most people have more trouble telling us apart." She giggled. Honestly giggled. At my date. I was going to kill her. With pain. Lots of it.

"You're not Macy. You smell wrong," Hudson said, his deep voice sending a shiver up my spine.

There was a long silence, one in which I simply stood in the hall, tried my best not to laugh, and waited for Stacy to respond. I wasn't disappointed when she did.

"Wrong? I smell *wrong*?"

Yep. That went over like a lead balloon. Figuring I'd better save my date, I turned the corner, a wide smile breaking out when I saw Hudson there. He grinned back and pushed past Stacy in a move that must have really pissed her off.

Hudson didn't seem to have a single fuck to give to my sister, though. "I have missed you, my Macy."

I sank into his arms, cuddling against his chest with a soft moan I could only hope no one heard. What? That chest was a goddamned miracle of nature. "I missed you, too."

"You two make me sick," Stacy said from somewhere behind us. Her voice was sort of sad, but I couldn't worry about her right then. I had a plan that involved Hudson, no clothes, my bed, and me. She was not invited.

"Thanks for stopping by," I called out, still clinging to my man. Still craving to feel more of him. "I'll talk to you tomorrow."

The slam of the door was her only response. I knew my phone would be blowing up later, but for the moment, I had everything I wanted. A moment of peace, a quiet apartment, and Hudson in my arms.

"Should we go?" Hudson asked as he nuzzled down the length of my neck. I arched my back, making sure he had plenty of room to do more than just nuzzle. Something he understood and took advantage of by biting along my trapezius muscles as he moved from my clavicle to my mandible. It felt so good, so arousing as his bites turned from soft to hard. From playful to demanding.

Who knew a neck could be an erogenous zone?

"Hudson," I whispered, clinging to his shoulders. He groaned softly, the sound something I could feel where I leaned against him. Something I wanted to feel in more places. Lots of places. I wanted him to live up to his promise from the first night we met.

So I pulled out of his arms with a firm, "No."

"No?"

"No," I whispered with a slow shake of my head. "I don't want to go."

Poor Hudson looked slightly confused and terribly turned on. A fabulous combination in my opinion.

"What do you want, then?"

"You." Taking a deep breath, I did the only thing I could to make sure he knew how committed I was to what I wanted. I pulled away and grabbed my phone, making a big production of turning it off before setting it back on the counter. Stacy be damned... For one night, I wanted some private time with my man.

Hudson damn near knocked me to my knees when he licked his top lip in a subtle, almost unconscious way. That flash of pink was deadly to my girly parts.

And no, I wasn't going to use anatomically correct names for them.

"You have me," he said, his voice a deep, seductive tone that did nothing to quell my need for him. "What more do you want?"

All of it. All the more you have to give. All of you.

But I didn't say that. Instead, I told him the truth.

"You. Naked. In my bed." I pulled my dress over my head and let the gauzy fabric fall to the floor. "Now."

HUDSON

My cock had never ached so much. Not even when I was a young cub and growing into my needs as a male had I desired release so badly. But this was more than sexual. This was esehhnce. This was an attraction to the woman in front of me on every level. One I refused to ignore.

I could smell Macy's desire, feel her need in the way her body trembled as I followed her to her bedroom. She was ready for me, and I was ready to make her mine.

The second we were over the threshold, I slammed the door and picked her up. Those legs I longed to lick wrapped around me, and the heat of her cunt warmed my skin even through my shirt. She made me ache for her.

And I had a feeling the future doctor knew exactly what to do to soothe that.

I devoured her lips with a growl, sliding my tongue inside when she gasped. Her mouth tasted sweet, and her body was soft but firm where it met mine. She was everything I could have wanted, and she was in my arms and ready to mate. Finally. Great stars, we'd waited so long for this. My cock was practically leaking for her.

"Hudson," she whispered as she gripped my mane. "I don't normally do this."

"Do what?" I nearly came when she tugged at me. That little sign of aggression fueled my own. I tossed her on the bed, yanking my shirt over my head before reaching for my pants. Luckily, my mate understood my rush.

"This," she said as she helped me pull my clothes off. "I don't normally sleep with someone I barely know."

"That's okay. You won't be sleeping." I ripped the thin, lace garment from around her hips, grabbed her bare legs, and threw them over my shoulders. Her cunt glistened for me, so pink and swollen I had to take a moment to marvel. To stare. To let my mouth water at the sight of her.

She made me so hungry.

I attacked her cunt with a ferocity born of being denied for so long. I needed her, craved her, had to have her...and she was finally ready and willing. I could not delay. I fell upon her cunt like a man starving. That soft flesh was sweet and warm, and I groaned as I licked her. There was nothing like the taste of a female, and especially not my female. I could have licked her for days, lived on nothing but the sweetness she gave me. My cock throbbed, desperate for her tight heat, but I resisted. I had waited too long to taste her—I would not deny myself the pleasure.

Macy trembled and shook, grabbing my mane, directing me to where she wanted my attention. And I took direction well. Some males refused. They wanted to believe their skills could override any desires their female partners tried to show them. Not me. I liked when the female took charge, when she showed me exactly what she needed from me to make her come. Because that was my goal. Make Macy come as many times as I could. It was a challenge I wholeheartedly accepted.

"Fuck, Hudson." Macy spread her legs wider, resting her little feet on my shoulders as I sank deeper into her soft cunt. I couldn't get enough, couldn't stop licking and sucking on her for anything. I spread her like a man in control, devoured her like an animal, and the entire time, she could only beg for more.

So more, I gave.

Her first orgasm crashed over her seemingly without warning. I slid two fingers inside as she came, groaning at the quivering flesh sucking me in, wanting to feel that pressure on my cock. I didn't stop lapping at her, though. Just kept sucking, licking, biting, pumping my fingers in and out. I worked that cunt hard, bringing her three more orgasms before she finally pushed me away.

"Jesus, how do you know how to do that?" she asked, her legs shaking and her breaths coming in pants.

I licked over her hip, practically rutting into the mattress due to my need for her. "I watch a lot of instructional videos on your internet."

Macy went silent, then burst into laughter. The sound was one I loved, one I enjoyed hearing her make. I had made her happy with my words and my mouth on her cunt. Next, I needed to make her happy with my cock. A lot.

She would not walk away from this night calling my cock junk.

I climbed up her body, kissing my way across her breasts. Licking up the column of her neck. "You find me funny?"

Her lips met mine in a sweet, soft kiss that only brought me closer to the edge. The female was dangerous to me, utterly enrapturing. Wild beasts set on defending their territory could have burst through the door, and I wouldn't have been able to tear myself away from her.

"Funny is a relative word," she said, smiling. Another kiss, a soft rubbing of her hand on my back, and I was ready to come. I'd been ready to come since the moment I saw her in that hotel room the first day we met. That need had only grown more urgent as the days had passed.

The urgency escalated when she slipped a hand between us and gripped my cock.

"Macy," I said, my voice almost a whine as I rocked into her hold. So close, so ready for more. But this sweet, soft, beautiful female understood my need. Must have known how badly I wanted to come inside her. Without another word, she rolled me over and straddled my thighs. My hands went to her hips as she reached and grabbed a foil square from the cabinet beside the bed.

"One second." With quick movements, she sheathed my shaft in something thin and cold, but then she was on top of me. Astride me. Bringing me inside her cunt.

And my esehhnce crooned.

CHAPTER EIGHT_

MACY

Hudson was huge. I mean, I'd known that for a while. You couldn't look at him without thinking about the size of the man. But he was huge *everywhere*. And I hadn't had sex in a very long time. My vagina was out of practice, and he was bigger than anyone I'd ever been with. Not the best combination.

"Hudson." My groan made him slow. My nails embedding themselves in his chest probably helped in letting him know I was overwhelmed.

With careful, almost choreographed movements, he rolled me over until he rested on top of me. Never missing a thrust. Something in his chest rumbled against mine, something much like a growl. Which wasn't possible, and yet—

"Are you okay?" he asked, his voice filled with a sensual, gravelly tone that did things to me. Things that melded nicely with the way he filled me. But was I okay? I had no idea. My entire body shook, alive and on the edge of something either amazing or terrible. It was as if my nervous system was rapid-firing signals to my brain, and nothing could keep up with the input.

"Just...so much."

"I know." He bit my neck, and that little lick of pain had me trembling for him. "You're cunt is so small around me."

That should not have been as hot as it was. "It's...been a while."

He grunted, pushing a little deeper, making my back arch and my toes curl and some weird animal-like bleating escape my chest. He was going to break my pussy. Not in a bad way, more in an I'm-never-going-to-be-able-to-have-sex-with-anyone-smaller way. And I was going to love every second of it.

"Shit," I hissed as a tingle shot right through my clit.

"You okay?" he asked, his voice breathless, his hips still rocking. Was I? I didn't know anymore. All I knew was push and pull and strain and the pleasure that sent rockets shooting up those bones in my back that I couldn't remember the name of anymore. And a need for more.

"Please," I whispered as I wrapped my legs around him and clutched at his shoulders. "More."

Hudson answered my request with gusto. He slammed into me, his cock pushing deeper than I had thought possible, bottoming out as his hips met into mine. I gasped and arched harder, pulling him into me, needing more. Wanting it all. And he gave it. He put everything he had into that performance. Thrusting deep, pulling almost all the way out to slowly slide back inside, rotating his hips so he added a bit of pressure to my clit. He worked me over good. There was no avoiding my orgasm, no escaping him to make it last. Nope, that sucker slammed into me like a freight train without brakes. One second, I was a gasping, sweaty mess clinging to the man on top of me. The next, I was...well, a gasping, sweaty mess clinging to the man on top of me while in the middle of the best orgasm of my life.

And then he did it all again.

By the time I collapsed on Hudson's chest after successfully completing a reverse-cowgirl round, I was a trembling blob of sensation and sexual satiation. Thankfully, so was he.

"That was amazing," I said, unable to catch my breath.

His chest rumbled as he laughed. "You almost sound surprised. Did you doubt my prowess?"

"No, I think I doubted mine." I squealed as he rolled me, and I looked up at him as he once more lay on top of me. As he surprised me with his nonexistent refractory period. Did he never lose his erection?

Damn, the man was heavy and thick. Everywhere. All the time, it seemed.

And he was a charmer. "You are so sensual, so sexy, so beautiful. There was no way that wouldn't have been, as you say, *ah-maessing.*"

I ran a finger over his cheek, smiling, unable to resist my utter and total attraction to him. "Your accent is so sexy. Where are you from again?"

He kissed down my sternum and over to my breast, biting the nipple softly. "A long, long way away. But we are here now. That's more important."

I groaned as his hand slid over my hip to my pussy. Yes, that was definitely more important. Looked like it was time for round who-the-hell-knew.

Somewhere around five in the morning, I'd finally had enough.

"I need a shower."

Hudson, apparently, wasn't as finished. "Why?"

"Because I'm sweaty and smelly."

He groaned and pulled me into his arms. And then he sniffed me. "Not true. Besides, I like you sweaty."

"That's so...weird." I laughed and rose to my feet, comfortable in my nakedness. The man had spent literal hours with his face smashed against my pussy. A little naked ass wasn't going to bother him. "Join me?"

Hudson grabbed my hand and followed me into the bathroom, keeping close. Really close. Like, I could feel him hardening against my ass close. This was going to be the best shower ever; I just knew it.

"I'm turning on the light," I said as we crossed into my little bathroom. "You'd better close your eyes."

"Why?"

I flipped the switch right as he asked the question, not giving him time to prepare. It wasn't intentional; I was just so used to the blazing bulbs over the sink that I knew to keep my eyes closed when I'd been accustomed to the dark. Hudson did not. He yelped and brought both hands to his face.

"Sorry. It's bright. Give yourself a minute." I readied the shower and made sure the water was nice and warm, a feat that took longer than it should have. Old buildings didn't have the best plumbing, but it gave Hudson time to adjust to the light. Or so I hoped. He spent the time leaning against a wall and rubbing his eyes.

"Why does your light cause so much pain?" he asked as I finished setting things up for us.

"It's too bright, I know, but it works to wake me up in the mornings when I've been studying all night." I grabbed Hudson's hand and pulled him into the shower before reaching for the poof and body wash. And then I frowned. "I don't have anything that smells manly."

He huffed a laugh, still with his eyes closed, and let his hands wander all the way to my ass. Surprising how that happened. "I will smell like your cunt before I leave. That's manly enough."

"You are such a guy." I turned my back to him to wash my hair. He, of course, moved on from washing my ass to giving my breasts a solid soaping. The perv. "I never thought I'd be okay with a guy using the c-word around me."

"The *see-werrd?*"

Oh gosh, he was going to make me say it.

"Cunt," I whispered, almost unable to get the word out.

"Why not?" Hudson dropped one hand between my legs, cupping the part of me in question. "That is what it is."

"True, but the word has negative connotations here. If someone called me that, I'd be ready to tear their face off."

"But I don't call you a cunt. I call this a cunt. A beautiful, wet, perfect cunt. My cunt."

I leaned back against him, rocking as his fingers explored my... Nope, couldn't do it. Pussy. He was exploring my pussy. But as he leaned over me and worked his finger against my clit, his chest vibrated in a way that wasn't quite...normal. The sound was one I'd heard from him earlier in the night, but this was louder. Longer and stronger. And decidedly not something I'd heard from other people.

"What's that noise?" When he didn't answer, I turned and looked up at him. "Hudson? I've heard that before. What is it?"

Hudson practically froze for a moment. Then he took a deep breath and opened his eyes. "Macy, I—"

"What the hell is wrong with your eyes?"

HUDSON

"Hudson? I've heard that before. What is it?"

Her voice washing over me sent chills up my spine. I kept my eyes closed, thinking. Worrying. She heard me croon for her. It wasn't the first time I'd done it, but this was louder and more insistent than before. There was no human way to explain the sound. I needed to tell her the truth. Crooning was supposed to be such a special thing, a moment a potential mate pair would remember throughout their lives. I wanted to share that moment with her, to explain the sound and what it meant. I wanted her to understand the significance. She wanted—needed—to know about me, about Reithharians and our mating customs, all of it. And I needed to tell her. I knew we would work out in the end, and yet the idea of upsetting her with the truth had me pausing. Something I was unaccustomed to doing.

Macy turned in my arms, rubbing her body against mine as she did. My little female was so beautiful and sexy, even when I couldn't see her. I let my hunter senses take over, basking in her scent, her feel, her heat. The curve of her under my fingers, the softness against my chest. The warm scent of her desire floating in the air. Perfect, all of her. I wanted to tell her my secrets, to have her know who and what I was. I wanted to mate with her fully and have her live with me like Cutlass and Klow-ee did. Marriage, they called it on Earth. I wanted it. I wanted so much. But first, she had to know...had to be told. So I took a deep breath, opened my eyes, and looked right into hers.

"Macy, I—"

She gasped and stiffened in my arms. "What the hell is wrong with your eyes?"

"What?"

"They're...yellow. Like, really yellow."

It took me a few moments to understand her words, but when I did, my stomach sank. The light...the pain in my eyes...the need I felt to keep them closed. The lenses making my Reithhar eyes more human must have come out at some point.

This was not how I wanted to start the conversation. "Macy, don't be afraid."

But she was already rushing out of the shower. Away from me.

"Why are your eyes yellow? That's not a normal color."

It was to me, but the human definition of normal was far different from the Reithhar one. "It is the eye color of my kind."

She blinked. Twice. "And what *kind* is that? Where are you from that yellow eyes are normal?"

And there it was. The question that I needed to answer, the one I couldn't run away from or try to sneak past. "Please, don't be afraid."

"Shit." She rushed out of the bathroom and across her bedroom, pulling clothes from a large piece of furniture once she reached it. "Telling me not to be afraid makes me afraid. Be honest with me, Hudson. What the fuck is going on?"

She threw my pants at me once she was covered, and I slid them on over my wet skin because it seemed to be what she wanted. A barrier. Something between us.

I hated that she wanted distance.

"My name is Hohddshoun, and I am a Reithhar Master Hunter from planet Xouthhgros. I am...not from Earth."

She stared for a long moment before shaking her head. "Nope."

"What?"

"Nope. I am nopeing out of this conversation." Hands up, she pushed past me and hurried down the hall.

"I don't know what *noe-pah* is, but I need you not to do it," I said as I followed behind her like the desperate male I was. "You are my mate, and I—"

She stopped and spun, her eyes filled with something akin to anger. She looked ready to attack. I had pushed her into predator mode.

"I'm your what?"

I didn't understand her question. "My mate. My kind, we croon for our mates, for the ones we want to spend our lives with. That's the noise you hear in my chest. I am crooning for you. I have chosen you."

"And if I don't choose you?"

Her words might as well have been a spear to my abdomen. I reached for her, seeking her warmth and touch. Looking for some sort of reassurance.

But she took a step back, taking away my chance. "So you want me to believe that you're an alien from planet Chowthgross—"

"Xouthhgros."

"Whatever," she said while waving her hand as if brushing my correction away. "You're an alien from planet Xouthhgros. You came to Earth for what...our natural resources?"

I wasn't sure how to answer that. Sort of, I guessed, if females were natural resources. But I had a feeling telling her that wouldn't work in my favor. So I stayed silent, something that only seemed to make her angrier.

Macy stalked closer, a huntress making her move as she gave me a death stare. "Let me get this straight. You came here and decided to join a dating agency? To use them to help find you a woman dumb enough to fall for this?"

The translation for *dumm* didn't fit my mate at all. "No, you're not *dumm*, Macy. I came here because of an ad for Ampetheia. I wanted her to help me find my mate."

She froze, her eyes going even wider. "They know? The agency knows you're...not human?"

That question seemed dangerous, but I answered it. "Yes."

She paced across the room, her voice much softer when she said, "And what? You were going to just enjoy my *cunt* and head back to the stars?"

I was across the room in a second, pinning her against the wall. "Never. I asked to find a mate because I wanted a female in my life. Someone to cherish and care for, someone to care for me as well. I have found that in you, my Macy. I would never leave you behind to go back out into the cold of space."

"No?"

"No." I ran my hand down her soft, dark hair. Crooning to her. "I would take you with me."

She jerked away from my touch. "You'd abduct me to your ship and drag me away from everything I know?"

"*Abb-duktah?* What is this word?"

"Take. Steal. Kidnap."

The images...women crying, children screaming. The translator could not have been right on what she meant. "I...no. That's not what I said."

"Might as well have been." She pushed me away and headed for the door. "Hudson, I don't know what game you're playing, but this ends now. I'm not dealing with your level of crazy, and I'm certainly not going to run away with some alien to the unknown wonders of space."

"Then we can stay here, with Cutlass and Klow-ee." I sighed when she reached for her phone. "Please don't turn that on."

"Why not?"

"Because your sister will call and interrupt us. We need some time alone to talk."

Her face grew redder as the song of the phone powering on played. "I think it's time for you to leave."

"Macy, no. Please hear me—"

"Oh, I've heard enough." She crossed her arms over her chest in a move that screamed defense. She was blocking out what she saw as a threat...which was me. "Please, go."

There was no doubting her words or meaning. With my heart breaking inside of my chest, I crossed the room. I didn't dare touch her for fear she'd completely curl in on herself, but I stood in front of her. And I let her hear my croon.

"My esehhnce sings for you, Macy. You are my one, the female I choose to be mine forever. I am a strong Reithhar, a good provider. I would take care of you."

"And what if I don't want to be taken care of?"

"Then I will stand beside you and listen to your stories of the people passing us by."

Macy sighed, her eyes softening a little. "Hudson, I just... I can't do this right now."

I risked a single touch, a finger to her wrist, before I made the hardest decision of my very long life and headed for the door. "Think about it, Macy. Think about us. We are good together. You know that."

I was halfway down the hall, forcing myself to keep moving away from her as I chanted *It'll all work out* in my head, when the huntress fired what seemed to be her fatal shot.

"I don't know anything anymore."

CHAPTER NINE

HUDSON

"You broke her."

If Maverick didn't stop saying that, I was going to throttle him like some sort of filthy, wily prey. "I did not."

"You must have. She doesn't choose you. You broke the bond."

His words made me ache, made my heart freeze and my mind spin. I hated them. "Shut up, Maverick. You have no idea what you're talking about. Everything will work out."

It was getting harder and harder to believe those words, though.

"Boys," Ampetheia yelled, snapping our attention back across the desk. "I am here to discuss your matches, not listen to you pick at each other."

"Sorry," Maverick mumbled. I nodded to go along with his apology, even though I didn't feel like agreeing with him on anything. Especially not when it came to my Macy.

But Ampetheia seemed satisfied with our sort-of apologies. "Good. Now, Hudson, your match hasn't refused you outright yet."

"She told me to get out and refuses to take my calls or sexts." No, I would not focus on that aspect. I refused. "But it will work out. I'm sure of it."

Ampetheia blinked her orange eyes at me before shaking her head. "Human women are sometimes fickle. She may come around yet, but that would affect Maverick and his match."

Maverick grunted. "Of course."

"Why would Macy choosing me affect him?"

She paused, locking her gaze on mine. The air in the room took on weight. There was no room to breathe, no space to move. I was captivated by those orange eyes as I waited for her to speak. To say something. To find—

"I think you and Maverick are matched to the same female."

The earth stilled. Nothing moved; nothing dared take a breath. Everything ceased to exist for a moment as those words settled over me. And then I was on my feet.

"What?" I roared.

Ampetheia put her hands up in some sort of defensive move. "I'm trying to see past it, but that mirror thing I told you about? Still in effect and tying the two of you together. I just don't understand it."

Maverick stood beside me, looking just as shocked and angry as I felt. "So if she refuses him tomorrow..."

"She could very well end up with you. Normally, I wouldn't tell two males this sort of information, but everything is still unclear and I want to warn you both."

The certainty that Macy would come back to me? The surety I'd had that this plan would work out since I first saw the flyer for the Intergalactic Dating Agency in a bathroom on some far-off space station? It shattered into a million pieces inside of me.

"But she refused me because I am not human," I said. "Maverick is not human."

Ampetheia shook her head. "I can only tell you what I see, and that's Maverick with the same woman I matched to you."

There was no holding in my snarl, no controlling my rage. I stormed out of the room, ready to kill Maverick but knowing I couldn't. If Macy didn't choose me, she would be his. She would need him to protect her, to care for her...to bring her pleasure. And I would be forced to restrain myself every second so as not to destroy the one man who could do all that.

The one man other than me.

"Yo, where's the fire?" Klow-ee asked as she came out of another office.

"No fire," I growled, not stopping. Not even pausing. I needed to get away, to find distance from Maverick before I acted on my rage and my pain. I needed to run, to hunt something, to find some wild and angry beast to work out the feelings inside of me. I needed time to figure out what to do.

But Klow-ee wasn't one to let us run away. She grabbed my arm, something that I normally could have brushed off, but I was so angry, so out of control, I could only stop. I refused to hurt the little female.

"Hey, what's up?" Klow-ee asked, looking at me in a way that only increased my pain. But as a human female, she had a different view than I did on the situation. Plus, I needed to expunge the feelings inside of me.

So I offered them to her. "My Macy may end up with Maverick."

Klow-ee's eyes grew wider. "What? How?"

"Some sort of mirror thing."

"That doesn't sound right. From what you told me about Macy, I can't believe she'd end up turning you down and getting it on with someone you see as a brother. That's like romance novel-level drama."

She never quite made sense to me, but it didn't matter. Nothing mattered. "Ampetheia has seen it. Or something that could possibly be it. I don't really understand the Freknal logic."

"So it's not for sure?" She bared her teeth in a smile when I shook my head. "Then there's still time to prove Ms. Ampetheia wrong. It's not over until the fat lady sings."

"What fat lady?"

"It's an expression. Never mind. Just...sit tight. Don't do anything stupid. I'll see what I can do."

I nodded even though I had no idea what could possibly make things better. But really, what more did I have to lose? I slid to the floor and pulled my knees against my chest. And I waited.

"Not here," Klow-ee yelled when she passed by me a few minutes later.

"But you said sit tight. I sat...as tight as I could."

She made that whooshing sound that meant she was annoyed. Again. I'd done what she asked.

"Sit tight doesn't mean sit...in any way. Go home. Hang out with Cutlass. Fix things if you need to stay busy."

"Humans are strange."

"So are you non-humans, big guy. Now, go. I have work to do."

———

MACY

The hours were unending, long and drawn-out in a way that only made me feel worse. I couldn't even look at my phone, couldn't stand to know if Hudson had been trying to reach me or not. The only thing I seemed to be able to make my body do was go to school. Though, I didn't study or do anything productive while there. Nope. I sat and I stared at all the dead bodies in the lab, the dead humans. All the people who'd lived their lives and given their physical forms to science for research. And I compared them to Hudson.

Bigger or smaller? Paler or darker? What made them different? What made them inherently human and him...not?

But the answers wouldn't come, and the pain just kept growing. Two days had felt like a lifetime; I couldn't imagine saying goodbye forever. But how could I not?

On the third day, the last full day before I was supposed to notify the agency of my decision, my seclusion ended with the throwing open of my apartment's door.

"Bitch, you'd better be alive in here." Stacy stormed into the room with another woman beside her. One I'd never met. One I didn't care to meet, so I huddled under my blanket and tried to be invisible.

"Leave me alone."

"Nope. Not happening." Stacy yanked the blanket away from me, exposing me to the brightest sunlight in the history of the world. And her award-winning glare. "What the hell? You get into a fight with your boyfriend and go radio silent? I thought you might actually be dead this morning."

I tried to grab the blanket, but she danced away and took it with her. The bitch. "I'm not dead. And it wasn't a fight. More of a...disagreement."

"Disagreements don't make people go all quiet and hermit-y. What's up?"

I glanced at the other woman. "Nothing."

Stacy rolled her eyes. "This is Chloe. She was looking for you, so I dragged her up with me."

"I don't know Chloe."

The woman shrugged. "No, you don't, but we have friends in common."

Doubtful. I didn't have any friends. Not really. Not other than Stacy. "Like who?"

"I'm married to Cutlass," Chloe said, looking particularly uninterested and completely focused at the same time. That was a serious skill.

Still... "I don't know a Cutlass."

"He's sort of a brother to Hudson."

That was enough to get me to go vertical once more. "Excuse me?"

"Yeah." She glanced at Stacy. "Think we can get a few minutes alone? I totally get where the hermit thing is coming from."

My sister glanced from one of us to the other before huffing. "Fine. I'm going to run down to the coffee shop. Anyone want anything?"

I shook my head, as did Chloe, and then Stacy was gone. Leaving me alone with a woman I didn't know. One who might be more than she seemed.

"Are you an alien, too?" I asked, curling farther into the corner of the couch.

"Nope. Fully human here." She sat down on the other end, keeping space between us. Whether that was because of my obvious retreat from her or because I hadn't showered in three days and probably smelled like death, I didn't know.

"So..." I said, searching for a way to ask what I wanted to know. Finding none, I went with blunt. "You married an alien."

She grinned. "I did."

"How?"

"You mean the figurative how or the literal? Because my guess is you don't need to know the steps to get a marriage license in Wayne County."

My eye roll would have been epic had I been able to find the energy to give one. "Figurative how."

She shrugged. "I fell in love, so I married him."

"That easy?"

"No, not at all. I did the same thing you did. Only I figured out the alien thing the first weekend."

I snorted a laugh, the kind that was more self-deprecating than funny. "You're smarter than I am."

"No way, Doc. I'm just observant." She shot me a wink and a small, almost crooked grin. "Cutlass can fix things with some sort of alien mojo thing, and I caught him. Scared the hell out of me."

"But you stayed with him."

"After I pulled my head out of my ass and decided he was worth it."

I stared at her, at the way she looked so...happy, pretty, and girl-next-door. Average, in a good way. And yet she had this amazing, fantastical secret. One that people probably never would have suspected. Not that most people would suspect a woman was married to an alien, but line her up with fifteen other people and tell me one had a huge, unbelievable secret, and she'd probably be the last one I thought about. I didn't know if I would be able to appear so...normal.

But hell, I might have been willing to try.

"*Is* he worth it?" I asked, unable not to, even though I felt like an ass for it.

Chloe's smile couldn't have gotten bigger. "Absolutely. He treats me like a queen—like a princess, but way dirtier. There's nothing G-rated about our relationship."

"Sex doesn't cure all."

"No, but it's nice. And being treated well cures a lot. Being respected, even more. Being loved unconditionally pretty much makes everything come up rainbows and unicorns and glitter. That's what you get with these guys."

I couldn't help myself. "Unicorns vomiting glitter?"

She shrugged again, rolling right along with my sarcasm. "Something like that."

But there was no glitter in my world at that moment, no rainbows in the sky, and I was afraid I'd killed off the last unicorn. Figuratively, of course. "I called him a liar."

"He's not a liar, he's an alien."

"I'm not sure that's much better." The words sounded harsh, and I regretted them almost the second they left my mouth. Of course it was better to be an alien. Hudson had never lied, not really. He'd hidden the details of his origin from me, but he hadn't lied. I needed to stop treating him as if he had, but I didn't know how.

And yet... "I didn't write my letter."

"I lied in mine." Chloe shrugged as my head popped up. "Ms. Ampetheia doesn't match off the letter. She senses connections. The mail order bride thing is sort of misleading."

"Huh." I hadn't expected that one. "Well, that's one thing off my mind. Though it doesn't help the fact that I was a jerk to Hudson."

Chloe sat back as I castigated myself, giving me a long look that made me want to curl up and hide. It was as if she could see into me, see through me. As if she knew all my secrets.

"Do you love him?" she finally asked.

I didn't even need to think about it. Not really. "Yeah, I do."

"Then what does it matter? He's here on Earth with you. He wants you. He loves you. Where he comes from shouldn't destroy what you've already built."

Ugh, I wanted to believe her, but...

"I don't know if I can deal with the whole alien thing. And I have school. And my sister."

"Your sister's an adult, and she never has to know. School is school... Once you explain things like match day and residency to Hudson, he'll be there one hundred percent to support you. It's how he's wired. And that alien thing is nothing more than what he is at the genetic level. He's still Hudson, the man you fell in love with. Why does his genetic structure matter?"

I wasn't sure if I could answer that question...or if I wanted to try.

CHAPTER TEN_

HUDSON

Hours. That was all I had left before my match ended and Macy was probably assigned to Maverick. I'd tried calling her, texting her smiling faces, doing everything I could to reach her but had gotten nowhere. My bond would die in a few hours, and I had no way to stop it.

Things would not work out for us.

For months, I'd focused on my plan. Come to Earth, work with the Freknal, find my mate. I'd done everything I'd thought I needed to do. And yet, I'd failed. The most important mission of my life, incomplete. I didn't know how to come back from that.

"Let's go," Cutlass said as he stormed into my unit.

I let my head fall to the side so I could see him. "Go where?"

"Hart Plaza. You need to get out of this room."

I held up my phone. "I'm waiting to hear from Macy."

"Klow-ee showed you how to use that thing. You can go places with it, and it will still work."

"I don't trust it."

"Well, too bad. We're going."

Maverick joined him in the doorway, both of them looking as if they wanted to start a fight. There was only one I wanted to do battle with.

"I don't want to be around you." I stared at Maverick, trying hard to hold on to my anger and not sink into the pain of my mate rejecting me.

Maverick grabbed me by the arm and yanked me off the floor where I'd been curled up clutching the phone for...I had no idea how long. Klow-ee had said sit tight. I'd followed her orders.

"Yeah, well, I don't exactly want to be matched to a female you're crooning all over," Maverick growled and pushed me toward the bathroom door. "Life sucks. Get your lenses in so you don't scare the humans, and let's go mingle."

I resisted until Cutlass joined in the pulling and dragging attempt to get me to move. At that point, I gave up and let them lead me. Macy was going to decide what she wanted to do, and there was nothing I could do to change her mind if she wouldn't talk to me. I might as well spend the worst hours of my life with my brothers before I started mourning.

We left the building and headed downtown, me complaining the whole way, Cutlass in a hurry for some reason, and Maverick sulking. No one seemed in the mood to be out or mingle as Maverick had said.

"Where is Klow-ee?" I asked as we reached the edge of Hart Plaza. It was too late for her to be working, and Cutlass would have never left her side without a good reason. I didn't believe I was a good reason in his mind.

"She's meeting us here." Cutlass glanced my way, looking more worried than I cared to admit. "She's been busy today."

Hart Plaza was filled with people as we headed toward the river. Music filled the night air, the scent of food cooking wafted past us, and humans ran around laughing and enjoying the beautiful weather. Me? I sulked some more.

This was not where I should have been. "I want to leave."

"No." Cutlass directed us to the fountain, then started peering over the crowd. It was as if he was hunting for something. Or someone.

"What are you looking for?"

"Klow-ee."

Not surprising. "Why? She knows how to find you."

"I want her with me." He gave me a side-eye. "You have to feel the same with Macy. That longing to be close to her?"

His words made everything hurt even more. Made me want to curl up in a ball and roar in agony. It was time for me to go back home. "Yes, I do. But she doesn't want me, and I don't want to be here."

But before I could move more than two steps away, Maverick grabbed my arm.

"Maybe Macy wants you, maybe not." Maverick pointed across the crowd, looking far less grouchy than before. "Why don't you go find out for sure?"

I looked to where he was pointing, and my heart dropped. Macy stood with Klow-ee on the other side of the park. And they were both smiling. My beautiful, lovely, amazing human female stood looking at me, not with hate or distrust but something lighter. Happier.

Something that looked like love.

I had never run so fast, never wanted to cross a distance so much. I ran toward that sunny smile with everything I had. Completely focused on my mate and ignoring the cries of the humans I had to push out of the way to get to her.

When I finally reached her, I didn't stop. I simply grabbed her, picking her up, and held her tight. She wrapped herself around me, her soft, warm little body embracing mine. Her scent relaxing every tense muscle I had. And I was home.

"I'm so sorry," Macy said, clutching me tightly. "I got scared and the whole not from around here thing and—"

"It's fine." And it was. She was in my arms, her scent making me croon once more, her body responding to mine. She was there, smiling at me in a way that told me everything would be okay. And I would never let her go again. "You're here."

"I am. I had to find you."

Joy exploded within me as nothing else ever had. I attacked her lips, mating her mouth with my tongue, unable to resist a taste of her sweetness. She responded just as vigorously, even wrapping her legs around my hips to bring us closer. My hands on her ass, her cunt pressed against my stomach, I gave in to the joy of having found my mate.

"Yo, there are kids around here," Klow-ee said as she smacked my arm.

Macy and I pulled apart, and she dropped her legs from around my hips with a soft flushing of her skin.

"Yeah. Sorry. I forgot," she said. Me? I didn't care. I needed to get my mate alone and naked, needed to reclaim her body, needed to thrust deep within her cunt. Needed it immediately.

"Been there," Klow-ee said, obviously knowing what Macy and I needed. "Okay, we're out of here. You two have fun."

She grabbed Cutlass' hand and strolled off, with Maverick trailing behind them. My brother gave me a single head nod before he left. A look of understanding. I hoped he would be matched soon, but not to my Macy. Never. She was all mine, she chose me, and I would fight to the death for her.

"I've missed you," Macy said once we were as alone as we could be in a sea of people.

"I missed you as well. You wouldn't answer my calls."

"I wasn't ready."

I nuzzled into her neck, pressing my body against hers so she could feel my warmth. My strength. My need. "Are you ready now?"

Macy looked up at me with an expression I wanted to savor, one I wanted to see every day for the rest of my very long life. "Yes. But you have to know, medical school will be hard."

"I know."

"And I might get matched to a hospital in another state. We'd have to move."

I pulled her tighter. "Okay."

"And my sister will never stop calling so much. I almost lost her once to cancer—I'm scared of something happening to her again. It's why she clings. We need each other more than most people do."

"Fine. She can move with us."

"Hudson," Macy said, cocking her head and looking up at me as if I didn't understand her. But I did. I understood her better than she did herself.

"You want to be a doctor because your sister was sick. I get it. It's your biggest goal, and nothing will stop you. Fine. We'll move. We'll struggle. We'll drag your sister with us and complain about how little privacy we have. I'm okay with all of that."

She looked even more confused. "You are?"

"Of course. So long as I get you, everything else will work out."

My crooning grew louder as we stood together, bringing a smile to her beautiful face.

"I love that sound," she said.

"Good," I said just before I pressed my lips to hers for a soft kiss. "You will be my mate?"

"I...yes." She kissed me back, sinking into my hold. With a soft moan, she broke the kiss, licking her lips before meeting my eyes once more. "But I don't know what I'm doing. I don't know how to deal with all this. I haven't had a relationship in ages, and this one...it comes with built-in *komp-lick-aesshuns*."

"I don't know what *komp-lick-aesshuns* are, but we'll slay them. We...both of us. If we're together, we'll be happy."

She smiled wide and bright. "I like the idea of together."

"Good. Now let's go be together. Alone and naked. Before your sister interrupts us."

Macy threw her head back and laughed, lighting up my world in a way even her harsh bathroom lights couldn't have done. "That sounds perfect."

And it would be.

Especially once I found her sister a mate of her own to help lessen the burden on mine. But we'd talk about that another time.

HUDSON

"We're going to be late."

"Don't care." I bit Macy's neck to get her attention. Not that I didn't already have it. I'd pinned her against the wall of the shower and slid inside her the second I could. If she wasn't paying attention to the way I filled her cunt, we'd have a problem.

I still made sure to please her well so she never called my cock junk.

Macy's chuckle echoed in the small bathroom, but that sound quickly died as I went deeper. I grunted with every thrust, pressing her ass against the tiles with the force. Her mumbled words of yes and please and close only drove me wilder, made me move faster and harder. I wanted her to come. Needed it. And I was going to get it.

"Yes, I...Hud—" Macy gripped my shoulders, moaning loudly as she came. As her walls milked my own release. My hips slapped into hers as I surrendered to that pleasure, and still, I wanted more. I could never get enough of my human mate.

Macy clung to me, limp and sated as her breathing returned to a normal pace. The water in the shower had long since run cold, but she didn't seem to mind. My mate's post-*lahhb* showers were her favorite part of the day, especially when I joined her. Most especially when I picked her up, pinned her to the wall, and slid my cock inside her.

Thank the stars my mate had agreed to move in with me in the *were-howss*.

"They're going to be mad." Macy's legs shook as I finally set her down on her feet.

"Still don't care."

"You don't care that Maverick is finding out who his match is today?"

I shook my head as my hand slid down between her legs. "Not as much as I care about licking your sweet cunt until you come on my tongue."

She groaned softly as I played with her clit. "You are so dirty."

"You love it."

"I do." She brought our lips together, kissing me deeply, and then pulled away. "We have to go support Maverick."

I wanted to argue, but I knew she was right. After Macy chose me, Ampetheia's mirror visions didn't stop. We'd all sat on edge the last week or so, waiting for news that she'd finally figured out what they meant. Maverick had downright avoided Macy, and she'd clung to me every second she was away from *skuule*. Me? I'd sat around growling at any male who came near my female. Especially Maverick. But the call had come in yesterday morning that Ampetheia had figured out the problem and found the correct match for Maverick. We were all looking forward to knowing what the mirror thing meant.

But first, I needed to drive my mate crazy with lust.

"Hudson," Macy moaned. She rocked her hips against my hand, trying to pull away and to work herself harder over my fingers. Such a needful thing. But we had news to hear before we could go again. And we would. Go again, that is

"Fine." I dragged her out of the shower and pushed her up against the edge of the sink, pressing my chest into her back. "But I'm licking your cunt when we get back."

She giggled. "Deal."

But I still didn't let her go, partially bending her over and working my fingers into her cunt instead. "First, you get my hand."

"They're going to be mad." But her voice shook and she didn't try to stop me.

"Still don't care."

Ten minutes and two quickie fingerings later—one as my mate tried to get dressed...not my fault she bent over and put that cunt right on display for me—we stumbled into Cutlass and Klow-ee's unit.

"You're late," Klow-ee said, fighting to hide the smile pulling at her mouth.

I raised my shoulders in what humans called a shrug before taking a seat on their couch. "We know."

But Macy was always much more shy about our bedgames. "Sorry."

Klow-ee just rolled her eyes. "Maverick should be back any second. I can't wait to see who he matched to."

But when Maverick walked in, he looked more angry than happy.

"What happened?" Klow-ee asked.

He paced the length of the room, glancing from me to Macy and back. "My match...she..."

A knock on the door interrupted whatever he was going to say. Klow-ee hurried to open it while the rest of us watched on. Waiting for more. Needing to know what was happening.

Unfortunately, Stacy raced in and overtook the conversation

"There you are," she said, ignoring everyone but her sister. "I have exciting news."

But Macy wasn't one to be distracted. She nodded toward Maverick as if to indicate he had control of the room. "Wait, we were just talking about something."

"I can't wait. Sorry, hot stuff." She shot Mav a huge grin. "So remember how I signed you up for the dating agency?"

"Yeah?" Macy shot Maverick a pained look, then joined me on the couch, sinking into my side as if needing reassurance. Something I happily gave her with an arm around her waist.

"Well, since you seemed to hit the hottie jackpot, I figured I'd give it a try as well."

The room went silent, and Macy stiffened in my arms. "But...you're dating Chad."

Stacy waved her hand. "Only sort of. Besides, if things work out, I could just break it off with Chad. New guy never has to know. Why not give it a shot, right? So I did."

"Oh, shit," Klow-ee said, looking from Stacy to Maverick. "Mirrors."

Which made no sense to me. "What about mirrors?"

"Mace!" Stacy squealed. "They matched me! I get to meet my Mr. Right tomorrow."

"What?" Macy glanced at Maverick again, looking almost horrified. "Oh, God. How? And who?"

"Some guy named Maverick. I mean, he has to be hot with a name like that, right?"

The quiet growl of a Reithhar on the attack broke the peaceful background noises of the room. I pulled Macy closer, jerking my head around to face the threat. Maverick had a death stare pointed at Stacy. He growled again, just once, and then he was gone, slamming the door behind him.

"Ugh, what's his deal?" Stacy asked, scrunching her nose in a disgusted sort of way.

"You are, you dumb cow," Klow-ee said, glaring at Stacy before rushing out the door with Cutlass on her heels.

Stacy looked shocked. "Well, that was rude."

"Stace, you just screwed up." Macy looked at me with a sadness in her eyes that ripped a hole in my chest. That look, knowing something something had cased her pain, was something I wouldn't accept.

"It's not your fault," I whispered in her ear, letting my Reithhar croon loud enough for her to hear.

Stacy, meanwhile, still looked lost. "What? How did I screw up?"

Macy sighed and faced her sister. "The guy who was here? The one who slammed the door? That was Maverick."

"What?" Stacy's smile fell, and her eyes went wide. "But...shit."

"Yeah. Shit." Macy grabbed my hand and snuggled into my side. "These next two weeks are going to be hard on all of us as we deal with his cranky ass."

"I'll be with you," I said, holding her close. "The rest will work itself out."

She smiled up at me. "How do you always know what to say?"

"Because I know you, my mate."

"Wait, what about me?" Stacy looked almost panicked. "What do I do?"

I kissed the upturned lips of my mate, unable to resist. "Let's go home."

Macy didn't even pause. We were on our feet and headed for the door before she even answered her sister. "Break up with Chad for good, apologize to Maverick, and hope he forgives you."

"You can't just disappear on me." Stacy lunged as if to grab my mate, but I stepped between them.

"She can, and we are." I made sure my words were understood. I couldn't growl or snap at the girl because she didn't know I wasn't human yet, but I wouldn't hold back if she threatened my mate in any way. Including upsetting her. And yet, if Stacy found her mate, she would be less reliant on mine. So I couldn't leave her with nothing. "I know you feel bad about your mistake, but you need to fix it. Not Macy. Not me. Take a few hours to figure out what you need to do, and come back for Maverick. He's a proud male. Keep that in mind, and everything will work out for you."

"But I need Macy to help me," Stacy almost cried. "Why are you leaving me alone?"

"Because I *can't* help you," Macy said. "Break up with Chad. Come back and apologize to Maverick. That's all you can do."

Stacy took a couple of deep breaths before setting her face in a determined expression. The mask of a prey animal trying to look brave. "Fine. I'll deal with Chad and then be back."

"You can do this," Macy said. "It'll be worth it."

"Good luck, Stacy." I rushed Macy out the door and to our own little unit. Last week, she probably would have held me back so she could deal with her sister. Would have tossed aside her own needs for those of Stacy. Not anymore. Even her phone stayed off when she was alone with me, a fact that proved more to me than anything else she could have done.

"That was rude," Macy said sadly as soon as we had the door closed behind us.

I refused to let her think she'd done something wrong. "That was the truth."

"She doesn't know he's not human, and I have no idea how to

prepare her for something like that. If I should at all." She looked up at me, her expression slightly lost. Something that wouldn't do.

"Let Maverick tell her. It's his job."

"So what do we do? Just...wait?"

I shrugged. I was really beginning to feel comfortable with that particular human tic. "We go back to bed, and I show you how good it is to be mated to a Reithhar."

Macy smiled. "Show me how?"

I grabbed the hem of her dress and pulled it up. She raised her arms for me, letting me tug the fabric completely off. My sexy mate wasn't wearing anything underneath.

"With my hands." I ran a finger along the curve of her breast.

"And my mouth." I leaned in to kiss her nipple, holding her close to me by the waist.

"And my cock."

"Hudson," Macy sighed as she grabbed my mane and tugged.

"Let me show you, mate. Let me distract you for a while."

And I did. Many times. The only thing Macy and I needed to worry about was Macy and me.

Everything else would work out.

Maverick wasn't a fan of the planet Earth. He also wasn't particularly fond of being matched to a human mail order bride. She was too bossy, too fake, too...everything he didn't want. Until he did.

Stacy spent a year of her life isolated from her friends and family, so she refused to spend another minute that way. That was why she signed up to be matched as a mail order bride. It worked for her sister; it'd work for her, too. As soon as she got past her match's broody ways.

One cranky alien with no clue how to be romantic, one clingy female who refuses to let her dislike of her match stop her, and one slip of the tongue that set the two on a crash course in how not to fall in love. What would you do if you found out the man from your fantasies was actually the man from your science fiction?

CHAPTER ONE_

STACY

Application 328F
Lead Generator: Referral
Species: Human
Planet: Earth
Breeding Rank: Receptacle
Intake Office: Detroit, Michigan, United States
Original Content: There are rules to dating me. A man must have
manners, he must treat me with respect, and he must be willing to feed me
at all times.
Translation: Human female seeks male with skills in the kitchen as well
as the bedroom.

There was something off about the woman from the dating agency. Something not quite normal or safe. She reminded me too much of the doctors who'd once ruled my life.

"Congratulations on joining us at the IG Dating Agency," the woman, Ampetheia, said. Her smile spread a little too wide across her face, her eyes a not-quite-normal color of brown. Definitely not safe.

"Thanks." I shifted on the chair, unable to hold still. Something about the way she watched me was making me uncomfortable even though I couldn't pin down the reason. It wasn't as if she looked dangerous in any way. The woman was wearing a brown cardigan, for Christ's sake. Was she a ninja in disguise? An assassin on the side? I couldn't tell, but she was still totally watching me with those beady eyes. Time to fake it.

I pasted on a bright smile and tried to keep my leg from shaking. "My sister had such success with the gentleman you matched her with, I figured you might be able to help me, as well."

Ninja lady looked about ready for the kill. Crap, how did one escape a woman in a cardigan? Throw cat food at her? Bring up the wedding episode of *Outlander* to see if she could be distracted by the kilt? Rip apart a book?

No, scratch that one. I couldn't be that evil. Macy would kill me for sure.

"Your sister was a prime candidate, and of course, I can assist you as well, dear." Ampetheia practically purred. Odd, that sound. "I already have the perfect man for you."

That didn't take nearly as long as I thought it would. "Already?"

Ampetheia laughed. "The match I set up for your sister caused me many headaches. Oh, not because of Macy, dear. Your sister was a dream client. More because... Well, when I see two people together, it helps if those people don't look like anyone else."

"Huh." I sat back and crossed my legs, suddenly a little less wary of the woman. That's what had to be setting off my bullshit alarm—she was another bullshitter. "So the whole mail order bride thing is a lie? Awesome. I cribbed that letter in the worst way. I'd hate to think you were matching me to someone off that drivel."

Her beady eyes went surprisingly round. Really, those colored contacts were the worst. "You...what?"

"Yeah, I get it. You do some voodoo magic thing to find a partner for your client, but you can't let anyone know about the voodoo magic thing because, let's face it, that shit's scary. It's okay. I won't tell. So, when do I get to meet him?"

"Meet whom?"

"My match. You said you had one for me."

Ampetheia shook her head. "Yes, of course. Maverick. I'll call him tonight. I don't see why you can't meet him tomorrow if you have the time."

"Sounds good." I rose, ready to get the hell out of her office. I might not be as worried about hidden ninja assassin skills anymore, but that didn't mean I wanted to hang around. Ampetheia was not someone to be trifled with. "Tell him I'll meet him at the immersive date hotel in the afternoon. He should wear black. I find black on guys very attractive. Oh, and no flip-flops or sandals. Man feet shouldn't be on display."

Ampetheia stared at me for a long, quiet moment. "Is there anything else, Stacy?"

I ran through the list in my head...black clothes, no feet, meet at hotel, be ready for nooky. Not sure I should mention that last one, though she had to expect there'd be a little bumping and grinding going on. No one set you up to spend two days in a single hotel room with a potential relationship candidate without understanding that those hormones would be racing. She knew exactly what was going to go on in that room.

And so I didn't need to tell her that. "Not right now. I'll call you if I think of something."

I tossed her a smile and a wave and left. Once I made it outside, I grabbed my phone and pulled up my favorite call recipients. With the number of times I called her every day, you'd probably think my twin sister would be in my top spot. Not the case. God before family—my number one call was my favorite Sunday brunch restaurant. Reservations could be hard to get, you know?

"Crap," I hissed when she didn't answer. That was becoming a habit —the not answering. I knew she had her boyfriend now, but still. Okay, fine... I mean, the man was sex on legs. Like, ridiculously handsome. If she weren't my sister, I'd totally go in for the steal. But she was, and that would make holiday dinners totally awkward. Anyway, Macy had Hudson—she'd even moved in to his loft—so I knew she was often busy with him. But I needed her. Immediately.

In fact, I was going to stop by her new place. She wouldn't mind.

I made it to the warehouse she lived in and up the stairs in a matter of minutes. The place was filled with men. I mean, there were a handful of women who lived there, including my sister, but all I ever saw when I visited were men. Handsome, buff men. It was like a housing facility for romance-novel cover models. Why couldn't I live in a building like that? The only man I saw in the hallways at my place was old Mr. Webster, and he definitely wasn't handsome or buff. He was old, bald, hunched, and wrinkled like a man who'd smoked cigarettes every day for half a century. Which he was, so...fitting

I counted the hotties loitering in the halls on my way upstairs, just for fun. It took me five solid, ogle-worthy specimens to reach her door. Five. This was like the honey hole of hotties.

But Macy wasn't in her place. Or at least, she didn't answer when I knocked. And the door was locked, so I couldn't go inside and wait. Crap. I yanked out my phone and tried calling again, but still no response. Where was she? My heart raced, and the hallway grew warm as I considered that question. Macy was my twin, my only family left, and we were tight. If she was gone...if I'd lost her...I'd be totally and utterly alone. I'd be—

Nope. Couldn't think that way. She had to be around here somewhere.

I shook off the anxiety nipping at my heels and checked out my hottie-less surroundings. Where did all the muscled men go when you needed them? Voices from the apartment across the hall gave me an idea, though. I knocked on that door with a smile and a cock to my hip, hoping they had some clue where my sister was and ready to make a great first impression. You only got one, you know?

But everything went a little wonky when the door opened.

Have you ever had the wind knocked out of you? Where you fall or hit something and go *whoosh,* and suddenly, you can't breathe? That was what happened to me when Mr. Tall, Dark, and Hella Sexy swung that slab of steel out of the way.

"Hi," I said on a tiny breath of air. The man stared at me, his face harsh and his eyes intense. Green eyes. Holy fuck, he had green eyes. And they were definitely locked on me in a way that was not quite wholesome. There was a feel to his look, a sense of being touched. I swear, he'd made my panties wet just by giving me the eye.

Well done, sir.

"Uh, I'm—" Before I could introduce myself, I heard my sister's voice coming from inside. Perfect! That broke me right out of my lust stupor and reminded me why I was there in the first place. I had a story to tell.

"There you are," I said as I pushed past the eye candy and headed for the couch where my sister was standing beside her new guy. "I have exciting news."

But Macy wasn't easily distracted. She nodded toward the man at the door. "Wait, we were just talking about something."

"I can't wait. Sorry, hot stuff." I shot a grin at the eye-fucker, just for good measure. I mean, the guy was delicious. Might as well hedge my bets a bit. "So remember how I signed you up for the dating agency?"

"Yeah?" Macy made a face then sat next to her future husband. He wrapped an arm around her waist and pulled her in tight. All possessive-like. How did she handle that crap so well? I'd be... Well, if I dated a guy who looked like Hudson, I'd probably be melting into his side just like Macy was right then.

Time to tell her my news so we could celebrate. "Well, since you seemed to hit the hottie jackpot, I figured I'd give it a try as well."

The room went silent in a bad way. In a this-isn't-good way. What did I miss?

Macy was the first to recover. "But...you're dating Chad."

Ouch. I mean, I'd never totally revealed everything there was to tell about my relationship with Chad, but hearing her bring him up stung. I didn't date Chad... I borrowed him occasionally when the loneliness got too hard to fight. But I wasn't about to tell her that, especially not in a room full of people I didn't know.

So I waved her off as if the whole thing were beneath me. What? I'd seen it done on TV. That hand wave totally worked. "Only sort of. Besides, if things work out, I could just break it off with Chad. New guy never has to know." And he wouldn't. My situation with Chad made me look bad in a hell of a lot of ways. No sense throwing my garbage in new guy's face. "Why not give it a shot, right? So I did."

"Oh, shit. Mirrors," Chloe, the woman who'd barged into Macy's apartment when she was being all woe-is-me over a misunderstanding with Hudson, said from where she sat on another couch. More like a love seat. And she had her own hottie with his arm around her waist. Damn, that lady had to have mad skills at something to snag a man who looked like him.

"What about mirrors?" Hudson asked, totally not paying attention to me. Neither was my sister. Damn it.

"Mace!" I squealed, making sure her focus was where it belonged for this reveal. "They matched me! I get to meet my Mr. Right tomorrow."

"What?" Macy's eyes flitted to the hottie by the door again, and her face fell into something that looked like the expression I'd make if I had to slice up dead bodies every day like she did. "Oh, God. How? And who?"

That didn't sound like joy. At all. "Some guy named Maverick. I mean, he has to be hot with a name like that, right?"

Something that sounded an awful lot like a growl reverberated through the room. The guy at the door was staring at me, that slow, rough rumble coming from him. And he definitely didn't look happy. Before I could ask him what his problem was, he stormed out of the apartment. He even slammed the door behind him.

"Ugh, what's his deal?" I asked, oddly sad that Mr. Too Good For This had left. I couldn't trust my feelings about him, though. Not when I was so close to a perfect match. I tended to make bad choices where men were concerned. Especially hot men. It was a weakness.

Chloe definitely had feelings about that guy leaving the way he did. "You are such an idiot," she said before racing out the door with her husband on her heels.

Shocked was an understatement for how I felt. "Well, that was rude."

But Macy wouldn't even look at me. "Stace, you just screwed up."

"What? How did I screw up?"

My sister sighed, finally meeting my gaze with something close to irritation on her face. "The guy who was here? The one who slammed the door? That was Maverick."

"What? But..." There were no words. Well, other than one. No. No fucking way. How bad of luck did I have? "Shit."

"Yeah. Shit." Macy snuggled into Hudson, pretty much rubbing her new relationship in my face as mine fell apart before it had even begun. "These next two weeks are going to be hard on all of us as we deal with his crankiness."

She and Hudson whispered back and forth, completely ignoring me. What was this? How had I gone from excited about possibilities to bereft within the span of thirty seconds? Any why wasn't Macy helping me when she knew this guy already?

Shit, I needed my much smarter, much more logical sister right then. And I wasn't afraid to fight for her attention. "Wait, what about me? What do I do?"

But there was no fight. Macy ignored me in favor of giving her man a little kiss before letting him pull her to her feet and lead her toward the door. Leaving me alone in a virtual stranger's apartment.

But before she could make it to the door, Macy came through. Sort of. "Break up with Chad for good, apologize to Maverick, and hope he forgives you."

I reached for her, needing more. "You can't just disappear on me."

Hudson jumped between us, looking fierce and ready for battle, as if I would ever hurt my sister. "She can, and we are. I know you feel bad about your mistake, but you need to fix it. Not Macy. Not me. Take a few hours to figure out what you need to do, and come back for Maverick. He's a proud male. Keep that in mind, and everything will work out for you."

"But I need Macy to help me. Why are you leaving me alone?"

"Because I can't help you," Macy said. "Break up with Chad. Come back and apologize to Maverick. That's all you can do."

She couldn't help me, my ass. She knew Maverick, was practically married to someone who seemed awfully chummy with the guy. There had to be something. But by the look of resolve on her face and the way she refused to step around her boyfriend bodyguard, I knew there was no use fighting for her help. Macy's mind was made up, and she didn't often stray from what she decided were her rules.

I was on my own with this one.

There were moments in every life where you knew you needed to pull up the big-girl panties and get shit done. I'd experienced my first moment like that when my cancer diagnosis had come in. No matter what my parents said or the doctors thought, I never once gave in to the idea that the disease would knock me down. Same thing when I found out about Chad's cheating ways the first time. I kicked that bastard into the friends-with-benefits spot so fast, his head spun. I didn't need to tell the world or cry over it; I simply got the job done and moved on.

This was just another one of those times.

I took a couple of deep breaths to focus myself before lifting my chin. Warrior face on. "Fine. I'll deal with Chad and then be back."

"You can do this," Macy said. "It'll be worth it."

I doubted her. A lot. But hell, what more did I have to lose?

Hudson gave me a soft, "Good luck, Stacy," before the two of them walked out the door and left me alone. In someone else's apartment. Probably that someone who'd called me an idiot. Wonderful.

I gave myself one moment to truly think about what had just happened. To wallow in it.

Oh God, I'd fucked up.

Mr. FuckMeEyes was my match, and apparently, he didn't like what I had to say about Chad. Not that he knew me or Chad or what our situation was. The guy was reacting before he could get the whole story. That pissed me off for a second. He was my match, the man meant to be with me, but he was also a crabby jerk with an anger complex. And he growled. Who the hell growled? What were we, animals? And why the hell had I been matched with someone who refused to listen? That just wouldn't work for me.

I was going to have to make a few adjustments to my plans.

Finally ready to face this issue head on, I took a deep, centering breath and headed back out the door. Nope. This wasn't going to end on Maverick's terms. I was supposed to be matched. That meant I got a weekend in a nice hotel with the man that creepy voodoo lady thought was right for me.

I was getting my weekend, even if the right man was all sorts of wrong.

I yanked my phone out of my purse and dialed as I headed back to my car. Time to turn the tables in my favor.

"IG Dating—"

I totally didn't have time for the welcoming speech. "Yeah. Hi. I need Ampetheia."

The woman paused. "Uh, is there something I can help you with? She's with a client."

"I'm sure you're super awesome at your job, but no. I need her. It'll only take a second."

Another pause. This one longer than the last. She was close to breaking. "Okay, well... Can I at least have your name?"

Jackpot. "I'm Stacy."

The line clicked and went silent as I slid into my car and started the engine. The humidity was too high, and the sun was beating down on my car like some sort of furnace. It totally didn't help that the wet, stifling heat made me think of Maverick and that eye-fuck at the door. What I wouldn't give to go back and change that entire script. I could be alone with him right now, getting to know him.

Maybe even getting naked with him.

Okay, not naked. I'd only met him a handful of minutes ago. But I could at least be fantasizing about him without wanting to smack him upside the head. That was totally allowed, right?

The AC had just turned cold when the phone clicked once more.

"Stacy? How can I help you?" Ampetheia sounded more worried than pissed, which was a good thing.

Good because I was probably about to piss her off. "I need you to call Maverick."

"Excuse me?"

"I need you to call Maverick. Tell Mr. Broody Growler he'd better show up for our date."

This time, she didn't sound so sympathetic. "Is there something wrong?"

Always. "Nope, but he's going to want to back out, and I refuse to let him. You tell him if he doesn't show up, I'm camping for the week at his place, even if it's in the damn hallway."

"This isn't how the IGDA does business, Stacy."

"No, it's not." Time to pull out my ace in the hole. "You do business by using your empathetic abilities to match people who perhaps shouldn't be matched. That high success rate you tout? Is that before or after the two-week time period you give us to decide our fates? And at what point do the people being matched find out that the whole setup is a lie?"

The silence that met me was long and heavy, almost deadly. I drove without really focusing on the roads, waiting to see if my bluff had succeeded.

Two whole minutes later... "I'll call him."

I nearly punched the roof of the car in my celebrating. "Good. Thank you. And have a great weekend."

I hung up the phone and tossed it back into my purse. Challenge thrown. That fucker thought he could growl at me, not give me a chance to explain an offhanded comment, get me all hot and bothered with a look worthy of some serious sexing, and then walk away? Nope. Not happening.

The man was too arrogant for his own good.

It was going to be so much fun breaking him down.

CHAPTER TWO_

MAVERICK

Application 5751SL
Lead Generator: Advertisement at Space Station PF456-G2
Species: Reithhar
Residence: Former planet Xouthhgros, Former planet BHG489
Breeding Rank: Inseminator
Intake Office: Space Station PF456-G2
Original Content: Reithhar Master Mechanic and Pilot from planet
Xouthhgros looking for female mate on the off chance the species on this
new planet meets my specifications.
Translation: Charming leading man perfect for that fantasy life every
woman wants.

The door slamming behind me as I left Cutlass' might have been one of
the most satisfying sounds on this ridiculous planet. For far too long,
we'd been waiting around for Ampetheia to work through these so-called
matches. Cutlass and Klow-ee had worked out well, and Hudson
seemed happy with his Macy. But my female? This mirror image of
Macy who was supposed to be my perfect match? She could not be the

right choice. How could they match me to someone so bossy, so arrogant as to assume control, and so hurtful with her words? Impossible was an understatement.

Even though my *esehhnce* had just crooned for her.

I rushed to the unit I'd claimed as my own, the one at the end of the hall. Far away from where the mated couples lived. I'd much rather have been sleeping in the ship we left half a solar system away than in the same building as two newly mated couples, but my training as a pilot was too ingrained to ignore. We needed to stay together for safety, so I'd joined my fellow Reithhars living on Earth.

The regrets did not take long to pile up.

When we moved in to the storage building Klow-ee had found for us, I'd moved in to a unit closer to Cutlass, who lived across the hall from Hudson. Safety in proximity, you see. But the sounds of Cutlass and Klow-ee mating at all hours were too much for me to deal with, so I'd moved. Add in Hudson and his half of the mirror females, and I'd been living in a constant state of arousal. Completion was only for the others, though. Not for me. I had no match or partner.

The sounds of their bedgames had driven me mad, made me sick with desire and longing for things I'd never truly contemplated before. Sure, when Hudson had found the flyer for this place and came to Cutlass and me with his stories of how Freknal beings were talented at seeing connections, I was intrigued. Not convinced, but curious. And seeing the matchmaker's prowess with my two shipmates had landed a bit of credibility to the legends. But no longer. Ampetheia was either losing her touch or her mind.

I would never accept Macy's sister as my mate, no matter what my esehhnce did.

"Maverick, wait."

Just what I needed. I paused, unable to hold back a growl or a glare as Klow-ee rushed toward me with Cutlass right behind her. Seeing them only made the sting of my own match that much more noticeable.

"What?"

Klow-ee wrinkled her forehead and brought her hand up as if to touch me. "Are you okay?"

"Yes," I said as I stepped out of her reach. "Leave me alone."

"No." The little human crossed her arms over her chest. I'd seen her do that a hundred times before. She was angry. Good. So was I.

"That was a shitty thing to happen," Klow-ee said, a fierceness to her voice that probably matched my own. "But she's your match. You need to talk to her."

I scoffed and gave Cutlass a head nod. "Control your human."

That went over about as well as I expected.

"Or what?" he asked, looking ready to battle. Picking a fight with a man I saw as my brother probably wasn't the best idea, but the rage inside of me needed a place to go. A good brawl would have relieved some of the tension I carried, but in the end, I backed down. This wasn't the time or the place. Nor was Cutlass the right sparring partner.

Though whoever that Chad guy was who Stacy seemed set on staying with could have fit the bill.

And didn't that just piss me off even more? I was ready to take down humans I'd never met because of some female who shouldn't have mattered to me. That was a new low.

I sighed and shook my head. "I need to leave now."

"What are you going to do?" Klow-ee asked, once again wrinkling her forehead.

I lifted a shoulder in a lazy sort of move that Hudson called a *schhr-uug*. "Wait two weeks and reapply. Or skip the whole matching thing and head off to another planet somewhere. Who cares?"

Klow-ee did that human thing where her bottom lip stuck out more than the top one. A pout, I think they called it. I hated her pout. I was a sucker for that pout.

"I care," she said in a soft voice that made me feel even worse than I already did. Oh no, was she going to drop water from her eyes? I'd seen that before, especially on the programs Klow-ee watched. The ones that were sent into the unit through the monitor on the wall. Things were never good when the characters made the water drop. I shot Cutlass a panicked look, hoping for a little guidance on what I was supposed to do with her. She was his mate, after all. He just shook his head and watched Klow-ee with wary eyes, probably as confused as I was.

Fine. Looked like I needed to be the male in this group. "I know you care, but this isn't about you, Klow-ee."

"No, it's about all of us. Our little family here." She grabbed Cutlass' arm and pulled him closer. "I worry about you boys."

Those words in that soft, unsteady tone of voice were like a punch to the gut. One delivered by a sneaky, worthy opponent. Still, there were things I couldn't admit yet. Facts I had to deal with that Klow-ee and Cutlass didn't need to know about.

"Don't worry," I said, sighing my frustrations. "I'll call Ampetheia and find out how to go about being reassigned."

Klow-ee frowned. "You won't even consider her?"

Chad would. Which is probably why I needed to stay the hell away from her.

"No." I snorted and opened the door to my unit, ready to be left alone for a while so I could stew in my unresolved rage. Maybe punch a few walls. Or stroke my cock to the picture of Stacy's huge, dark eyes looking up at me. The way the black centers dilated and that breathy little gasp came sneaking out. I'd felt her attraction at that moment, her need, and I'd returned it. I'd even crooned for her. But then she'd opened her mouth, and that moment disappeared into the atmosphere.

But no one else had heard my esehhnce croon, and I needed to keep it that way. That would be my secret, because if either of my Reithhar brothers knew, they'd push me to accept her, simply because denying my esehhnce would be painful.

Mating to a female who chose to take another to her bed would be worse.

"Take her home, Cutlass," I said as I walked through my door. "I can't deal with being nice right now."

I didn't slam anything because it would have upset Klow-ee, and there was really no reason to get her going. She was a nice female, kind and funny. I gave her a hard time, but I enjoyed her being around, and Cutlass had never seemed happier. The old grump had perked up since being matched. Not Hudson level of perked—that male was a constant source of good mood—but more than the normal cranky bastard I'd gotten used to on the colony.

His mating had worked wonders for him.

Mine?

Well, my match had a Chad and a demanding attitude that wouldn't work with my own.

The words of my match filtered through my mind again, realigning in ways that only added to my anger. She was playing with the system, applying to match while being with someone else. Another male. Was he bigger or stronger than me? Human males didn't seem to be, but I never knocked out a possibility without all the facts. Perhaps he wasn't good at bedgames, and that's why this female was looking for a new male. I was good at bedgames and enjoyed licking cunts like the rest of the males in my breed. I could make that little female scream for sure.

But I wouldn't get the chance to prove that to her. Because she had a Chad. My crooning meant nothing to her.

My phone rang as I paced the length of my unit. I almost ignored it, but something inside of me longed to know who was calling.

The name on the screen took me by surprise.

"Yes?" I said once I connected the call.

Ampetheia's deep, direct voice crackled through the speaker. "Maverick, dear. Your match called me a few minutes ago."

Of course she did. "So you're canceling the match?"

"What? No. That's not what she wanted at all."

That...wasn't possible. "So what did she call for?"

"She said to tell you to show up. And to wear black. Oh, and no sandals. She has a negative response to naked male feet."

It took me almost thirty seconds to put all those words together and have them make sense. I didn't think I'd been so shocked in all my years. "She said what?"

"Is there something I need to know?" Ampetheia asked, sounding anxious. "Do I need to get involved?"

Did she? No, not really. We already had someone standing between us. No sense adding Ampetheia to the Chad pile. No, she definitely didn't need to be involved.

I could handle the little human female on my own.

I grinned as plans began to take shape in my mind. "Not at all. Just a translation error. I'll show up for the date, no problem."

And I would. I had two weeks to set the woman straight on why playing around with a male's feelings was a bad idea. Why pitting two males against one another was a dangerous proposition. She wanted me to go on a date? Fine. I'd go.

And she'd hate every second of it.

CHAPTER THREE

STACY

I walked into the hotel with my head high and my favorite dress on. This Maverick guy thought I'd take it easy on him. Not happening. Strappy, short, flirty, and fun was the look I needed to knock him down a peg or two. Plus, the striped sundress I picked made my not-quite-normal breasts look spectacular. Again, not making it easy on him. Let him try to resist checking me out. The guy at the front desk certainly couldn't.

"You'll be in room 730." His name badge said Derrick. The way his eyes kept wandering a little farther south than was polite said *nice rack*.

See? Perfect dress for the job.

"Thanks." When his eyes popped back up to mine, I gave the guy my best smile, the one I'd practiced for hours on end. The one I knew got the most response from men, "I appreciate your help, Derrick."

So maybe saying his name in a phone-sex voice was going a little far. The guy blushed. Not quite what I was going for, but I'd take that response as a positive. Time to get ready to deal with Maverick.

Which, by the way, wasn't really a name. Maverick was an old car, just like Hudson and Cutlass. I Googled that shit. Something I'd worry about after I dealt with the particular car I'd been saddled with. Talk about a lemon.

Key in hand, I headed up to the room. The view overlooking the Detroit River and Windsor, Canada was phenomenal, but I closed the curtains on it. If I was going to teach Maverick a lesson, I needed to set the scene. He could *not* be distracted by the scenery.

It took a good fifteen minutes to prep, but at the end, I thought the result was worth the time spent. The bed was made correctly, the cover crisp and inviting, the room a little darker than normal, candles lit, and me... Well, I was ready to look my best. To make sure Maverick understood what he was giving up if he walked away.

Seriously, who names their kid after a car? I'd never heard of a child named Fiat or Toyota or Escort.

I really needed to get over the whole car thing. All three guys I'd met through Macy were named after cars. Hudson, Cutlass, Maverick...it was a trend. One that pricked at me like a puzzle.

A puzzle I didn't have time for.

At two minutes until our assigned meeting time, I sat on the edge of the mattress and posed. This was another thing I'd practiced—how to look my absolute best wearing the sundress and sitting down. You couldn't blame me for the sitting part. I had superhigh heels on, and standing in them made my feet hurt. Bedroom heels were not meant for being vertical for long.

So I sat and I posed and I gave the door a sultry, sexy look. And I waited. And waited. And waited some more.

After half an hour, I knew I'd screwed up. I was pacing—barefoot, of course—at that point because posing was hard. I'd end up with a crick in my neck if I tried to keep up that position for too long. Trust me, I'd done it.

At sixty minutes, my confidence was gone. All of it. Crap.

What had I been thinking? Why had I even brought up Chad and implied this match guy would be a second choice? I wasn't with Chad— we hadn't been together in years. He was just...convenient. A fuck buddy, if you will. And while that probably wasn't the best or healthiest thing for me to be doing, it worked. He was there when no one else was, when the days got too quiet and the nights too lonely. When my life reminded me of the silence of the hospital from when I was sick. That year had been brutal—months on end of living in a hospital bed could play tricks with your mind for sure. Chad knew that. He knew me, my secrets and my needs. And he knew about my scars and was way past judging me for them.

Still, if I had someone else, someone solid and sure to help me through those dark times, I'd have left him behind. We didn't work well together, and he knew it. But comfort was comfort, and with my parents gone and Macy always so busy in school, I took comfort where I could get it. I refused to feel bad about that.

Until Maverick...

At the ninety-minute mark, I accepted the fact that my plan was a failure. Maverick wasn't coming. I'd need to figure out another way to be in his face that didn't involve swanky hotel rooms and dinners bought and paid for by the agency. With Macy dating Maverick's friend and living in the same building, bumping into Maverick shouldn't be too hard. Not ideal, but doable once I ate a pint of ice cream to get over the sting of rejection and got my head back in the game.

Still, this immersive thing would have been better. Perfect, really. A chance to show and tease and force a response. I was probably going to have to camp in the hallway outside of the apartment like I'd threatened, though. Long nights on a hard floor with nothing to entertain myself as I waited. Ugh. Maverick was a jerk for making me do such a thing. Did he think I was kidding? Did he not understand how resolute I could be once I set my mind to something? The man was in for some serious surprises, apparently.

Resigned to defeat, I tucked my bedroom shoes back in my bag. Sad, really. Those leopard-print stilettos made my legs look amazing, but no one had ever seen them in action. Just my shoe salesman, but he didn't count. Shoe guys were like therapists—it was part of their job to keep your secrets. Those shoes were my favorite secret. Someday, I'd wear them for someone who would appreciate the beauty and understand the pain enough not to make me walk in them.

I was just about to blow out the first candle when the door swung open. No knock, no polite warning. Just a beep and a swoosh before the man of the hour walked in.

The windblown hair looked good on him. Too good. I needed shields up for this conversation.

"Thanks for showing," I said as I crossed my arms over my chest.

That move pushed my girls up enough to make a really awesome cleavage line. Not that I did it on purpose.

Fine...it was totally on purpose. Dress, rack, good...remember?

Maverick busting in like this, when I was totally not prepared for him, wasn't what I'd wanted to happen. I'd planned and plotted and practiced to get everything right, but there was no unshining that shoe now. The man was in the room, looking at me.

Looking *hard* at me.

His eyes, the light jade color and the intensity of his stare, made me almost uncomfortable. There was something so different about him. Unusual. And not just because the jackass didn't smile.

"You demanded. I showed."

See? Jackass. "Good. Now how about we head out for a bit? I'm starving, and the minibar's empty."

Maverick looked positively dumbfounded. "You're serious? You actually want to spend time together?"

"One, the dating agency is paying. And since they're a big bunch of fakers who lie to get customers, I'm totally okay with taking advantage. Two, you need a lesson in dating. You're cranky and rude, which isn't going to win you any Mr. Michigan contests. Consider it my public duty to prepare you for the next gal. And three, I don't joke about food. Ever." I grabbed my purse, slipped on my sensible-but-cute flats, and headed for the door. "Coming?"

Maverick grumbled but followed me out the door and down the hallway. I saw that as a major accomplishment. In fact, I was almost ready to think the man had potential, but when the elevator arrived, that opinion tanked. He didn't wait to let me on first. In fact, he practically jumped in front of me to get in. Lord, this was going to be tougher than I thought.

"For the record," I said as I pressed the button for the lobby. "Women prefer men with manners, which means you hold the doors for her and let her enter first."

"Why?"

I glanced over my shoulder, just catching him as he adjusted from staring at my ass to glowering at my face. I seriously loved this dress.

"Because it's polite," I said, keeping my voice steady even though I wanted to let it drop into the sexy range. Don't judge...we all do it. But just because I kept my voice on the G-rated spectrum didn't mean I couldn't make my words a little PG. "And because it gives you a chance to check out her ass without getting caught. Take advantage of those moments."

"And that's what females want? To be leered at?"

I shrugged and faced the door, unable to deal with his glare any longer. "Women like to be wanted."

Maverick grunted. "And if I don't want the particular woman?"

Oof. Okay, that hurt. A lot. More than it should have, really. I closed my eyes and took a breath, pushing back the ache his words caused me. One weekend, and I could get rid of him. I could stop this charade and go back to my normal, boring life. This would be fine. I had a plan.

"You can still be nice to her," I said, proud that I'd kept my voice from shaking. "It's good practice for the next woman in your life."

He grunted again, which was about as much of an approval as I'd get. And I was okay with that. Maverick didn't want me? Fine. I'd still make him behave like a gentleman this weekend and teach him a few things so the woman he ended up with could reap the benefits. Might as well help out the next girl in line, because it wouldn't be me putting up with him for long.

Screw that.

MAVERICK

She was lecturing me on human culture. Courting rituals, to be exact. The rules and expectations of males in her society that needed to be followed to attract an eligible female.

What had I gotten myself into?

"Manners. They're so important because..."

I wished, for the first time in my life, that my hearing was not as sharp as it was.

As Stacy continued talking to me about everything from holding doors to how to help a female into a coat, I fought to keep my eyes anywhere but on her body. The female was loud and bossy, way too direct and mouthy for me, but she was attractive in a way that called to my male side. I didn't care for her, though. Not in the least. Not even in that dress that drew my eyes to her breasts of their own volition. Or the way my cock grew hard at the glimpses of her legs under the strips of fabric that made up the bottom. No, I didn't care for her. Not even though I couldn't keep from sneaking glances at all that extra skin on display.

"And another thing..."

Yeah, she had another thing. And two more after that. Meanwhile, I kept my eyes dancing over her body since she was so distracted by her own speech. She was spunkier than I'd assumed, filled with drive and purpose and strength that overshadowed most others of her kind. And she smelled good. Like sex and sweetness and something natural that appealed to the male in me. Every whiff of her fragrance caused my cock to grow harder. To the point that I worried I'd need to stroke myself to completion before the night was through.

I could not deny my physical attraction to her. And then there was the fact that I'd crooned for her almost the second I saw her. Not that I was going to admit that to anybody. In fact, I had to bite back the sound every few minutes as we made our way outside. What was I supposed to do with that when she was not available for me?

"I mean, the thing is—"

I was done with her things. "How about you stop talking for five minutes so I can take you to dinner?"

Stacy stopped in the middle of the sidewalk to give me an odd sort of look. One that made my groin tighten with something close to desire.

"You want to take me to dinner?"

Want to take her...yes. I wanted. Deeply, though not to dinner. "No, but I'm hungry and you're here. You can come with me."

A pain unlike any I'd seen from a human flashed across her face. Something about that expression, about causing my supposed mate to hurt, killed me inside. I ached to wipe that look away and soothe whatever damage I'd caused. I hadn't meant to injure her, not really. Okay, maybe what I'd said was a little over the line, but I didn't think she'd respond with pain.

But then the hurt morphed into something close to fury, and my cock practically leaked because of it.

"Fine. But I'm choosing the restaurant."

See? Bossy. And sexy. Though, at that point, I respected her for it.

I'd hurt her, and she'd come back strong and direct. That trait was admirable.

Ignoring my desires, I gave her a quick nod. "Whatever pleases you, boss."

"Are you always so fucking grumpy?"

"Only when people piss me off."

"You should work on that. There are breathing techniques and things to teach you to control your anger."

Of course there were.

As she moved on to give me more detail on how I could change to fit her ideals, I continued down the street. No matter how beautiful she was, and how hard her little body made my cock, or how much I wanted to know what her cunt tasted like, she was too bossy for me. We would never find peace together. Only conflict and fighting. And bedgames. Angry, hard matings that led to broken furniture and bruises. I could almost feel the ache she'd leave behind. Chad would see my bite marks on her skin and know she was not truly his.

Which was enough of a warning to force me to act.

"We should stop this," I said, grabbing her arm. "Let's forget we were matched and go on about our lives. We obviously don't get along."

But that fury was back, and a look that shocked me took over her pretty face. The female was a warrior for sure. My warrior.

"Oh no, mister. We're staying the weekend. I deserve a few days of fun in a luxury hotel, and you need a few lessons on manners for... whomever you end up with."

That should have sounded like torture, but I found myself almost relieved. I didn't want to spend a weekend dealing with her rules and trying to keep my cock on stand-down, but I also didn't want to see her walk away just yet. The smart decision would have been to go back to my apartment, rub my cock until I was spent, and forget the beautiful woman whom my esehhnce had crooned for in record time. Fate was wrong—she was not for him.

But smart decisions were not what I was after, apparently.

"You sure your Chad won't mind you having dinner with another male?"

Stacy's lips turned down, and her eyes held a serious expression. "I'm not with Chad."

I took a step back, my mind spinning. "But when you came to—"

"I know what I said when I was at Cutlass'. It was...well, not a lie, really. But it kind of was. I'm not with Chad or anyone else. I haven't had a *boie-frahhnd* in years."

The translator in my brain threw images of couples at me for the word *boie-frahhnd*. Huh.

"So you have no male in your life?"

"No," she said. "Not one like that. My past with Chad is...complicated. But he's not someone in the way. He's not anyone important to me."

Not important. That didn't sound as final as I'd like, but it was something. An opening of sorts. If this Chad wasn't an impediment to our mating, a match was possible.

Except for her bossy, demanding attitude that did nothing but piss me off. I was a pilot, a leader, and I would be the boss of our mating. If we made it that far. Everything was still too precarious to know for sure.

But possibilities had opened up.

"Fine," I said, growling slightly as the word exploded from between my lips. "We'll go to dinner. Maybe using your mouth for something other than talking will be a good thing."

She frowned, those plump, pink lips turning down, bringing my attention right to them. Caught my focus and left me not thinking about food. At all. Her mouth...on my cock. That picture didn't help the situation.

Dinner was going to be hell.

CHAPTER FOUR_

The man ordered a hamburger.

A well-done hamburger.

At a restaurant famous for fish.

Jackass.

"You know, they have great seafood here," I said as Maverick handed his menu back to the waiter.

"So?" He sounded gruff, but I didn't miss the way his eyes drifted lower. He was talking to my boobs. Of course.

"If you wanted a burger, we could have gone to a different place."

He seemed confused...and seriously irritated. "They have burgers here."

I sighed. "But if you didn't want seafood, why would you agree to come here? To a seafood restaurant?"

He sat back, eyeing my face for a moment. "You demanded to be able to choose."

Well...huh. I couldn't exactly argue with the truth, now could I? Plus, he was smiling, sort of. Half smiling. Not frowning. That little tilt to his mouth was almost charming.

And made me think of his mouth...on mine...and other parts.

"Besides," Maverick added as I reached for my ice water. It was suddenly stuffy at our table. "This city has burgers no matter where I go. I assumed this place would as well, so I didn't need to argue with you over something so small. You argue enough on your own."

Aw, well, that helped. Charmingness...gone.

"We could have gone somewhere else."

"But you chose here."

"I didn't think you'd want a burger."

"How could you? You don't know me."

And for some reason, those words hurt. A lot more than they should have. I didn't know him...and I probably never would. Not with the way we fought.

"You're right," I said as I laid my napkin across my lap, trying hard not to look at him. I didn't need to see him gloat.

But when he spoke again, Maverick didn't sound gloaty. In fact, he sounded almost resigned. "Don't worry. You'll be rid of me soon enough, and then you won't have to deal with a man who chooses a burger over insects."

I wanted to break, to tell him I wouldn't mind getting to know him, that I figured his gruff exterior was an act for some reason. But I couldn't because...

"I'm not eating insects." When he didn't respond, I leaned forward. Pissed. "I am *not* eating insects."

The look in his eye, the tilt to his lips. Things just got interesting.

MAVERICK

She looked completely surprised. And maybe even a little angry.

"I am *not* eating insects."

Definitely angry. This might be fun.

"Sure you are," I said as I sat back in my chair, looking forward to seeing a little fire from her. "At least, that's what you told the waiter to bring you."

If she had been a Reithhar female, she would have been growling at me. "I ordered crab legs, jackass."

Time to pull out the big guns, which happened to be my knowledge of things far removed from construction and piloting ships across the stars. While Cutlass and Hudson had been busy with their mates, I'd been studying. A lot.

"Look at your choice of prey, sweetheart. In the overall hierarchy of your oceans, crustaceans are the insects of the ecoverse."

Stacy was silent for a moment, and I could almost see the wheels turning in her head. She was thinking it over, which caught me by surprise. I expected her to fight more, to dig her heels in and refuse to back down. I did not anticipate her being logical.

"They're not insects."

Ah, there was the stubbornness I'd expected. "They are in their world."

"We're all in one world."

I snorted a laugh. "Keep telling yourself that."

She slammed her napkin on the table and stood up, almost knocking over her chair. "If you'll excuse me, I need to find the restroom."

I almost felt a little guilty as she stormed away. Almost. I could have been nicer, could have chosen not to point out what she was eating in the overall scheme of life on her planet, but she'd been abrasive since the moment we met. Plus, there was the whole Chad issue that appeared to be a non-issue, though I wasn't sure about that yet. I was on edge and ready to fight back, even if I did hate myself a little bit for it.

But her zeal and fire certainly didn't make my cock feel bad. On the contrary, he was ready to push her even further just to see where we'd end up.

Stacy arrived back at the table at the same time as the waiter who brought us our food. I watched with interest as her plate was placed in front of her, fascinated by her reactions. Her lips turned down, and her brow pressed together a bit, giving her the look of someone in deep thought or serious disgust.

My money was on disgust.

"You see them as insects now, right?" I had to ask. I couldn't help myself.

Stacy sighed and ignored her crab to eat the green plant life on her plate instead. "I hate you."

Yeah, I hated her, too. Though a little less with every minute, it seemed.

CHAPTER FIVE_

STACY

"Well, that was fun," I said as we walked back to the hotel. I mean, it was a total lie—dinner had been a train wreck that left me tired, aggravated, and hungry. Like, really hungry. Stupid man and his stupid insects comment. I'd never be able to eat crab again. Or lobster. Or... anything with insect-like legs.

There went my seafood dinners on Christmas Eve.

But on top of all that, there was something else brewing inside of me. Some emotion I wasn't too happy to have to deal with. I felt almost fearful. I couldn't put my finger on what exactly that meant, but something had knocked me off my game. It could have been as bad as having to listen to Maverick all night or as simple as dealing with what I ended up eating. Steamed vegetables reminded me of hospital food. Hospital food reminded me of hospital beds. Which reminded me of fear and pain and a loneliness so big, it seemed to want to swallow me down and never let me go.

For the first time that night, I had been thankful for Maverick's company. If I'd have been alone when that feeling hit, I don't know what I would have done. Something stupid, probably. Maybe even reckless. I never did handle those sorts of memories well.

"You have a strange idea of fun," Maverick said, reminding me that I'd been trying to start a conversation. Sort of.

"It's sarcasm, you might want to try it."

"What is *ssar-khaashem*?"

Great. More jackassedness. I was about to make a smart remark about his making fun of me, but the look on his face stopped me. He seemed serious. But how could that be?

"Don't pick on me," I said, trying really hard not to get taken in by his curious expression. "I'm hungry and cranky."

"I'm not picking. I don't know this word, *ssar-khaashem*. But if you can't explain it..."

Well, shit, that sounded like a challenge.

"Sarcasm is using words that mean the opposite of your intent to mock or make fun of something."

Maverick's brow furrowed. That look should not have made my panties wet, but did. How did someone end up that hot? And why was I so attracted to such a jackass?

"So it's mean-spirited?"

"Well, no. Not really," I said, but my mind spun on all the times I'd used sarcasm in the past. All the times it had been used against me. "It can be, though. I guess."

"I'll not use it then. Where I'm from, being mean-spirited to others was frowned upon. Here, it's almost normalized."

He wasn't wrong. But as we started walking again, slower this time, the rest of his words came to be more important.

"Why did you leave?" I asked. I still didn't know where he was from. Hell, I might never know. We weren't exactly friends or anything.

"My home was destroyed."

"Your house?"

"No," he said, his voice softening. His face falling a bit. "Everything."

That was something I could actually imagine. When I got sick and ended up in the hospital, it had certainly seemed as if I'd lost everything. My life, my freedom, even my own body. My opinion of Maverick slid off course with that one bit of truth.

"Was it because of a war?" I stopped again, reaching for his arm.

Needing connection and assuming he did as well. Even if he did hate me. "Is that how your home was destroyed?"

He shook his head, staring up into the sky as if the stars peeking through the clouds meant something to him. Something important. "Natural *dee-sahhster*."

"Oh." *Oh.* Sudden and without reason. Yeah, that would leave scars I could relate to. "I'm so sorry."

I ran my hand over his arm, not really thinking about the move, just offering whatever comfort I could. The muscles were solid under my hold, his skin warm beneath my fingers. I shivered a bit at the thought of the man's strength.

Maverick stared down at my hand on his flesh, but he didn't pull away. And neither did I.

"Thank you," he said, his voice little more than a whisper. That thanks was more than I could have asked for, more than I'd expected.

Perhaps there was hope for him yet.

We started walking again with me hanging on to his arm. For protection, of course. Detroit was a dangerous city. There was no comfort in that hold, no desire being granted.

It was only for my protection.

MAVERICK

Her hand on my skin made me excited in ways it shouldn't have. Something about her touch, about the feel of her skin, stirred my esehhnce and made me want to croon for her all over. I'd been fighting that particular need, but I didn't know how long I could hold off. She was so close, so desirable, so beautiful.

But it was her quietness, her comforting demeanor and acceptance of my truth without arguing, that truly drew me to her. She'd calmed so much since the disastrous start at the hotel, and she seemed like an entirely different person than the one who'd stormed into Cutlass' unit just a few days before. But which was the real Stacy? Bossy and brash, arrogant and rude, or soft and kind? I had no idea, and that kept me on edge.

"What about you?" I asked, seeking more knowledge about her. "Tell me things."

"There should be a please there," she said, though a small smile turned those pink lips up. My people didn't mate mouths like the humans did, so that was something I'd never experienced. I was curious for sure, though. Especially after seeing so much mouth mating being enjoyed by my brothers once they met their mates. Curious, but not quite enough to make that move.

"Please," I said, drawing the word out and letting the air drag over my tongue. "Tell me."

Stacy didn't seem able to focus, and a lovely flush spread across the tops of her breasts. I longed to touch there, to run a finger from one side to the other to see if they were as soft as they appeared.

She sighed. "What do you want to know about me?"

Everything. "You have a twin sister."

Her eyes narrowed, and she suddenly seemed far warier. "Yeah, I do."

"She looks very much like you."

Stacy bristled, her shoulders squaring and her eyes hardening right before mine. No longer intrigued by my teasing, this was a woman ready to attack. Or to be attacked and defend herself.

"Yeah, well...twins."

The tone of her voice seemed to be an ending, but I needed more. I wanted to understand. "I have no recollection of multiple births where I'm from. In fact, I didn't know such a thing was possible. What was it like?"

"What...to have a twin?"

"Sure. To have such a close bond from birth to another person must be something unique."

She looked up at me, almost shocked, it seemed. "Really? You only want to know what it's like to grow up together?"

"Yes, really. Why?"

She shrugged. "Most guys who find out I have a twin sister want to know if we've ever had a *thhree-sum*."

That word didn't translate well. Or at least, the images thrown at me from the communication core were a little...confusing. "What is a *thhree-sum*?"

Stacy stopped in her tracks, yanking her hand from my arm. I missed her touch immediately, something I wasn't about to admit.

"Don't mock me. I won't be sarcastic with you again, but you don't get to make fun like that."

Fiery. Hot. Determined. There was a Stacy that intrigued. "I don't know mock. I asked a question to get to know you."

"You asked me to explain a threesome."

"Yes? Why is that wrong?"

She crossed her arms over her chest and glared. "Fine. It's when three people have sex all together. Most guys have some weird fantasy about getting with my sister and me at the same time simply because we look alike."

My growl was loud and unstoppable. That sort of thing wasn't done on planet Xouthhgros. Sure, until a mate was found, bedgames were casual and varied, but no mated male would ever allow such a thing with his female. We gave ourselves fully to our mates—and expected the same back. No wonder my asking about her sister upset her.

"I had no idea that was an issue for you and Macy," I said as I held open the door to the hotel for her. I made sure to grab a good look at her ass when she passed me as well. These manners she spoke about seemed like a fair trade in the end. "I understand your rules here are far more lax than where I'm from, but we don't seek extra partners that way. We find the one person meant for us, and we don't ever let anyone come between that bond. We honor our mates, cherish them. Asking others into a mating bed just isn't done. I'm sorry if that's what you thought I was looking for when I asked about being a twin. I can assure you, it was not."

There was a moment of quiet, a handful of seconds where Stacy stood and did nothing but look at me. The corridor was shadowed and quiet, the back hallway where we stood nearly empty. And she stared. I wasn't sure how to react, had no idea what the look on her face meant.

But I knew exactly what to do when she lunged for me and jumped into my arms. I grabbed her and pulled her close, giving myself over to the desire that had been building within me all night. Stacy wrapped her legs around my hips and planted her lips against mine in what had to be the most brutal mouth mating of all time.

Kissing...it was called kissing on Earth.

When Stacy's tongue slid between my lips to stroke against mine, I no longer cared what the hell the right word was. I was done.

Completely overtaken by the sensual power of the little female with the big attitude. She was mine, and I was going to claim her with my cock.

But mouth mating was definitely going on my list of favorite things about being on Earth.

CHAPTER SIX

STACY

I jumped. I had to.

Maverick's hands grabbed my ass in the most perfect way imaginable, and his lips practically crushed mine. That little bit of pain was okay, though, because I wanted him like that: strong, gruff, and taking what he wanted. I wanted him to be a little rough with me. He'd just said he wouldn't be trying to finagle a threesome at any point along the way. He deserved a present.

God, the boys I hung around before him really *were* assholes.

I had no idea how we managed it, but somehow Maverick got us up to the hotel room without breaking the kiss. At one point, he even had me pressed up against the wall in the elevator, his hands sliding under my skirt in a way that made me want to cry.

I truly did love a man with callused palms.

As soon as the door to our room was open—he really was good at multitasking—he carried me through and kicked it closed behind us. And then he took that kiss to the next level. His tongue tangled with mine, his soft grunts and moans making me want more. Need more.

Shit, hate sex was hot.

"This doesn't change anything," I said as we finally broke apart long enough for me to pull my dress over my head. Not caring about my scars. Only wanting to feel him, to be with him.

"Fine." He yanked his shirt off and dropped his hands to his pants. "You tell yourself that."

He spun me around, yanking open the curtains and pressing my chest against the windows. The river was a sea of blackness, and the lights of the Canadian shore were far enough away to seem almost from a fantasy world. As if the place wasn't real. Maverick had me on display, though I doubted anyone could possibly see me from so far away. Still, doing this, being shoved up against the glass in my simple, lacy lingerie, was so dirty and exhibitionist. I loved it.

The glass was cold beneath my skin, hard and unforgiving. The only sounds in the room were those of our breaths. I shivered from the chill in the air and the heat in my blood. Anticipation for what was next, what Maverick would do to me now that he had me pinned, kept me quivering and excited. This was going to be so much more than just sex. I knew it. Could sense something important hovering nearby.

This would be life-changing.

When Maverick slid his fingers into my panties, when he sent shivers up my spine with a mere brush of his fingers against my hips, I had to rest my head against the glass. I was too keyed up, too needy, too fucking wet to do anything other than shake for him. And talk.

"You going to fuck me against the windows?"

Maverick grunted, the sound making me moan. "No. I'm going to lick your cunt until you come on my tongue."

Dead. I was dead. Or about to be. Not until he made good on his promise. Because seriously, I wasn't going to say no to that.

He slid my panties off with more care than I expected. His large, rough hands running from my waist all the way down the length of my legs in a slow slide. That calmed me, allowed a bit of relaxation in. Pushed aside the anxiety and tension a little. That slowness and care faked me out as I assumed it showed me how Maverick would treat the rest of the act. Sure, I was against a window, but that didn't mean he couldn't be slow and careful. He'd warm my body up for him before diving in. I'd have a warning of some sort about what was next.

It was almost funny how wrong I was.

That slow, careful removal of my panties was nothing more than a lie. The second I lifted my leg so he could remove the fabric from one side, he grabbed my hips, yanked me back so I was bent almost in half with my hands still against the glass, and he licked a filthy, wet trail from my clit all the way to my asshole.

The porn-star moan that dropped from my lips was unavoidable, really.

"Maverick." I spread my feet farther, giving him enough room to do...whatever he intended to do. Because who wouldn't? The man had his tongue on my clit, circling and licking and—fuck me running—nibbling, even as his fingers slid inside my sopping wet pussy. No one in their right mind would say no to him. Not when his mouth was too busy to make me hate him.

Maverick growled against me as he pushed his fingers in deep. Really deep. I may have even gasped at that delicious pressure. Still, he growled. There was no other way to describe it. The sound seemed all sorts of wrong and right at the same time. Animalistic and needy but totally him as well. And the vibrations it gave off against my skin. Yeah, he could growl all he wanted. That sound was better than a finger vibe for sure.

When Maverick scraped his teeth over my clit, I plastered myself against the glass and moaned again. Uninhibited and completely at his mercy. He felt so good on me. Every touch, every lick, every push of his fingers—so perfect. I couldn't help myself—I reached back and grabbed his hair, pulling him in tighter against my flesh. Needing more. Wanting to get him to make me come.

But Maverick wasn't having it.

"Demanding, aren't you?" He knocked my hands away, keeping his lips close enough to my pussy to tease me as he laid down his rules. "Hands back on the window. Watch me in the reflection if you can. I want you to see what I do to you."

Shaky and with a little whine, I did as I was told, even though I wasn't ready to give in yet. "But you're so close to where I want you."

"I'll get there."

Fuck, his confidence and low, rough voice were so damn hot. "Maverick—"

He smacked my ass. Just once, but harder than anyone ever had. A true hit. The sting sent fire through my body, the surprise making me gasp and groan in equal measure. That really shouldn't have made me even wetter, but it totally did. And Maverick didn't miss that.

"You like me being in charge, don't you?" His dark chuckle was enough to bring out a low moan from me, but his fingers spreading me wider so he could lick a path along the inside of me was what really brought out the trembles.

"Please," I whispered, watching his shadowy form in the glass below me. Almost ready to surrender completely.

Almost.

And Maverick knew it. "It's my face in your cunt, princess. Let me do what I know how to do. I'll get you off."

"You'd better."

He pulled me closer by my hips and kissed my clit in the sweetest, most debauched sort of way. "Trust me."

Oof, that was a hard one. I didn't trust many people. I mean, sure, I was staying in a hotel room with a man I barely knew, who currently had his face between my legs. There was trust there. But giving up control? Letting him lead me to wherever he chose to go? That was different.

It was also sort of...titillating.

"Fine, but you'd better be good," I hissed as he went back to spreading me open so he could focus on my clit.

I could feel him smile against me. "I'm more than just good."

And he was.

My first orgasm swept over me as I pressed my face and chest against the windows, my yelp loud and sharp from the pleasure. But Maverick didn't stop. He didn't even give me a break. He kept licking, sucking, fingering, pushing, spreading...he kept bringing me more. Over and over, he pushed me right to the edge and kept going. Rolling me through multiple orgasms until there was nothing but his mouth, his hands, and the cold glass.

Still, every girl had her breaking point.

"Please," I huffed, my legs shaking and my breaths coming too fast to be normal. "I can't. No more."

Maverick pulled his mouth away but kept his fingers inside me, moving all slow and curling them until he made me moan. "I win?"

"We weren't competing."

He chuckled again, dragging his thumb over my clit in a way that made my knees go weak. "Everything is a competition with you."

He growled again, this time with his mouth pressed hard against my pussy. The vibrations almost made me scream, but I was done with this. I needed him, needed to feel him inside me, was so fucking desperate for it.

Too desperate.

I slammed my hand against the glass, my own version of throwing the white flag. "Yes. You win this one with your ridiculous tongue and magic fingers. Now fuck me so I can make you come, too."

I hadn't expected him to pick me up and smack my ass as he tossed me over his shoulder. I also hadn't expected him to throw me on the bed. That said, I didn't know if you could set expectations for a man like Maverick.

"A little rough, don't you think?" I tried to look irritated at the man, but he was shirtless, his jeans undone and hanging just enough over his hips for me to see the tip of his cock peeking out. And he was looking at me like I was something worth his time. In fact, he looked at me as if I was wanted and precious. That might have been the hottest part about him.

But then Maverick grinned a cocky, one-sided sort of smile. And he dropped his pants.

Sweet mercy.

My knees fell open of their own accord as he approached, an automatic response to the glory that was his cock. It was hard and long, positively thick. A true fatty with just the right amount of curve to hit the good spots inside of me. Maverick's cock was dildo-model good. Perfect, really. And just so wonderfully big. I wasn't one of those girls who said crazy shit like, "Oh my gosh, I don't think it will fit." They all fit. It was just a matter of how comfortable they could fit once all the way in.

Maverick's cock was going to hurt in all the right ways.

My brain positively short-circuited when he placed a knee on the mattress and took that beautiful, glorious cock in his hand. My mouth watered and my body clenched on nothing as he stroked from base to tip. We needed to move this along because I didn't want to wait another second to feel all that.

"Let me help you," I said as I leaned back to grab a condom from the nightstand. That's right—I'd made sure to stock up on the prophylactics. My sister was in med school, and she'd shown me the slide shows of nasty, STD-infected genitals. I wasn't about to play that kind of game. Besides, I'd had time on my hands. The time I'd waited for Maverick earlier in the day had been put to good use.

Maverick watched as I tore open the package, stared at me as if he was waiting to pounce. And I was totally going to let him. His cock was hot and weighty in my hand, the skin softer than I would have expected. I couldn't help running my fingers along the length. Just once. Okay, fine. Three times. When he groaned that soft, manly rumble that meant my touch felt good, I practically beamed at him. Yeah, this was going to be good. Unable not to, I placed a sweet, soft kiss right on the tip before rolling the latex over him.

"Ready," I said as I lay back against the mattress and let my knees fall open. If I got so much time to look, he should as well.

Maverick cocked a smile, following me down until he was right on top of me. "Good. Because I'm not wasting more time."

I dropped my legs open more as he settled between them, hooking a calf over his hip to give him better access. "You think that time spent with your face between my legs was wasted?"

Instead of answering me, Maverick held my gaze as he pushed in slow. There was no pausing, though. No nudge or back-and-forth. Just one long, slow glide as his cock practically split me in two. Owning me as no man ever had. And I loved it. I might have even moaned his name as if I was on some cheesy soap opera.

What? You try not to.

"Not wasted," he said, grabbing my leg and pulling it so my calf rested on his shoulder. He even placed a quick kiss on my knee, something so sweet before he used his shoulder to open me up. He was so built, so thick and muscular all over. Thank God for Pilates.

"You don't think so?" I said on a breath of air, trying to stay in the conversation even as I wanted to reduce our talk to yes and please and more and fuck.

"No." He grunted as he slid all the way home, his eyes falling almost closed in what had to be pleasure. "But I've wanted to know how your cunt feels with my cock inside it since the first time I saw you."

I grabbed his shoulders as he started to really move, hanging on as my heart pounded through my ears. Such a sweet comment. Such a naughty moment. "And what's your verdict?"

He groaned and slid almost all the way out before thrusting back in. "On what?"

"You know what."

He grinned and licked over my top lip before whispering. "Let me hear it."

Oh, he was going to make me say the dirty words. As if I was somehow too delicate. Silly man. "How does my cunt feel wrapped around your cock? Am I wet enough for you?"

He grunted in what sounded almost like a whine, moving faster, leaning down to kiss me hard and deep before pulling away. "Your cunt feels like home."

Yeah, okay. He had a little charm, still.

Between his words and the phenomenal things his cock did to my pussy, there was no holding back. I came before he did, shaking and trembling as my entire body seemed to seize around him. Maverick followed, grunting and biting my shoulder as he pressed in deep. Both of us clinging to the other as we rode out the explosions.

And when he rolled me over, when he dragged me up his body to lay across his chest, I knew sex hadn't been a mistake. The man may have driven me crazy, but I didn't care. He wrapped me in his arms and held me as if I mattered. As if he cared about me in ways beyond the physical. He held me close and gave me comfort I'd never experienced.

"Sleep, princess. I want to wake you with my tongue in your cunt."

Comfort and filthy fucking promises. What more did I need?

MAVERICK

The single sun of Earth wasn't all the way over the horizon when I awoke. Stacy rested in my arms still, her head on my chest, her eyes closed and her breathing even. Asleep. Quiet.

Unmasked.

This was the female I'd wanted to see. The real one. She'd shown herself to me in flashes on our date, and I wanted more of that person.

I ran a finger down her cheek, unable to resist touching that soft, sweet-smelling skin. Her eyes blinked open as I reached her chin, and she smiled. That look devastated me.

I crooned for her. Again. Unable to hold back the purring sound of my people.

I had no idea what made me open my mouth, but when I did, the words that came out were not at all what I'd expected.

"I'm not who you think I am."

She blinked but didn't look surprised. "Neither am I."

"I am not from Earth."

No reaction. Just that same soft look in her eyes. "I knew something was different, but I didn't expect that."

"We weren't allowed to tell." I still wasn't by Ampetheia's rules. But if I was going to possibly claim this female as my mate, if I was going to ask her to stay unmasked with me, I needed to be able to do the same for her. No hiding for either of us.

Stacy stayed quiet for a long moment, eyes unfocused, hand still against my chest. But then she frowned. "Is Hudson like you as well?"

"Yes."

"My sister still loves him."

"And he loves her."

She snuggled closer. "Okay, then."

That was...too easy. "Okay, then?"

"Sure. My sister's smart. Smarter than I'll ever be. If she's okay with the whole not-from-Earth thing, then I can be too."

"That's it?" I pushed her back so I could see her face. "No argument? No demands for information?"

"Maverick, do you know what these scars mean?" She rolled slightly, showing me what looked like wings along her back. I'd noticed them the night before, but I had been too worried about pleasing her and myself to ask. The harsh, dark pink lines stood out against her golden skin in the morning light. Undeniable marks from severe wounds. Obvious signs of a battle fought.

"No," I said as I traced one around her ribs. "Tell me."

"I had *kan-sserr*, which is a sickness." My translator threw many images to define cancer, all of them ugly and hard. Whatever that particular threat was, I never wanted it near my mate again.

"I don't like this *kan-sserr*."

"Nobody does. *Kan-sserr* is a horrible, cruel disease that takes over your body and destroys you from the inside out. Mine spread to a few areas, one being here." She grabbed my hand and settled it over her breast. "See the round scar? It's not as easy to spot as the ones on my back."

I traced the line in question, noticing another matching one on her other breast. A pale, near-perfect circle around the darkened area in the middle. "What is this from?"

"I had breast *kan-sserr* as a teenager. It's super rare and hard to treat when you get it so young, but I got it. And I beat it. The doctors removed flesh from my back to rebuild my breasts once all the sickness was gone, but it was a really long process. I spent almost a year in a hospital bed fighting every single sick cell of it."

I brushed the back of my fingers over one of her scars. "You're a warrior."

She shook her head. "Maybe. But I'm also uncomfortable with people seeing my scars because I'm afraid they'll disgust them. And I'm scared of being alone because of how hard being isolated from everyone was that year. And I have a hard time letting people tell me what to do because I prefer to be in control. Of everything."

"Bossy."

"Whatever."

"But that's how you deal with your past."

"Yeah. It is. I know not everyone likes that, but—"

I pressed my lips to hers, needing her silence. Not wanting to hear her say bad things about herself.

"Stop," I whispered when I finally pulled away. "It's your hunting mask. I understand."

"You do?"

I hummed and nuzzled into her neck, hiding behind her as I admitted my hurt as well. "Back on Xouthhgros, the men wore masks on their hunts to help them feel braver. There were creatures on other planets that could take a warrior down with a single strike. The masks gave them courage and strength. Just like yours does."

Her smile fell, and she seemed to grow almost sad. "What happened to your planet?"

"There was an explosion. On Earth, it would be something like a volcanic eruption. It happened while I was hunting. I wasn't there to help them."

"I'm sorry." She ran a hand through my mane, holding me close. "That had to be so hard on you to lose everything so quickly."

"It was. There were five of us on that trip. We moved to a colony across the solar system, but it was destroyed as well. We'd been hunting again, Cutlass, Hudson and I—the other two had stayed behind. When the colony exploded, the three of us remaining headed farther out to get away from the chaos. We ended up in this space station where we found a flier for the Intergalactic Dating Agency. Hudson, he wanted to meet his mate, so he came here. Cutlass and I came with him because we didn't have a reason not to."

"And you signed up to be matched, just like Hudson and Cutlass."

"Yes."

"But you were matched to someone you don't like." Her voice wobbled, and her breaths came faster. I couldn't stand the thought of her in pain, so I pulled back. Looking her in the eye.

"To someone who pretends to be someone I don't like."

She stared, her eyes deep, her mind obviously spinning. And when she spoke, her words were so true they actually hurt.

"I'm afraid of being weak."

"I'm afraid of losing everything I care about."

"We're quite the pair."

"Yes, we are. And we've been matched." I licked along the seam of her lips, seeking entrance. Wanting nothing more than to mouth mate with her for days. She accepted me, giving in to the kiss with a soft exhale that only made me want to hear more of them.

"I crooned for you," I said as I moved from her lips to her chin.

"I don't know what that means, but I have a feeling it's important." She grabbed my mane, pulling me back up. Demanding more kisses.

I couldn't answer, could only press my lips to hers and roll her under me. Important wasn't a big enough word for crooning. Vital, necessary, amazing...those held more meaning. And still, they weren't enough.

Her legs wrapped around my hips, and her arms pulled me closer as I mated her mouth with human-type kisses. Her body called to me, inviting me inside. And I responded, as selfish as that may have been.

"Maverick," she whispered when I slowly slid into her wet heat.

I shook my head, unable to speak. Too weighted down by the moment to use words. Instead, I crooned for her, singing my desire and needs with my people's song.

Stacy curled closer and wrapped her body around mine, watching me as I mated her with long, drawn-out strokes of my cock. As I pressed her body into the mattress and loved all over her. This was my match, my mate, my female. This was a person I could see myself with for the rest of our days. Not the brash, bossy person she pretended to be when she was upset or scared. The Stacy who'd woken up in my arms, admitted her secrets, and accepted mine was the real one. The true one.

The one I wanted.

The one I probably didn't deserve but would keep by my side always.

CHAPTER SEVEN_

STACY

Sunday afternoon came far too soon. Two days of sex and snuggles, of getting to know the man behind the bad attitude—it all left me feeling slightly raw. I liked being with Maverick, and the idea of sitting around alone once again after having that closeness almost killed something inside of me. But I left Maverick in the parking lot at the hotel after a long and hot kiss good-bye like I was supposed to. Because I was an adult.

And then I called my sister in tears as soon as I pulled onto the freeway heading home. She didn't judge. Okay, she sighed and seemed a little patronizing when she told me things would work out, but she didn't judge. Much.

And I didn't mention the fact that I knew her soon-to-be husband was an alien. Some things needed to be spoken about in person, and I wasn't ready to fully break my Maverick-and-me bubble just yet.

I spent Sunday evening on the couch thinking of Maverick and trying to find a way to snuggle with a pillow. Spoiler: it's not nearly as awesome as snuggling a man like Maverick. Not even close. I went to bed itching for a set of arms to hold me, for the weight of a man on top of me, and for the quiet sounds of another person nearby. I was officially lonely.

Monday morning was back to the old grindstone, so I was up and rolling with the sun. And a text from Maverick.

Try not to miss me too much today.

Still a jackass, even though he made me grin like a middle schooler with a crush. But if he could banter, so could I. I sent back a text before heading into the shower.

Try not to be grumpy today. Impossible; I know.

When I grabbed my phone after getting ready, there was another text from Maverick.

Not as impossible as you not missing me, princess.

Arrogant, but true.

———

"Someone had a good weekend."

My head spun away from the awful spreadsheets I'd spent my morning fixing—for the love of God, VLookup is not that hard—to find my coworker Patricia smiling at me from the entrance to my cube. She was a nice enough lady and a bit of a gossip. We got along just fine.

"I have no idea what you mean."

She leaned a hip against the corner of my desk, looking very much like she was about to hear something juicy. "Oh, please. Either you got yourself a man, or Ben & Jerry's bought back that chocolate-covered potato chip ice cream you liked so much."

Ouch, that hurt. I really did miss that ice cream. "Now I want something sweet."

Patricia tossed me a Milky Way. She knew the way to my heart. And to get me to unzip my lips.

"Spill."

I waited a good five seconds—a fact that should be lauded, by the way—before I broke. And then I gushed. "He's...amazing. A real cranky bastard, and he totally made my favorite food completely inedible to me forever, but I like him."

She grinned. "You *do* like him."

"I do." And I did. A lot. Maybe too much considering the small amount of time I'd known him. Add in the fact that he wasn't really human, and there were some serious red flags. But hell, who cared? I looked amazing in red.

Patricia, though, didn't seem as overjoyed as I would have expected. In fact, she looked at the floor, purposely avoiding my eyes.

"What?" I asked, the weight of whatever she felt she needed to say hitting me hard.

"Has he met your sister yet?"

Stomach, meet your shoes. "Why?"

"Nothing really. Just..." She sighed and shrugged. "You two look so much alike. You're both so personable and pretty, but she's going to be a doctor. That sort of drive can be attractive, if you know what I mean."

I did. I hated thinking about it, but I did. Still, Patricia was talking about Maverick, about him going after my sister. He'd given me the whole mating-to-just-one-person speech. He'd told me he was mine.

And then he'd left me in the parking lot and only sent me two texts in twenty-four hours.

"She's dating his friend," I said, my voice too soft. Too weak. Too full of doubt. "I'm sure that's not going to be an issue."

Sure...I was really, really sure.

Sort of.

———

My day totally sucked after that conversation. My phone remained silent—no calls or texts from the man I'd spent the entire weekend with. I couldn't calm my nerves and ended up eating three Milky Ways just to keep functioning. And a couple of icy, sweet, coffee drinks. And a cake pop or two.

My hips didn't lie—it was going to be a busy week at the gym for me.

I was so far gone, so anxious and edgy, that even a text from Maverick at the end of the day didn't help. He wanted me to come over to his place. I was getting what I wanted—more time with him—so why couldn't I breathe properly?

Still, I went. Driving across town and fighting traffic the whole way until I pulled up outside the old warehouse that had been converted into loft-style apartments. I trudged up the stairs to his place, trying hard to calm myself. Trying and failing.

"Hey," Maverick said when he opened the door. There was a smile on his face, one meant just for me. One that said he was happy to see me, happy to be near me. That he was still mine. I fell into his arms, suddenly feeling so silly for spending my day stressing out.

"Hi," I said, sighing when he squeezed me tighter. As if he knew. As if he'd missed me just as much.

"You okay?"

"I am now." And I was. Patricia had thrown me for a loop, but Maverick straightened me back out. One look, one smile, one hug, and all was right with the world.

Well, maybe not all...

"Hey, you two," Macy called from the doorway of the apartment she shared with Hudson. "Dinner's just about ready. Come on down once you've said hello."

I clung to Maverick even as the cold wall of doubt slipped between us once more. "We're eating with them?"

"Yes," he said, pulling away so he could see my face. Give me that intense stare he'd somehow mastered. "Why?"

I didn't know how to answer that without sounding needy and clingy and...unattractive. How did I explain that I didn't want to spend time with my sister? That I worried about the two of them in some crazy sort of way? That I needed time alone with him and just him?

I didn't have any idea, so I ignored everything. "No reason."

"Come on." He grabbed my hand and pulled me behind him as he headed down the hall. "She promised no insects."

My eye roll was huge.

———

Later that night, after dinner and chatting and making a ton of excuses on why we needed to leave so early, Maverick pulled me into his bed. Into his arms. Just the two of us, finally.

"I needed this today," I whispered as he stripped me bare. He didn't respond with words, though his hands were gentle as they touched me.

Loving, almost. There was a sweetness to his touch that spoke to me, and a dirtiness to his kisses that drew me out.

"Maverick," I hissed when he slid inside. My hands clutched at him, my fingernails pressing into his shoulders.

He grunted, kissing me, pulling me close as he began to move. As he filled me over and over again. "You missed me."

"I did." A whispered truth, a moment of pure and utter openness. Bared to him in more ways than one.

"Good." He kissed me again, deeper this time, as his hands ran long, smooth trails over my body. As he lay on top of me, pressing me into the mattress, every inch of me covered by him.

And still, I doubted.

It hadn't escaped my attention that he didn't say "I missed you" back. That he didn't say anything more than good. But instead of focusing on that, I paid attention to the feel of him. To the push and pull between us. To the need that only he seemed to ignite in me.

Sex wouldn't cure all, but I could at least feel good for a little while before I dealt with the turmoil brewing between us. The one I couldn't quite put my finger on.

MAVERICK

Something felt off.

I'd been the pilot of our hunting party, which meant I led them into dangerous territories. And got them back out. Always. I'd developed an instinct for knowing when to set down and when to keep flying, had earned it after many rotations around the suns of flying, fixing, and risking my life.

Feeling that sense of dread, that impending doom looming over me, from my possible mate was unexpected. And unwanted. But some things were unavoidable.

Stacy had started to put her mask back on, spending far too much time seeking something I didn't know how to give her. I wanted her to be open with me, to be herself, but she blocked me most of the time. She refused to open herself up to me, telling untruths and avoiding my eyes instead. That person was not my Stacy—that was the fake Stacy. The one who had to hide, who feared too much.

I didn't like the fake Stacy.

And I missed her. The real her. Every second of every day that we spent apart was torture, but every moment in the presence of the not-real Stacy was agony. But I couldn't avoid her, couldn't miss a single second when the real Stacy might show up. So when she invited me over to her place the night after the tense dinner with Hudson and Macy, I went.

I would always come when she called for me.

"Hey," Stacy said as she opened the door. Her long, dark hair was stacked on top of her head in some sort of messy pile. It revealed her neck to me, the bones of her shoulders, the delicateness of her structure. I loved when she wore her hair up. There was something so sensual about her neck, so decidedly feminine. It stole my focus every time.

I didn't speak—couldn't, really. Instead, I grabbed her around the hips and pulled her closer. Nuzzling into her neck and placing kisses along the length. Tasting her. Showing her how much she attracted me, how much I wanted her.

She smacked my chest and giggled. "Quit before we skip dinner and end up in bed all night."

Perfect. "And the problem with that is?"

She pulled away from my hold and rolled her eyes, but the soft smile of my Stacy remained even as she moved into the kitchen.

"I grabbed steaks and potatoes, figuring we could make steak *free-tes*."

"What are *free-tzzz*?"

She grinned at me over her shoulder. "Frites. One word. And they're fries, basically, but frites sounds fancier. Plus, I have truffle oil for them. Truffle oil makes everything better."

I didn't know what truffle oil was, but it didn't matter. Stacy was looking at me with pure joy on her face, no mask, no hiding. I would have eaten her insects if she'd asked me to at that moment.

"Okay." There was raw meat resting on a board on the counter and small, white strips to the side. "What do I do?"

"Do you cook?"

"Not here, no. Your food is very different from my home."

"Oh. Well, it's okay." She moved across the kitchen to the oven.

"The broiler's ready, so I can get the steaks on. The fries will only take a few minutes."

"So I was right on time."

"I was early." She shook her head, a weird, almost sad look on her face. "I had a lot on my mind, and staying busy in the kitchen helps me focus."

That was understandable. I often took on some small project when I needed time to work out a plan or strategy. That was the logical side of our brain working its way through the chaos we tended to put in front of it.

Stacy placed the meat into the oven. Then she moved the white strips to a tall, round vessel beside the stove. When she dropped the sticks inside the vessel, a roar unlike any I'd heard on this planet boomed through the space.

I was in front of her before I could breathe, ready to kill anything that could harm her.

"Uh, Mav?"

"What?" I leaned over the vessel, taking care not to put myself directly in harm's way. If something came out and attacked, Stacy would be alone. I would not leave her undefended. "Why does this thing scream?"

"It's the hot oil. It does that."

I leaned farther over the pot, still keeping Stacy secured behind my back. The liquid inside was bubbling and obviously hot, but contained. Human cooking was something I didn't understand.

"Oh."

Stacy chuckled and bumped me with her hip so I'd move out of her way. "Go relax. I've got this."

"Have you always cooked?" I asked as I left her to her odd cooking monsters and explored her apartment. There was so much of the real Stacy in this place.

"No. In fact, I hated it. But then I spent a year eating hospital food and another six months on a bland diet as my body recovered. After that, I learned to cook because my taste buds had changed. Which is weird, you know? No one tells you when you go through chemo that you'll love *strah-bah-reehs* one day and hate them the next."

"So you hate these *strah-bah-reehs*?"

"With the fire of a thousand suns."

I would be sure never to have them in our home. Moving through the area where I deemed she spent a lot of time, I found small details about her life scattered on tables and shelves. I grabbed a picture in a jeweled frame, one of her and Macy as small children.

"You two really did look a lot alike."

"Yeah, so?" Stacy said, her voice harder than before.

I held up the picture. "It's easier to tell you apart now, I think."

She shrugged. "Macy has bigger boobs."

"Yes, she does." Larger breasts, a different set to her eyes, smaller lips. The two were quite different, really. Macy was nowhere near as beautiful as my match.

But my response seemed to dim something inside of Stacy. Her face fell, her entire body practically sagging as if I'd said something wrong.

"Oh."

"What is oh?" I asked, setting the picture down.

"Nothing." She waved her hand and smiled once more, but it wasn't my Stacy's smile. It was fake Stacy's. Smaller and less vibrant, not reaching her eyes.

I didn't like that smile.

"Stacy, why—"

A loud buzz interrupted me and made her jump. "Oh, the steaks are done. Come sit, and I'll get the plates ready."

I did as she asked, but I wouldn't let her get away with avoiding me. I would ask her about this all later.

———

But later never came. Not really. After dinner, Stacy dragged me to her bed, stripping my clothes off along the way. I was weak...I couldn't resist her when she started whispering about all the things she wanted from me, what she wished for. So I followed, and I ignored the fact that I needed to know what I'd said to make her sad.

Later, I told myself. Later.

Naked and on top of her, I sighed and kissed her sweet lips. Running my hands along her skin to show her how I cherished her. How much I cared. How much she meant to me.

"Maverick," she gasped. "I feel so connected to you."

I grunted my agreement, squeezing her closer. Needing to touch every inch of my Stacy. Then I slid lower, running my lips along her chest and stomach. Along her hips until I could place her legs over my shoulders and focus on her sweet cunt.

"Mav," she sighed, her hands rough on my shoulders. I licked her from top to bottom, spreading her open with my fingers so I could get to that little piece of flesh that made her shake. I loved that piece of flesh. Loved how she reacted when I sucked on it.

But Stacy was impatient. She pulled and tugged until I crawled back up the length of her, then she grabbed my cock and placed it at the entrance to her cunt. I did as she seemed to want, thrusting inside, my lips meeting hers in a frantic sort of kiss.

"Please," she said when we broke apart. "Please tell me."

"What?"

She shook her head.

"Stacy," I said as I slowed my thrusts. "What do you need?"

"This. Just this." But her eyes didn't meet mine, and I knew she was lying. Still, if my cock was what she wanted, I would give it to her. I would give her anything.

I grabbed both her hands and held them over her head. Pinning her. And I thrust hard and full until she shook. Until she screamed. Until her mask broke and the real Stacy was back.

But later that night after our bedgames were over, she didn't curl into my side. In fact, she kept a good amount of space between us. I hated that space, so I rolled toward her and pulled her into my arms. To show her I cared. To protect her. To make sure she knew how much she meant to me. Clinging to my Stacy as I fell asleep.

CHAPTER EIGHT

STACY

Things were falling apart.

I knew this, could practically feel the end coming, but there was nothing I could do to stop it. I'd tried to no avail, and I was getting more and more worried. Desperation wasn't a good look for me, that was for sure.

And Maverick...well, he wouldn't budge on the whole emotional response thing, of which there was none. Did he care? Did he want me around? He asked me to come over sometimes. Did that matter? Did his calling me to say he wanted to spend time together mean anything?

If calling meant something, then what did it mean when he didn't call? When it fell on me to ask and invite and cajole. Like today... Today was all on me. I'd called Maverick from work to see if he wanted me to come over for dinner. Being forced into a spot where I wasn't sure if I was wanted was harsh. His response had been heartbreaking.

If you'd like.

I didn't care about what I liked, I wanted to know what he liked. Would he care if I chose not to call for days? Would he notice? Did I want to know?

Still, I went because I didn't want to be alone—and because I missed him when he wasn't with me. After work, I headed to the warehouse. I was just about to open the front door to the warehouse when my phone rang. For a moment, I had this horrible, almost panic attack thought that it was Maverick calling off our food-Netflix-and-chill night, but no. It was worse.

It was Chad.

"What's up, hot stuff?"

"Shut up, Chad. What do you want?"

"You busy tonight?"

Which meant sex. He wanted sex. Because that was all we were to each other—fuck buddies with a hell of a lot of history. But no more.

"Sorry, killer, but I have a date. With my boyfriend."

"Oh, look at you getting all serious. Do I know him?" He sounded happy and confident, not at all bothered by the fact that I had a boyfriend. I hadn't had one since him, to be honest. Not that he cared.

Not that I wanted him to care. "No, you don't know him. He's not from around here."

Understatement. Literally.

"Has he met your sister yet?"

I froze, my stomach dropping into my shoes and ice water running through my veins. "What?"

"Has he met Macy?"

"Yeah," I said, feeling like I was going to throw up all over my pretty, peep toed shoes. "She lives in the same building he does."

His chuckle was a lot less friendly. "Well, that's convenient."

"What are you implying, Chad?"

He raised his voice in a mocking way. A very un-Chad way. "Oh gosh, Stace. I swear, I thought she was you."

"Macy's in a relationship with his friend. She wouldn't do that."

"But does he want to?" Chad's tone ate at me. His words sank in deep in a way only he knew how to do. Because with all our history, he knew every button to hit to make me doubt. And he hit them hard. "Or are they going to share you? Is that what this is? Some plan between two guys for the twin threesome of their fantasies? Her guy gets you two one night, yours the next?"

"You're sick."

"I'm realistic and a guy. I know how men think. No guy can resist the pull of identical twins. It's practically an obsession."

"Not for him," I said, but doubt hit me hard. The whole living situation *was* awfully convenient. I knew Macy would never—and I mean *never*—even think about doing anything like that. One, she had Hudson, but two, she was a good sister. She wouldn't hurt me that way.

"Oh, so you were the backup?" Chad asked. "Macy hooked her guy first, right? Yeah, I can see that. She's such an aggressive chick with her career shit. It's hot. I've known you since high school, and I still have no idea what you actually do."

Data processing and project analysis, but who the hell knew what that meant? Obviously not Chad. Definitely not Maverick.

Everything inside of me shattered like glass. My hopes, my feelings for Maverick, my confidence...all gone. It couldn't be true, but the doubts fed off Chad's words. His accusations. And doubt lied. Doubt lied hard. Maverick claimed he wanted me? That he was matched to me and took that seriously? How could I know for sure?

What if he hung out with Macy and Hudson just to be around my brilliant, driven sister?

What if he wished he had her instead of me?

Was I just the backup plan?

"I hate you, Chad," I said, my voice weak and wobbly as I fought back tears.

"Don't be like that. You know you can trust me. I don't want your sister. But other guys? I'm telling you. That fantasy might as well be an instinct."

"Shut up," I hissed. Hating him. Hating myself. Hating everything.

"Yeah, okay. I'll back off. Good luck, Stace. Call me if things crash and burn, though. You know I'll be there for you, baby."

I hung up, closing my eyes against the sick feeling burning in my gut. I hated him, hated the way he undermined everything, hated how he always brought up those old doubts of mine.

But what if he was right?

No. Maverick wasn't like that. True, he seemed to have trouble expressing his feelings, but he showed them, right? He hugged me. He held me at night. He showed up. That had to count for something.

If I needed to hear the words, I'd have to tell him that. Tell him I was on edge and unsure. Seek some solid ground with him. This was a relationship, one that needed a good foundation of trust and honesty to grow. I just had to tell him how I felt and hope he felt the same way. And I'd do it tonight.

I hurried up the stairs at the lofts, needing to see him. Wanting to feel his arms around me so I could calm myself. Ignoring every other person who walked past me in my hyperfocused need to get to Maverick's place and have the conversation I'd been avoiding like a child.

I was a grown-up. I could do this. Adulting sucked, but worrying about something I could easily get an answer to was worse.

But before I could reach Maverick's apartment, I had to walk past Hudson's. The one he shared with my sister. The door wasn't closed all the way, as the guys tended to come and go like family. Normally, nothing I'd really think about. But Maverick's voice coming from inside had me stopping in my tracks.

"I want yours."

"They're the exact same," Hudson replied. The two were obviously arguing, their voices a bit louder than usual.

"No, they're not." Maverick sounded pissed, which wasn't like him. He was broody and had a bad attitude at times, but he never really got angry with us. At least, not with me.

"There're only a few minor differences. They are the same." Hudson's words sent a chill up my spine. What the hell were they talking about?

"Yeah, I know. I've seen the differences. Yours is cleaner with less damage."

I leaned closer, that sick feeling reigniting. Damage? Were they talking about Macy and me? Was he equating my scars to...damage?

"So what do you want to do?" Hudson asked. I pressed myself against the doorframe, waiting for Maverick's answer. Wanting to know the same thing. What did he want to do with his damaged...whatever?

"I don't know," Maverick said, sounding even more irritated. "But I need to figure something out. They may be similar, but they're not exactly the same. And this one, mine, it may work right, but it looks defective. I don't want something so ugly."

MAVERICK

I held the drill someone had obviously been chewing on. The damn thing had teeth marks all over it. It ran, but it looked ugly and was disgustingly slimy. I was ready to throw the damn thing out the window.

"They may be similar, but they're not exactly the same. And this one, mine, it may work right, but it looks defective. I don't want something so ugly."

At that moment, Stacy came rushing into the apartment. And she looked furious.

I dropped my arm, the drill falling to my side. "Stacy, what—"

"I'm not fucking defective, you *bas-stahrd*."

That word didn't quite translate, though the images thrown by the communication core were enough to make me growl. "*Bas-stahrd*? Are you insulting my family?"

That only seemed to make her angrier. "No, dumbass. I'm insulting you."

Macy appeared from the back bedroom, her eyes red and bleary from all the reading she seemed to be doing lately. "Stacy, what's going on?"

"Nothing." My match huffed and spun, looking ready to attack her own sister. Even Hudson seemed on edge by her anger. "Nothing's going on. I've just had enough of trying to fit in around here."

Macy glanced at her mate, shaking her head a little when he scowled at Stacy. "What are you talking about?"

"This. All of this. I was supposed to get a match like Hudson, but instead, I get this jackass."

My brow went tight, my chest aching. "I'm not a jackass."

Macy's eyes darted my way, looking almost apologetic. "Stace, maybe you should—"

"No. Don't tell me what to do. Maybe you should worry about your own man and how he's just another guy who sees us as commodities instead of human beings."

"I don't understand," Macy said.

"Oh, that's right. It's just me. You're the blessed Macy. The perfect one. I'm the one who's apparently defective and up for trade."

Macy's eyes went wide, and Hudson responded to her obvious

distress with a warning growl aimed at her sister. I stepped between them, just in case. There was no way I'd let him put a hand on Stacy, no matter what words came out of her mouth.

But at the same time, I'd heard enough. "Why don't you calm down so we can figure this out?"

Stacy's mask locked into place, her anger almost palpable. "Stand still, look pretty? Is that what you need from me to find me attractive? What, I'm too dumb to know what's going on?"

She'd lost her mind. "I never said any of that."

Stacy headed for the door, her eyes leaking and her face red. "Fuck off, Maverick. I thought you'd be different being as you're not even human, but apparently, men are the same no matter where they come from."

"Stacy, wait." I rushed after her, but she slammed the door in my face.

My match, my potential mate, had walked out on me in a fury.

Stacy was gone, and I was still holding a defective drill without any clue what had just happened.

CHAPTER NINE

STACY

It took me three seconds to start to cry.

Eighteen minutes to make it home.

Two hours to open the ice cream.

Half a day to open the vodka.

After that...well, things got cloudy.

I wasn't a drinker. Having spent so much time sick and not in control of my own body sort of killed that need for me. But there were times when nothing else would do. Hearing Maverick call me defective was one of those times.

So I spent a lot of time making martinis and crying into my ice cream. I didn't bathe, didn't get dressed, and really didn't even leave the couch. Well, except to brush my teeth every day. Ice cream and vodka did not contribute to good oral hygiene.

Basically, I was a sloth. A sad, angry, drunk, sugar-coma suffering sloth for a couple of days. It was a good thing I tended to hoard my sick time at work in case of an emergency. A two-day bender due to being called defective seemed like an emergency for sure.

But two days of staying in bed hiding from the world with my phone on do-not-disturb left me feeling worse than ever. I was lonely; there was no shame in admitting that. I hadn't even called Macy because...well, what if Maverick was there with her? Or what if she told me something supportive like *good riddance* or *you'll find better*—those awesomely hurtful words laced with good intentions that never did seem to help. If she'd started a conversation with something about the number of fish in the sea, I would have lost my mind. That would be like the final nail in the coffin of my relationship. The end. Do not pass go. Do not collect two hundred dollars. Do not expect to be brought back from the dark side. Ever.

So I refused to call her or even look at my phone for fear of what I'd see there. Of course, she hadn't come by, so I guess I wasn't as much of a concern for her as I'd always assumed. Or maybe she was just too caught up with her new alien heartthrob to worry about her sister anymore.

Ugh...way to drop the depressive bomb again, Stacy.

So I wallowed. Not going to lie. It was hard-core, solid wallowing for sure. But wallowing never got you anywhere, so on the third day post defective conversation, I got up, turned my phone off without looking at a single message, and went back to work. After I showered, of course.

Being back at my desk was soothing in an odd sort of way. Distracting, maybe. I worked hard, completely focused on my projects and reports so I didn't sink into thoughts of my sister or my alien or defective anything. I functioned to the best of my ability, which really was pretty damn good. Cell phone off, emails only accepted to my professional account, no social media. No outside life to worry about.

It was oddly freeing...and wholly terrifying.

For the first time ever, I honestly thought about moving out of Michigan. And by thought, I meant researched other places to live. Maybe Detroit just wasn't the place for me. I'd almost died there, had barely *lived* there, and had my heart broken more times than I cared to admit there. I could go someplace else, start new. Find a life away from my twin and my cancer history and...him. Both hims. Chad and Maverick. I could walk away and be free of all the old baggage I'd been hauling around for years.

But deep down, I hated the idea of leaving Macy behind. Maverick, too, if I was being honest. My mind may have hated him, but my heart hadn't gotten the memo just yet. I missed him while I was wallowing. I craved him. The very idea that we'd reached the end of our coupledom physically hurt me as nothing else ever had.

So while I scanned apartment listings in places like Portland, Austin, and Chicago, I gripped my phone, thinking about turning it on to see what sort of alerts I had. Wondering if anyone had called or texted. Wondering if Maverick had reached out to me.

But the phone stayed off, and I locked down any hope of some sort of grand romantic gesture from my alien mail order boyfriend. If he'd wanted to talk to me, he could have. He knew where I lived. Hell, he knew where I worked.

But no one showed up.

And nothing else mattered, because showing up was ninety-five percent of success.

At least, that's what the inspirational picture hanging in the lunch room told me.

MAVERICK

Two days was a long time to go without seeing my mate, without talking to her, without knowing what had happened to make her so angry.

Two days was agony.

"You're an idiot," Macy spat for about the tenth time since she'd shown up at my unit. Yeah, her sister wasn't too happy with me.

Not that I was willing to admit her insults bothered me. "I'm a male."

"A male idiot."

"What do you know?" I asked, stamping down the fire of my anger. Macy wasn't the one who'd hurt me, but she was close and an easy target. I had to walk a fine line to keep myself under control.

Macy didn't hide from her words like her sister did. Those dark eyes so much like my Stacy's pierced right through me. "I know you really care about her."

I grunted, unable to say anything to that. Of course I cared. How could a mate not care? And she was my mate. I'd crooned a hundred times for her, but she'd pulled away from me. Hidden herself behind that mask. And then she'd slammed the door in my face.

"See?" Macy said, sitting up as if excited and pointing at me. "That was a positive grunt. You care, so why not reach out to her?"

"She threw a tantrum like a child."

"So now you're going to be stubborn like one? Yeah, that'll work out." Macy sighed, looking so much like her sister it made my chest ache. "I need to talk to her."

"No. This is my decision, Macy. We let her be for a few days." My decision, but not one I felt confident in anymore. Every day, every hour, had worn on my certainty that this plan would work. Stacy needed to come back, to make the effort to figure out what had happened. She was in the wrong.

Macy said I was being stubborn.

Hudson said I was being a glutton for punishment.

I knew I was being cautious. But it hurt. A lot.

"She's going to think we abandoned her," Macy said, looking so heartbroken, I almost caved right there.

"She hasn't called us either." And that was something that bothered me. Stacy always called and texted. Every day. All the time. If not me, her sister. But she'd gone completely silent.

"She's turned off her phone," Macy reminded me. "She does that when things really hurt her. She also turns to ice cream and alcohol, so I guess we can only hope she stays sober enough not to drive anywhere. Or make bad decisions."

I growled, unable to stop myself. I needed to be with Stacy, to protect her, but feeding into her behavior wouldn't help anything. She needed to reach out, to make the first move. She'd screwed up.

Hadn't she?

"I don't know what to do anymore," I said. Voicing my doubts was a hard admission. I was the pilot of our ship, the one who led the way and made all the decisions. But in this? Dealing with a human mate I hardly knew? I was lost. Adrift in a world I barely understood with a female who turned my life upside down and inside out.

I was clueless.

"You've got until seven tonight," Macy said, standing up and heading for the door. "She's my sister, and if you don't fix things today, I'm going over to her apartment and dragging her out. I've played your game because it's your relationship on the line, but I won't lose my sister in any way, for any reason. Get your head out of your ass, Maverick."

She turned her back on me as if to leave. Just like Stacy had done. Her dark hair flying out behind her as Stacy's had. Her arm reaching for the door like Stacy's had. Another stab to my already wrecked heart.

Another reminder of the day my mate walked away from me.

Everything I had on the inside broke as I relived my mate leaving me behind. Every ounce of strength and resolve, every bit of wisdom I'd learned, gone. I had nothing left, no way to resist the call to simply be angry. To hate myself for how many mistakes I'd made.

I had failed my match, and I wasn't sure if I could fix it.

Frustrated, I growled and grabbed the first thing I could get my hands on. It was a hammer I'd left on the counter, one with good weight and a nice handle. One that fit my hand perfectly. I didn't care. I threw that hammer in the opposite direction of Macy, embedding it in the drywall next to me. White dust flew into the air, grit and dirt mingled into particles that would gum up any engine. Would destroy the smooth glide of any piece of machinery. I usually hated grit, but this time, I didn't care that those particles would soon be making their way into everything around me.

The cloud was just another mess to clean up, but the situation with Stacy was more important. More vital.

More dangerous.

Macy spun at the noise, her eyes wide, even though the hammer hadn't been anywhere near her. "What are you—"

Before she could finish her sentence, Hudson came crashing through the door. He snarled and set himself between Macy and me, guarding. Protecting.

I didn't blame him.

"What was that?" he asked, keeping his eyes on mine.

"I threw a hammer."

He softened, looking almost confused. "Why?"

"Because I screwed up. Because I hate myself for how I've acted. Because I miss my mate."

It was Macy who responded. "Why don't you tell her that?"

"Tell her what?"

"All of that. Tell her how you feel."

"How I feel?" I gripped my mane, pulling my head back to stare at the ceiling, digging past the hurt and the pain and the anger. Past the defensiveness I'd developed over years of loss. Past everything to the very core of my being. "I want her as my mate. I want her here with me forever. I want to take care of her and make her laugh every day."

"So why don't you *tell her that*?" Macy asked. "You're such a guy. You think she somehow magically knows how much you care about her? She doesn't. You need to use words to confirm your feelings. You need to express what you want and how she fits into your life. You need to talk, Maverick."

I let go of my mane, dropping my head to meet her gaze once more. "But she won't talk to anyone."

Before Macy could respond, her phone rang. And she smiled. "Yeah, she will, apparently."

CHAPTER TEN

STACY

You know how, when things get really bad and you just want to feel something other than pain again, you sometimes do stupid things?

I did stupid things.

Well, one stupid thing. But it was a doozy.

I didn't intend to do it, not really. I mean, I turned on my phone to see if Maverick or Macy had contacted me. Totally innocent, right? I was lonely and sad and unsure what to do. I was also tired of avoiding them and figuring I should act like an adult. So I *turned on my phone.*

And the first text that popped up was from Chad.

I shouldn't have done it. I should have ignored his stupid message and carried on with my plan. But I didn't. I was weak and hurting and needing someone, anyone, to be in my corner. So no, I didn't ignore him.

I texted him back.

Nothing dirty, no offers to hook up or anything like that. A simple note of "It's been a bad week. I'll talk to you later." Which seemed so innocuous and safe at that moment.

And then I saw all the texts from Macy and Maverick and even Chloe. I saw how upset they all were, how much they seemed to care about what was going on with me. I saw their concern, and I knew I'd screwed up.

Especially when reading the texts from Macy.

Macy: *Dumbass. Why'd you race out of here that way? The guys were arguing about tools, and you went nuts. What happened?*

Oh, shit. Tools. Defective tools. Maverick had been holding on to something big and yellow when I walked in, but I wasn't sure what it was. Nor did I take the time to find out. I really was a dumbass.

Macy: *I've got labs and study sessions all week. Please call me so I know you're okay.*

Macy: *I'm going to fail my finals. I'm skipping one on Wednesday if you don't get back to me. I mean it.*

It was Wednesday. My sister, the studyaholic and overzealous future doctor, was about to skip a final because I'd been too hurt to talk to her. I needed to call her. So I did.

"Hey." Simple, but the only greeting I could get out at the moment. I knew she'd be pissed.

"You are such a dumbass."

See? Pissed.

"Don't skip your final," I said, my voice soft even to my own ears.

"I'm not. I was seriously going to, but Hudson got all growly with me about it."

I huffed. "The fun of dating an alien, right?"

Macy was silent for a long, almost tense moment. I closed my eyes, waiting for something. I'd almost forgotten we hadn't talked about that fact. I'd gotten so caught up in Maverick and trying to find my place in his life that I'd neglected my twin. That was new.

"Is that why you ran off?" Macy finally asked. "Because he told you?"

"No. I knew before our weekend together was over."

"And you're okay with it?"

Was I? I gave that question the attention it deserved. It wasn't a hard answer. "Yeah, I am. I wish you would have told me about Hudson, though."

"I know, and I'm sorry. The guys are cautious with who can know about them. I would have told you eventually, but it all happened so fast." Something clicked in the background, a thump that sounded an awful lot like a door closing. But she didn't make mention of anything. "So if it wasn't the whole not-from-around-here thing, what made you storm off the other day? What happened? You never gave anyone a chance to explain anything."

My eyes burned, and I pulled a blanket around my legs as I curled into the corner of the couch. Hiding. "I thought they were talking about me. And you. About my scars and me being...less." I took a deep breath, fighting to get the words out that were the worst. "About sharing or trading or something."

Macy was quiet for a long moment before she sighed. "You know I'd never even think about such things."

"I know *you* wouldn't, but they're guys. It's almost ingrained to think stuff like that."

"One, no, it's not. You really need to spend some time around decent men. And two, our Reithhar men don't think that way. At all. They are not human. If I told Hudson I wanted to have sex with another man or woman in our bed—"

The roar that came from the other end of the phone hurt my ears and practically made my phone vibrate. Apparently, that noise I'd heard was Hudson entering the room with Macy. Wonderful.

"See?" Macy said once all was quiet once more. "No possibility of threesomes or moresomes. Maverick wouldn't want that. He wouldn't want anyone but you."

Ugh, that last statement was like a knife to the heart. Her words rang so true in even my addled head that I couldn't deny them. Maverick had said that to me, had promised me that was not what he'd ever want. They'd been talking about defective tools, and I'd assumed they were talking about me. And worse, I acted on that assumption without asking what was going on first. Which meant I was an idiot.

"I screwed up."

"Yup, you totally did," Macy said. "You should call Maverick so you can fix this."

"I should," I said, pulling the blanket over my head. Creating a cocoon of safety as I asked her a question I was sort of afraid of knowing the answer to. "Will he even answer my call, though?"

Macy didn't answer me because she didn't need to. From

somewhere over the line, from what sounded like he had to have been standing in the same room with her, Maverick said yes.

And that yes was more soothing to my frazzled nerves than anything else could have been.

"Will he come over so we can talk?"

There was a silent pause, one long enough to make me feel sick. To bring back all those feelings of dread and loss. One that I couldn't stand to sit through for long.

"Macy?"

"He left," she said. My world stopped, tears falling down my cheeks as those words reverberated through my mind. He left. Like, left or *left*? Because there was a difference in how far his leaving would take him.

"Where?" I asked, squeezing my eyes closed to keep the sound of crying out of my voice. "I wanted to talk to him. Where's he going?"

"He didn't say, but if I were to guess, I'd think he was on his way to your place."

CHAPTER ELEVEN_

MAVERICK

I ran downstairs, racing for the vehicle Klow-ee drove. I didn't have keys, but it wouldn't matter. The thing was falling apart and easy to steal.

Luckily, though, I didn't need to.

"What's the rush?" Klow-ee said as I ran out the door and into the space where the vehicles rested.

I grabbed her by the arm and directed her back the way she'd been coming. "Stacy. Now."

"She called?"

I didn't bother answering, simply jumped into her junk heap of a vehicle. Klow-ee followed, not hesitating. She was definitely a good human to have around.

"Same place I dropped you off last time?" she asked as she squealed the tires and took off for the road.

"Yes."

We were silent for most of the trip, but Klow-ee never could hold her tongue for long.

"You know, you guys should learn to drive." She frowned as she pulled onto Stacy's street. "You'd have to learn to read first, though."

I didn't care. Didn't even bother to answer her. I simply grunted and jumped from the car as it pulled against the curb in front of Stacy's building.

Klow-ee hollered, "You're welcome," to me from the car, but I just kept going. My Stacy had called. She was ready to fix things, so I would show up. I would tell her everything. I would make sure she knew exactly how much she meant to me.

She'd called, so I'd do anything I could to help clean up the mess between us.

I didn't care that there were humans on the sidewalks or cars in the streets. I ran across the sidewalk and up the steps to the door, desperate for my mate who had finally reached out. Too afraid she'd change her mind before I got to her to slow down. Once we worked through this rough patch, I would never again let her run from me. No matter what, I would make sure she knew how much she meant to me. I would pull that mask off and tear it into a million pieces.

I would make sure my mate knew I was utterly and totally devoted to her.

Up three flights of stairs, and I was almost there. In fact, the door to her unit was swinging open when I reached her floor, but the hall wasn't empty in front of it and the door wasn't being opened for me.

A male stood, looking like he was about to enter.

"Hey, babe," he said, moving as if to walk past Stacy. I couldn't see her yet, didn't know what her face looked like, but it didn't matter. He had to be Chad.

"What are you doing here?" she asked, sounding sad and sweet...and surprised. Good.

"Got your text." The guy leaned closer, his face hidden by the wall. That was okay. I could kill him without looking at him. "Figured I'd come make your bad day better. I've got about half an hour to take care of you, then I need to bolt. I'm meeting up with the guys for drinks in a bit."

She'd texted him. Not me, not her sister until today. But she'd texted Chad. Time slowed as I waited to see what she'd do, how she'd handle this. Would she choose Chad? Had I screwed up so badly that she'd take another male to her bed and leave me standing outside?

Stacy's hand reached for him, palm up, resting against his chest once she could touch him. My heart burned, and something inside of me crumbled.

But she didn't pull him inside.

On the contrary...

She shoved him across the hall.

"Hey," Chad said as he stumbled back.

"No, Chad," Stacy said, confirming my suspicions of who the male was. "I don't want you here."

That was all I needed to repair every broken piece inside of me.

"What?" Chad asked, looking as if he was about to push past her. "Quit playing around."

"She's not." I shoved past the human, pushing him into the opposite wall from where Stacy stood, and slammed the door in his face. Something he deserved. "Is that what you want? Some boy who will give you thirty minutes before he leaves you for something better?"

Stacy stood before me, looking so small and scared. I didn't know what to do with her like that. I was too angry, too hurt, and yet hopeful. Plus, she looked so beautiful, she made my cock hard and my body ache for her. A confusing place to be for sure.

But then Stacy raised her little chin, and she made her decision.

"No."

I stalked closer, forcing her back. Pushing her into the wall behind her door. "So what do you want?"

She licked her lips. "You."

"You want me?" I kept my eyes on her mouth. Wanting it. Needing it. Craving a taste of her.

Her plump, sweet lips formed a shape like a kiss, and she whispered a quiet, "Yes."

"Good." I nuzzled closer, scenting her neck. "I want you, too."

Her hands landed on my chest, warm and soft, sending a shiver up my spine. "Even though I annoy the hell out of you?"

I bit the place where her neck met her shoulder. My favorite part of her other than her sweet cunt. "I'll take the good with the bad."

She pushed me away and rolled her eyes. "I don't want to be called bossy."

I shook my head, holding back a smile. "Never again."

"I hate being compared to my sister. I can't reach the bar of perfection she's set, and I don't want to have to try. It hurts me to think I'm second to her all the time."

"You are not second to anyone, my mate."

Her smile bloomed bright and beautiful and all for me. But then she pursed her lips, attempting to look serious once more. "Good. And there's no sisterly loving allowed—not even as a joke. In fact, don't even think of my sister as a female."

"I didn't, but I know you thought I did. Next time you're unsure of what I mean, ask me. Don't you dare storm away from me."

"Fine. But I need reassurance."

"Of what?"

"This. Us. Our connection."

"Words mean nothing. I show you how I care."

She glanced down, suddenly seeming less brave. "Sometimes I need words."

And there it was. The thing she needed from me to stay my Stacy. To drop her mask and be true with me. If only I'd known.

"Then you'll have them." I crouched down so I could put my face even with hers, so I could force her eyes on mine. "I care deeply for you. I want you in my life, in my bed, and as my mate. Forever. Will you be that for me? Will you accept me as yours?"

She smiled, so bright and beautiful there was no holding back my return one. "Yes."

I growled and stepped closer once more. "Good."

"You're still an asshole sometimes." But her body accepted mine, her hands gripping my arms and holding me tight. She may have meant the words, but that didn't keep her from wanting me.

I yanked her close by the hips, pressing her shoulders against the wall. "Yes, but I'm your asshole."

"Totally." She wrapped her arms around my neck and pulled me in for a deep, delicious kiss. Which led to another. And another. Which was fine by me. There was nothing left to say. She was mine and I was hers and we were going to stay together.

Wait, there was one more thing to say.

I pulled away on a gasp. "Lose Chad's number."

She nodded, her eyes unfocused and heated. "Already done."

I yanked her pants down and pulled her by the thighs so I could wedge my hips between her legs. Needing her. Ready to take her. Lying down, standing up, bent over backward…didn't matter. I needed to feel her cunt wrapped around my cock. To reconnect. To claim my mate.

"Good," I said as I lined myself up with where she was hot, wet, and ready for me. "Now quit talking. I only want you screaming my name when you ride my cock."

She groaned, rocking her hips against me, coating me in her wetness. "So bossy."

But she didn't say no.

MAVERICK

There were times when the fact that I wasn't human seemed almost unnoticeable. Other times, it was far more obvious—at least to me—than it should have been. Arguing with my mate was one time when those differences seemed to stand out.

"No."

Stacy put a hand on her hip and raised an eyebrow. "Yes."

My little mate was feeling feisty. I loved it when she got like that. "You can argue all you want, but the answer will still be no."

She huffed and slapped her hand against her thigh in a move that almost made me laugh. "Mav, you said I could decorate."

I looked over the decoration she held. "I did. But that picture is a lie."

Those lips I loved kissing so much turned down. "How is it a lie?"

I grabbed the picture from her hands and wrapped an arm around her waist, yanking her off her feet and against me. "Because that solar system does not exist."

She smiled, her eyes locked on mine. "How do you know? You can't have seen all of them."

"Many."

"But not all."

"No, not all."

"Then you don't know."

She was right—I didn't know. Not about the validity of the solar system depicted in the picture she wanted to hang. And though it was pretty, with the swirling colors and spots of light, it wasn't what I wanted to see. Space was not what I wanted to remember.

But maybe she didn't realize that.

I sat my mate back on her feet, making sure she didn't trip over the boxes and bags of things from her apartment. She was moving in with me, and I'd never been more pleased. Even though the unit was a mess with all the clutter. I would take a mess every day so long as it meant I had her with me.

"I don't want the picture to hang," I said, fighting to find the words I knew she needed.

"Why not?" She stared up at me all wide-eyed and open. My Stacy. No mask, no hiding.

I brushed her hair over her shoulder and pressed my lips to her forehead for a moment. "Because I was alone in space. I would rather fill our unit with pictures of us together, of the places you want to go and that I'll follow you to. I don't want to remember my time before you as much as I want to celebrate our shared experiences."

Stacy stood quiet and still, the gears of her mind turning away. My logical little mate thinking everything over.

And then she sighed. "I'll take it back in the morning."

"Thank you." I ran a finger down her arm, smiling when she shivered. "We could have Klow-ee take a picture of us in her unit instead."

"Why her place?"

"Because that's where we met."

She bit her lip, obviously fighting the smile my words brought out. As if I would ever forget that moment.

"You hated me." Her words were said in a warning tone, but her smile was strong. Something in that look, in the way her eyes practically dared me to argue with her, made my cock stand up and take notice of how sexy our mate was. And how long it had been since we'd touched her how we wanted to.

Carefully but with purpose, I pushed her until she took a step back. Then another. Herding her toward the couch, which was the only free spot I could see that was close enough. We'd been moving boxes all morning, not spending nearly enough time in our bed. I couldn't wait any longer for her.

"Hate is a strong word." I leaned over her until she fell onto the couch, her hair in disarray over the cushion and her legs hanging off the side. Perfect.

She licked her lip, inviting my eyes to that slip of pink. Teasing me with it. "You really disliked me."

I dropped to my knees and grabbed her calves. "My esehhnce crooned for you."

"Your esehhnce is brilliant."

I would have agreed with her, but I was too busy sliding her panties off. Hidden under the skirt she wore, her cunt glistened, swollen and pink and looking absolutely delicious in the warm, afternoon glow.

I couldn't resist her.

"You know," she said as I ran a finger over her softest flesh. "We could hang that picture—"

"No," I said with a pinch to her thigh. "No space pictures and no more talk of decorating. I'm the pilot of this unit, and I say it's Stacy-Maverick time."

She chuckled, cutting off with a moan when I ran a knuckle along the edge of her cunt. Teasing her the way I loved to do.

"And what happens during Stacy-Maverick time?" she asked, smiling down at me with a knowing look in her eye.

Again, I didn't answer her. Just leaned forward and licked a wet trail from the bottom of her cunt to the tip. Stacy groaned, her knees falling farther open and her head tilting back.

"Fine," she said as I pressed two fingers inside her. "Stacy-Maverick time. But then, decorating."

"Fine." I pressed a kiss right over her bundle of flesh, adding a twirl of my tongue at the last minute. "But that picture is still a no."

She grabbed my mane and pulled me against her as I attacked her cunt with my lips and tongue. Her heel pressed into my shoulder, and she arched and shook as I made sure to hit all the right spots. As I drew out every bit of pleasure I could from her. As I pushed her toward her release.

But my mate was nothing if not stubborn.

"Fine," she gasped. "You win that one."

She was right. I had won, starting the day she'd come storming into my life with her bossy ways.

But as she came around my fingers, her body quivering and my name on her lips, I knew she'd be winning, too. Every day, if I had my way about it. I'd wake her up with my tongue and make sure she fell asleep safe and warm after I took care of her with my cock. I'd let her win with every orgasm, every shake and moan, every single lick and touch and sweet word I had for her.

She'd be the winningest human in the history of Earth with me as her mate.

I'd make sure of it.